FORGET ABOUT ME

a nostalgic romantic comedy

Boston Classics
Book 2

KAREN GREY

Published by HOME COOKED BOOKS

A division of Jasper Productions, LLC

Cover art and design by Lana Pecherczyk

Subjects: | BISAC: FICTION / Romance / Romantic Comedy.|

FICTION / Romance / Historical / American.|

First edition, October 2020

Content guidance for this book can be found at www.karengrey.com/contentguidance

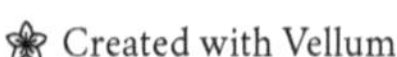 Created with Vellum

Praise

Boston Classics Series

★★★★★ "A rom com set in BOSTON in the 80s?? Yes please!"

- NYT bestselling author Erin Nicholas

★★★★★ "This author is truly a master at creating likeable, three-dimensional characters."

- Laurie Reads Romance

★★★★★ I'm always happy to read Karen's books that transport me back to the 80s and 90s. I love her snippets of music, TV, current events of that time period sprinkled throughout the book for that hit of nostalgia."

- Pixiedust reads

★★★★★ "I super, highly, and absolutely love and recommend this series! Readers who love the 80s/90s nostalgic era and maturing "broken" characters will be captivated with the characters, the plot, and the unforgettable era of the 80s/90s - the good, the bad, and even the ugly side of things."

- Currant7recommends

★★★★★ "I am loving this series, each book is entertaining and contains plenty of laugh out loud moments and heartfelt ones."

- Bookbub review

★★★★★ "Karen Grey has a lovely, deft touch with her characters, the plot, and with the world she's created."

- Bookbub review

★★★★★ "I love these retro romance reads!"

- Bookbub review

★★★★★ "I'm all about this semi-historical genre. The music, the radio, the phones with cords. Every bit of it."

- Goodreads review

Content Guidance

The content notes below are meant to give readers a generalized view of potentially triggering subjects within this novel.

- Use of expletives: frequent but not mean-spirited
- Sex/Nudity: several sex scenes
- Violence: none
- Death: death of secondary character and mention of an animal's death
- Other: struggles with religious faith

If you'd like a more detailed list of content warnings (which may include spoilers) they are available at:

https://www.karengrey.com/contentguidance

August, 1988

"Jack shall have Jill. Naught shall go ill."
Puck, A Midsummer Night's Dream, III, ii

Chapter 1

"You May Be Right" - Billy Joel
Lucy's Keep on Truckin' Mixtape, Song #3

BEN

Falling in love, killing a guy by accident and mortally wounding myself when it appears that my bride has taken her life is a lot. Doing it six times in four days is just too much. The addition of two weekend matinees to Shakespeare Boston's *Romeo and Juliet* schedule must be taking its toll. Still, I wouldn't trade it for anything. This year—just like the past seven—began in Los Angeles, where modeling work has dominated my life, keeping me far from home and too busy to do theater. Six months into 1988, due to circumstances I never expected to face, I'm back in Boston performing for a live audience. It feeds my soul, so I don't care if I'm exhausted.

I'm tired at the end of every weekend, but on this particular late-August Monday morning, I might be hallucinating. Adrenaline spiking, heart in my throat, it takes a few beats for me to figure out what just happened. My hands grip the railing that kept me from falling off my second-floor porch as I take in the lump I just tripped over on my way out the door.

It's a mottled gray color, and I think that's fur. Not moving, though. Wondering if it's alive, I step closer. It makes a snuffling noise, unfolding itself, and I release the breath I've been holding. It's not some weird package from a mega-fan; it's a dog. With tufted brows and a whiskery muzzle, he looks like the dog in that movie when we were kids—*Benji*.

"Where the heck did you come from, little guy?"

Where *did* he come from?

My heart takes off again, and I scan the backyard. Thankfully, no rabid fans or paparazzi seem to be lurking in the shadows. I've worked hard to keep this address a secret. I don't want my dad or his neighbors to have to deal with that level of crazy. Habitually, I check one particular neighbor's back yard, but as usual, it's empty. No one at that house is a fan of mine, that's for sure.

Eyes back on my visitor, I squat and hold out the back of my hand, just like Lucy taught me to do back when we were kids. He sniffs it, gives it a polite lick, then holds up his paw like he wants to shake hands. When I reach for it, though, he whimpers.

"It's okay, buddy," I say soothingly, but it actually looks like he's not okay. The paw is bleeding.

"Sorry, dude. I guess we should do something about that." Looks like my run isn't happening this morning. Maintaining a contractually mandated body- fat ratio and weight and muscle definition was way easier out in Los Angeles, where I had access to Callum Keen Enterprise's in-house chefs and gym along with a daily routine full of go-sees, meetings and shoots. I could skip today's workout, but that's a slippery slope. Next thing you know, I'll be eating steak and pasta.

Ah, pasta. I miss you so. Not as much as a certain former neighbor, but at least there's a chance I'll have *you* again.

An image of a steaming plate of spaghetti and meatballs presented to me with the most beautiful smile I've ever known hovers in my mind for a few precious moments. A guy can dream. But right now, this guy needs to take care of a mutt.

"Come on in, buddy."

The dog looks at me before limping over the threshold. I have a few first aid supplies, but I have no idea how to take care of a wound on an animal.

Three wasted Band-Aids later, I give up. "I think you need a vet."

Seven summers ago, the love of my life worked at an animal hospital over in Somerville, Massachusetts—one of the many satellite towns surrounding Boston—and just a couple miles from my dad's house here in Arlington. I gave her a ride to work most mornings. Spending that time together led to a whole series of incidents. Some are the sweetest memories I have.

Some still give me nightmares.

The dog lies down with a harrumph.

"I don't even have anything to feed you. Unless you like brown rice?"

He rolls over on his side, his tail thump lacking enthusiasm.

"Yeah, I didn't think so."

That vet's office is the only one I know of. Lucy probably doesn't work there anymore. I have no idea what she's doing now.

I'd likely know everything about her—heck, I'd probably be married to her—if I wasn't responsible for her brother's death.

HALF AN HOUR LATER, I'm in an antiseptic waiting room, filling out forms on a clipboard. The dog is on the chair next to me. I'm not sure if that's allowed, but nobody has told him to move. I've never actually been inside a vet's office. I always just dropped Lucy off out front, and my dad and I never had a pet growing up. I would've loved a dog, but my dad always seemed to have enough on his plate with running a business and taking care of me.

It feels pretty much like being at a regular doctor's office. The floor is linoleum instead of industrial carpet and the posters and artwork on the walls are of dogs and cats instead of humans, but the feel of nervous anticipation is pretty much the same.

I give up on the forms and go back to the middle-aged receptionist with the heavy Boston accent. "Since I just found him this morning, I don't know the answer to any of these questions."

She gives me a look like she doesn't quite believe me and makes some sort of notation before sliding the papers into a folder. "Have a seat."

"Do you have any idea how long it'll take? I have to get to work soon."

"Would you prefer to come back?" She flips through a large datebook. "I could get you in tomorrow or call you if we have a cancellation today."

"Yeah, I drive a delivery truck, so there's no way to call me." I look back at the dog, who's got quite the baleful look on his face. "I'll wait."

"Someone will be out as soon as we have an opening."

When I sit back down, the dog sighs quietly. He's remarkably calm, despite the rabbit scrabbling in a cage next to us and a yappy little dog across the room. Even the cat stalking along the top of the reception counter doesn't seem to faze my guy.

I check my watch. Maybe I should make an appointment and come back tomorrow. His wound is still oozing blood, though, and I don't want it to get infected. I've had a few like it myself, growing up in and around my dad's woodshop. Do dogs get tetanus shots, too?

After I've gone through all the magazines in the waiting room—which, thankfully, are pet magazines, so I don't have to encounter photos of myself—I go back to the desk. The gatekeeper's on the phone, so I give her my most winning smile, hoping she can do something to get us in soon.

"Porter?"

I turn from the receptionist's frown to face the girl I wasn't sure I'd ever see again, and it's like one of those movie moments where the music swells and the light gets rosy.

For half a second. When I really look at her, it's like the needle scratches across the record and the light blinks back to harsh fluorescent.

I do catch a flash of something in her wide-set, brown eyes.

Luciana Maria Minola taught me what passion looked, felt and sounded like when we were barely adults. I've never encountered anything as intense with anyone else. There's a half second where it zings back and forth between us, as strong as ever.

Until the dog interrupts our staring contest with a sharp bark.

She closes her eyes and takes a quick breath. When she opens them again, a cloak of professionalism smothers any remaining fire. Quickly dropping her eyes to the chart in her hands, she asks, "Does the dog have a name?"

All I can think is *please Lucy, just yell at me* because this fake niceness will kill me. "Uh, no. I just found him. Or her. I'm not sure."

She takes a quick look at the dog's undercarriage. "Okay, little man, let's take you to a room so we can figure out what's going on here." She slips a leash that doubles as a collar over his bare neck. She heads out of the waiting area, the dog limping at her side.

I hesitate. "His foot—I mean, his—uh, paw." I seem to have forgotten how to speak English. I could probably recite some Shakespeare. Mercutio has a few lines about a cat and a rat that might be appropriate since I'm pretty sure the latter is how Lucy would describe me.

"You can go with them." The receptionist's amused tone breaks through the fog Lucy's left me in. "You're the dog's owner, right?"

I stare at the woman, not sure of how to answer the question.

She shakes her head and points, as if she understands that just being in Lucy's presence makes all men act like idiots. "Just follow them down the hall."

"Oh. Yeah. Okay."

A few wrong turns later, after I surprise an old guy holding an enormous hissing cat and a goth girl with what I think is a ferret, I finally stumble into the correct exam room. The dog's on his back on an exam table. Lucy is rubbing his chest, cooing sweet nothings. My privates jolt with jealousy. Moving across the country, immersing myself in work, even dating other people—none of it has dimmed her effect on me.

I perch on a bench, again not sure if it's for humans or animals or both, and clasp my hands in front of the one part of my body that's sure of itself at the moment, willing it to sit, stay and behave. Lucy was my best friend's sister. Taking advantage of her in the past had disastrous consequences. I don't deserve to even *think* of how delicious her soft skin tasted or how beautiful her hair looked sprawled out on a pillow.

"So, we've got a puncture wound." Her voice is sharp. "He's a stray?"

I sit up, begging my frontal lobe to work. "Yeah. He just showed up at my house this morning. I opened the front door, and there he was holding up his paw." I imitate the dog's pose. "It was bloody, but I couldn't find anything in there. Maybe he got it out himself."

"Yeah, that happens. No collar or anything?"

"No, and I haven't seen him around before."

"Okay, well, you have a couple of choices here." Eyes on the chart, her tone grows even more businesslike. Each clipped word erases another chunk of our past. "You can take responsibility for him financially, as well as take care of him until you find the owner—assuming you're able to find them. If no one claims him, you can either choose to adopt him or look for someone else to adopt him. Or you can surrender him to us, and we'll take care of him and try to find him a home. Or you can take him to the shelter, where they'll deal with him, which may include euthanasia, depending on how many dogs they already have on board."

Finally, her face reveals some emotion. It's crystal clear what she thinks of options two and three. If I choose either, anything good she ever felt for me will be buried forever.

She may be right, it's definitely crazy, but maybe it's a lunatic she's looking for, as Billy Joel would say. The song, featured in one of the many mixtapes Lucy made for me, echoes in my mind as I try to find words. "You know I never had a dog. I have no idea whether I can take care of him or what to do—"

She snaps the chart closed. "Okay, then. You can either take him to Animal Contr—"

"No. I don't—" I swallow whatever I was going to say and wipe damp palms on my shorts. I'm fucking this up already. "I'm just saying, I might need help. I can pay. I just don't know what to do, how to take care of a dog. Like, can he ride around with me in the delivery truck?"

She finally looks directly at me. "You're still delivering cabinets? Didn't you finish college and move away?"

"I did. I'm… helping out my dad right now." I'm kind of surprised she doesn't know more about my situation. Her mom always had a finger on the pulse of Arlington gossip, plus it seems like half of Boston has read or heard all kinds of things about me. A few of them are actually true.

"Huh." She gives me a cryptic look before pulling something out of her pocket and shifting the dog's position on the table.

"In fact, I'm actually kind of late to do some deliveries. Do you know how much longer this will take?"

As I watch her go through the dog's fur with a fine-toothed comb, it burns to be treated like just another customer, but also, it's pretty cool to see little Lucy all grown up. The way she moves is different. Precise. Self-assured.

"Well, he's got fleas, and he's a bit underweight. Since it's possible he's been on his own for a while, I would recommend that we keep him for a few hours—give him shots, do a test for worms, which he likely has, and treat him for those as well as the fleas. The vet will look him over and decide whether this wound needs an antibiotic. You can pick him up anytime between four and five o'clock."

"Wait—you're not the vet?" I look around the room for the answer, as if the posters on the wall warning of the dangers of diseases I can't pronounce might enlighten me.

She drops the comb in a box on the counter, keeping a hand on the dog. "No, I'd still be in vet school if I'd gone that route. I dropped out of UMass after—after Tony—and moved back home." Her eyes don't stray from her examination of the dog. "I've worked my way up from assistant to animal technician."

My heart plummets. I'm such an idiot.

She scratches out a few notes on the chart. "Just a warning: the tests, the shots and everything? It's not going to be cheap."

I'm still grappling with the fact that the accident robbed her of her future, as if losing her brother wasn't bad enough. "Yeah, uh, sure. That's fine."

She shifts the dog to the floor.

Even though each pained look from her is another punch in my gut, I'm not ready to lose her again, so I start babbling. "I guess I need to get some supplies, but I don't know what he needs. I suppose I can just ask the people at the pet store and they can tell me. Maybe there's a book I can read on—"

She groans, placing a palm in the space between us. "Stop. Pick him up at five, and I'll meet you at the Pet Palace after dinner. Without me there, they'll upsell you on everything. Seven thirty. Got it?"

I squelch a triumphant smile and give her a thankful one instead. "Okay. Great. Thanks."

Halfway out the door, she turns back. "Do you want to give him a name or should I?"

"Oh." Another chance to do something right. "I can do it."

Problem is, I never was good at improvisation. My brain is full of Shakespeare, so I sift through some of those names, mumbling, "Uh... Romeo? No... Paris?" Then it hits me. The mischievous fairy that brings lovers back together. "What about Puck?"

This gets the dog barking, but Lucy isn't impressed. "Like in hockey?"

Her confusion's warranted. I never played the sport, though Tony and I were on a ton of other teams together. "No, like the character in *Midsummer Night's Dream*. Remember, we did that in high school?"

She nods curtly, her mouth tight. Tony was in the play, too. "Puck it is."

When the door shuts behind them, I sink back onto the bench. "I'll see you guys later. I'll miss you." My voice drops to a whisper even though I'm alone. Again. "I've been missing you."

I've met hundreds of drop-dead gorgeous women since leaving

Arlington for Los Angeles. Not a single one measured up to Lucy. Not a one had her easy, musical laugh. Not a one had skin as soft as hers or curves that I couldn't resist. Not a one had caramel-colored eyes that lit with pleasure when they caught mine or cheeks that turned from olive to rosy when she said my name.

That ease, that softness, that color—they've all disappeared.

And it's all my fault.

Chapter 2

"Treat Me Right" - Pat Benatar
Lucy's Right On Rock On Mixtape, Song #2

LUCY

"Oh, for Pete's sake!" The dog flinches at my outburst. "Sorry, little guy, you're okay." Making sure he's secured to the grooming table, I grab a dustpan and broom to clean up the shards of a test tube I just dropped.

Cindy, a fellow animal tech, pauses in the doorway. "Everything okay?"

"Yeah, just slippery fingers." I do my best to sound normal. Unfortunately, my stupid body has chucked normal out the window. "Luckily, I dropped the test tube *before* I filled it with blood."

Cindy smirks as she leans into the room. "Still full of sexual tension after your up-close-and-personal with Ben Porter?"

"What? What are you talking about?"

How in the heck does Cindy know Ben's name? Or about my history with him?

The petite redhead arches a perfectly shaped eyebrow. "I'm

talking about you in an exam room with Ben Porter." She may as well end the sing-song sentence with K-I-S-S-I-N-G.

I dump the broken glass into the trash and stare at the swinging lid. "How do you know him?"

"Uh, any woman with a pulse knows him." She points at me. "You picked up that chart out of turn. I assumed it was because you're a fan. I mean, I don't blame you. I'm just jealous." She puts a hand on her chest and moans. "Those ads where he's just wearing briefs? Oh my god."

"What are you talking about?" We can't be talking about the same person. My Ben studied theater, but he isn't in underwear ads.

At least I don't think so. I guess it's possible. But… unlikely.

She narrows her baby-blue-shadowed eyes at me. "Are you saying you don't know who Ben Porter is?"

"I know who he is. I grew up with him." Puck whines. I put the dustpan away and return to his side. "Easy boy." I blow out a breath to steady my hands, pick up a new test tube and set it carefully in its holder before picking up the hypodermic needle.

Cindy sidles in to hold the little dog for me, though he hasn't moved. "You grew up with him?"

"Yeah, he lived on the block behind us." I draw blood from the base of Puck's neck, carefully set the sample inside the tube and discard the needle before massaging the spot. "Good boy."

"So you *know* him know him. Is he gay? Everyone says he's gay."

"Ha-ha!" My blurt of nervous laughter earns me a strange look from Cindy. "No, I'm pretty sure he's not gay. Not that there's anything wrong with that, it's just… never mind." Setting the dog on the floor, images of Ben's naked body tangled with mine storm through my mind. I have got to get myself under control. "Okay, boy, let's see if we can get a fecal so we can find out how many worms you've got inside you."

The promise of parasite-filled poop doesn't seem to deter Cindy, who follows me out of the exam room.

"Really? Wow. So, do you still hang out with him? Do you have his phone number? Maybe he needs someone to bring this cutie home for him."

I hold up my free hand. "Sorry. I only have his old number, and I doubt it's still good. I haven't seen him for a long time, and I have no idea where he lives now, not that we're likely to start delivering pets back to their owners."

"Jeez, calm down. I was just kidding." She sticks out her lower lip in a pout. "I thought Deanna was the grouchy one and you were the nice one."

Deanna's the senior vet tech with over ten years at the practice. Cindy is brand new. I'm the Mama Bear in the middle, so I soften my tone. "I promise I'll let you know if I find out anything. Right now, I'm taking Puck outside."

"Puck? Is Ben a Bruins fan? Oh my god, I would so love to go to a hockey game with him!"

"Hold your horses, missy. It's Puck after the character in a Shakespeare play."

She slaps a hand to her forehead. "Buh doi! He's in a Shakespeare play right now. He's Romeo. Isn't that so rad?"

"I thought you said he was an underwear model. How do you know so much about him?"

She rolls her eyes. "I can read, duh."

My face must make my confusion clear.

"He's been in all the big magazines. *Teen, Tiger Beat, Bop.* Even *People.*" She says the last in a reverent whisper, and I have to stifle a laugh. Her delivery's so dramatic, she's the one who should be onstage. "The story of how he got started is choice. He was an intern at this big agency in Los Angeles and just, like, getting people coffee or something when Callum Keen saw him and was like, I want *that guy*. And the rest is history. He's been modeling ever since." She grabs my arm. "And he was in our waiting room. I cannot wait to tell my friends. They are gonna freak."

The bell sounds, indicating that a tech is needed to handle another patient. I tip my head in the direction of the exam rooms.

She huffs out a breath. "Okay, I'm going, but I want some dirt on him!"

When I open the door to the kennel, the familiar scents and sounds remind me of my purpose here. I've got a homeless dog to take care of. It's a tight space between the cages full of boarders, and they're all eager to say hello. When Puck hesitates on the threshold, I lift my chest, keep my breathing even and give a quick tug on the leash. "Let's go, buddy."

He trots calmly by my side, so I coo, "What a good boy." Since he isn't freaking out, I pause to say hello to one of the calmer dogs. As I talk to the older lab mix, Puck stands calmly next to me.

Sometimes I wish I could spend my whole day back here, like I did when I started out. Cleaning cages isn't fun, but the animals' needs are so simple. No office politics, no owners making impossible demands, no wishing I were the vet instead of just a tech.

Right now, though, I get to go outside for a few minutes with a surprisingly well-behaved little stray. I scratch under his bearded chin, and he licks mine. "Okay, buddy. Let's go make a poop so we can see what kind of worms you've got in there. Pretty sure there'll be a nice variety." He barks, tail wagging and eyes bright, like he agrees.

As we walk along the edge of the hospital's parking lot, he follows his nose and I revel in the warmth of the late morning sun. It was summer when Ben and I got together. I thought I'd successfully shoved everything about that time so far into the corner of my heart that I'd never see or hear from it again. Just like I haven't seen or heard from Ben in the seven years since he moved across the country without saying goodbye to me or my family.

A song sneaks into my head. Pat Benatar's "Treat Me Right" was at the top of the mixtape I made for Ben the day after I talked him into helping me lose my virginity.

Come to think of it, he did a disappearing act then too.

RUSHING DOWN *the walk because I'm late to catch the bus, I trip over an uneven brick and my bag goes flying.*

"Goddamn it!" Now I have to scramble to pick up purse crap strewn across my front yard. "Fuckety, fucking, fuck!"

If it's not obvious, my frustration isn't just about being late.

A hand appears in front of my face. When I jerk upright, my forehead collides with a sharp chin. "Ow!" I rub my head. "Jesus, Ben!"

"Sorry." He hands me a tampon and a Chapstick. Perfect. I snatch them away and stuff them deep inside my handbag. "What are you doing here?"

"Giving you a ride to work."

"You are?"

He hasn't given me a ride to work since we had sex. Ten fucking days ago. I figure it must've been so awful for him that he couldn't face me.

He jogs over to pick up a receipt that's flying across the grass. "Yeah. Uh. Sorry about the last couple weeks. The van was in the shop."

I side-eye him. "It was?"

"Didn't your brother tell you? I called and left a message."

"I didn't get any message."

He grabs my hand and pulls me toward the curb where the van waits, engine running. "C'mon, let's go. You're gonna be late."

Completely discombobulated, I somehow make it to the passenger side without tripping again. Before I know it, the engine's roaring. I instinctively grab the panic bar as Ben pulls out into morning traffic. Still running his words over in my head, I bleat when the van swerves to the right and into a parking space on a side street.

Before I can ask what the heck is going on, his mouth covers mine. I'm still braced on the panic bar, but his hungry kisses strip away the layers of anger and hurt that I've wrapped myself in since he disappeared on me.

Apparently, my hands don't give a shit about pride, because when the slam of a car door startles me out of the kiss, they're fisted in his shirt and have pulled him almost into my lap. Who knows what my mouth and tongue have been up to, but the pulse pounding in my nether regions tells me they were getting frisky.

When he pulls away, it's like ripping a bandage off an open wound.

He flops back to his own seat, eyes on the van's ceiling, hands in the air. "I'm sorry. I'm so sorry, Lucy. I've tried so hard to stay away from you."

"Wait." I brace myself in more ways than one. "Was the van in the shop or not?"

"It was. For a few days. But after that, I just—I couldn't be alone with you again."

"Why not?"

"Because... because this would happen." He gestures to the space between us and then grips the steering wheel, hard. Lucky van. "When Tony came home from boot camp last week, I couldn't even look at him without feeling guilty. I knew it was wrong to have sex with you, but I—"

"Whoa. Why was it wrong?"

"I took advantage of you. You were—"

"I asked you to have sex with me, Ben. And I'm eighteen, in case you forgot."

He drops his forehead to the steering wheel.

I shift in my seat, suddenly uncomfortable. "I guess... if you weren't into it, that's a whole other thing. Which I get; I mean, I don't know what I'm doing and"—I gesture to my lumpy thighs and belly—"I'm sure this isn't the sexiest body you've ever seen."

His eyes fly to mine, and he shakes his head. "No, Lucy. That is not it. You are... you're beautiful."

Anger, confusion and shame compete for top-dog status. Anger wins. "Then what the hell? Why have you been ignoring me? I thought you thought the sex was terrible but you were afraid to tell me!"

"That wasn't it." He faces front again, holding that steering wheel like the car might take off on its own if he lets go. "It was so good I didn't think I could be near you without touching you." His voice is so growly and low I can barely catch the words, but his intent is loud and clear. "Like right now. I just want to climb in the back and get naked with you."

I check out the back of his van. "Too bad it's full of cabinets, 'cause I'd be up for that."

He looks at me, blinking slowly.

"Ben, come on! I had an orgasm my first time out. Don't you think I'd want to do it again?"

He's looking at me with such shock that it's almost funny. "You don't feel guilty?"

"No, that's Catholic bullshit. I do not have a Fear of Flying, if you know what I mean."

He looks even more confused.

"It's a book? By Erica Jong? I'll lend it to you. I got it from Susan. Her mom lets her read all these cool books. The Sensuous Woman. Our Bodies, Our Selves. The Joy of Sex. I've been doing research."

His head moves slowly side to side. "So... you want to... do it again?"

"Have sex?"

He nods.

I smack him on the chest. "Duh! Why wouldn't I?"

"ARF!"

"Agh!" My eyes pop open. A familiar scent brings me crashing back to the present. "Oh. Thanks for the poop, buddy."

I shake my head, still hazy with memories, as I collect a sample. It's hard to believe that foul-mouthed, forward girl was actually me. It's like the summer I was eighteen is a chapter from somebody else's story. I think of that girl as Bad Lucy, but I was so free, so confident, so... sexy, even. It wasn't just the sex, though there was a lot of that. We had so many silly, stupid jokes. All the songs in every mixtape I made for him—for us—meant something to me because I listened with him.

Now, instead of dreams of college and being a vet, or of the next time Ben would make my body shudder with pleasure, my daydreams these days are filled with to-do lists. Get to the store after work, make sure my younger brothers Sal and Vinnie are on top of their schoolwork, ask my dad if he ever got his car inspected, take my mom's suits to the dry cleaner's. It's not like I'm my family's version of Cinderella. I like taking care of them. It makes me feel like I'm a better person. That pleasure junkie I used to be caused a lot of people a lot of pain. And one unrecoverable loss. Things have been better since I got her under control. For everyone.

And Ben? Ours was probably just one of many sexual flings for him. I'm over him, but that doesn't mean I won't get a little revenge by making him pay for a huge cartful of supplies at the pet store.

I look down at the dog as I open the back door. "Good boy. You did your job. You did your business, and I've got my head on straight. Thank you."

Pat Benatar's right. I'm no martyr, and there's no way Ben Porter and I can be lovers *or* friends ever again.

Chapter 3

"Our Lips Are Sealed" - The Go-Go's
Lucy's May the Force Be With You Mixtape, Song #7

BEN

Later that afternoon, I pick up the dog from the vet and when I open the passenger door to the van, he hops right in like he's done it a hundred times, which reminds me of Tony riding shotgun in this very vehicle—including the drive we took after we found out we'd have to audition for our first play.

IT'S A PERFECT FALL DAY. *There's a clear blue sky that goes on forever, and the air whipping through the open van windows is brisk but not cold. Tony and I are driving out Route 2, killing time till we have to go back to school. And to be honest, both of us need to calm down.*

Tony smacks the dashboard. "This is bogus, man. Just because Coach is doin' the nasty with Miss Barbetta, we gotta try out for the dipstick play." He finishes his rant by stomping a foot against the glove compartment.

I've got a good grip on the wheel at ten and two, so when I flinch, the van only swerves slightly. You never know when Tony'll yell or hit something. "Give him a break, Tony. She's wicked hot. And like he said, there are a lot more girls in the drama club than on a football team. You'll be scammin' in no time."

He puts his feet up on the dashboard. "Dude, they're all Joanies. And the guys are fags. I don't want people thinking I'm a fairy."

"Chill out, man. Since Coach is making everyone try out, no one's going to think that. And get your feet off the dashboard unless you're gonna clean it off."

"Your damn dad and this van. It isn't even the good van. It's his crappy, old one." He's grumbling, but he moves his feet and half-heartedly swipes at the footprints.

"Hey, at least I have something to drive."

"Yeah, yeah. So you can drive us to practice with the drama geeks. We're hosed."

Just a few weeks later, it's a different story. Tony can't wait to get back to school for play practice. Of course, he spends most of it making out with his leading lady. The stage manager's constantly having to hunt them down. They're experts at scoping out every hidden corner.

I'm in love too, honestly. Not with a girl. A girl settled into that part of my heart a long time ago. Of course, no one knows about that. Not even her.

Nah, what I've fallen in love with is this whole thing of being in a play. My goofing around suddenly fits somewhere. Plus, I can spend time with a bunch of people and feel like I'm part of something without worrying about getting tackled or elbowed or having to slide home to gain approval. Instead, I just have to make people laugh. Which, as it turns out, I'm kinda good at.

Every day, we Mechanicals—that's the name for the group of clowns in the show—go practice our parts with this student teacher—a hilarious guy— and then we go back to where the drama teacher rehearses with the rest of the cast and perform what we worked up. It's killer. We get 'em falling off their seats laughing every time. I can't wait to do it in front of a real audience.

Tony can't wait till we get our costumes. Not because of his, but because Tory, the girl playing Titania to his Oberon, talked the director into letting her not wear a bra under her already skimpy outfit. Tony's so stoked that he doesn't seem to notice he's playing the role of a fairy or be worried about the teasing that'll follow. He even stopped calling the drama geeks posers. He's so in love with Tory that she actually got him to memorize his lines—mostly in the right order.

When I pull up in front of his house, Tony's already halfway down the front walk. He swings into the passenger seat, mouth running. "Let's bounce. Time to get to rehearsal. You get to wear your dress, and Tory gets to leave her bra behind. My dick's itchin' just thinkin' about what's gonna happen at halftime." We finally learned to call it rehearsal instead of practice, but Tony refuses to call the intermission anything but halftime.

"You're such a horndog, Tony."

"Yeah, but she loves me anyway. I kid you not, that girl wants me."

I give him a look.

"She says if I get my lines perfect tonight, I can touch her boobs. And if I do the whole run perfect, we can get horizontal."

"For real?"

"For real." He laughs. "Dude, you're lucky you're funny. Otherwise, you'd be in deep shit for being caught on stage wearing a dress."

"Cheeuh. Totally." Even though I'm trying to be cool, I am a little worried about it.

"I'm so bad in this play that I'm fresh. I'm not a drama geek, I'm making being in the play cool so I'm a drama zeek."

"You wish, you asshole."

"Yeah. I know I suck." He sighs. "But Tory loves me anyway." He shoves my shoulder. Again, the ten and two save me. "You're really good, though. I gotta tell you, it takes some serious gonads to do what you're doing."

"Thanks, man. I was kind of wiggin' out about it at first, but now I'm stoked."

"Listen, if anybody gives you shit, you let me know. I'll have 'em eating their shorts." He turns up the stereo, which is playing "You Sexy Thing" by Hot Chocolate, the third song on the mixtape his sister Lucy made for me this week. Then he turns it down again. "Hey, this reminds me. What about that Letitia? She's choice. She's got some perky little ta-tas."

"Bite me, Tony. Letitia's nice." She's the only girl in the Mechanicals. I like her, but not like that.

"I'm not sayin' she's a slut. But you're with her every day. You should ask her out. We could have, like, a double date. I've been promising to take Tory out for dinner at Brigham's."

"Yeah, maybe."

And maybe I should. Since Lucy got recruited to work backstage, I've also been spending a lot of time with her... usually when Tony's off feeling up Tory. If I'm being honest here, Lucy has the best breasts in the whole show—they're literally awesome. Like, I'm full of awe when I get a chance to stare at them. Just the thought of being able to touch them has me hard. But I need to cap that. She may look eighteen, but she's only fifteen. And even if she was my age, she'd still be off limits.

"Hey space cadet, did you see that asshole talking to her yesterday?"

Sometimes it's like Tony can read my mind. *"Uh, no. Oh shit. Was I supposed to give Lucy a ride today?"*

"Nah, she stayed after school to work on the sets. But you gotta help me keep an eye on her, man. That stoner who works backstage with her was practically drooling over her. I mean, make me barf."

"Yeah, what a dickweed."

"If he gets too close, his dick's gonna be in the weeds. As in, no longer attached to his body."

"Totally." A sound escapes my mouth. I hope it sounds like indignation instead of terror.

MY HANDS ARE at ten and two, but I'm not driving down Route 2 any longer. I'm parked in front of my dad's house. Guess I got back home on autopilot during my trip down memory lane.

Up in my apartment, Puck bumps his head against my calf before scooting past me to run to my room, where he takes a running leap onto the bed. Turning around, he slaps his front paws low while his rump and tail stay high.

I wasn't kidding when I reminded Lucy that I don't know anything about being a dog owner, but this seems like an obvious invitation to play. Jumping on the bed, I roll him and pretend growl before letting him jump on my chest. He takes the hem of my sweat-shirt in his mouth, matching my growls. Before I know it, I'm howling with laughter. When I collapse back on the bed to catch my breath, Puck stretches out next to me, panting, belly up. I give it a rub and then pull him in next to me.

I haven't wrestled like this since me and Tony used to tackle each other in leaf and snow piles, ruining all our hard work but having a blast in the process.

I haven't laughed like this since... I don't know when.

All kinds of memories have been bubbling up today, not just of Tony and Lucy but of every time I went to the Minolas' house, which was pretty much as often as I could. Food tasted better there. Some-body was always yelling or laughing or crying. Mrs. Minola's hugs could squeeze the breath out of you. At my house, everything was quiet—had been since we'd moved here from my grandmother's, where we'd lived after my mom's death. When Grandma died, too, it was like my dad kind of gave up.

I'm a little afraid he's going to give up now.

Puck sighs next to me. Hm. My dad. "I guess we ought to make sure it's okay with the old man for you to be here, huh?"

Knocking on the kitchen door as we enter the house, I call, "Dad?" The lingering scent of Hamburger Helper Beef Stroganoff greets us. I'd recognize it anywhere, along with Shake 'N Bake chicken. I can't imagine eating that crap now. "You home?"

I follow what sounds like a baseball game to the den, where my dad's snoring in his Sofa with a Secret from Jordan's furniture. At least there isn't a cigarette burning in the ashtray. He finally gave up smoking a few years ago after one of his employees tossed a butt and almost set the shop on fire. The doctors said quitting probably kept the heart attack from killing him. Still, it'd been close. When I got that call back in June, I cabbed straight to the hospital from the airport after taking the red-eye from LA. Seeing him in that hospital bed scared the shit out of me.

He looks better now, but nowhere near as vital as the man who raised me. The man I just assumed would always be there for me. By avoiding the Minola family, I'd inadvertently avoided him.

Maybe all that needs to change.

I should probably let him sleep now, though. He had a long day today at work, out courting potential customers to give them estimates, something he doesn't trust anyone else to do. He can meet Puck tomorrow.

"Come on, pup, let's go outside," I whisper. Before we make it out the door, my dad lets out a loud snort, which sets off the dog.

My dad struggles to sit up straight. "What the hell is that?"

I try to shush Puck, but he keeps barking. He just doesn't listen to me like he does to Lucy. "It's a dog, Dad. He showed up at the apartment this morning." When I pick him up and wave his bandaged paw, he finally quiets. "I'm keeping him until he gets better and I find his owner. If it's okay with you."

My dad looks around the spotless, orderly room where built-in shelves and oak floors gleam. "Long as you clean up after him."

"Oh, sure." I shift the dog in my arms, trying to get him to stop wiggling. "So, you feeling okay?"

"I'd feel better if the Sox would score."

I nod at the TV. "They're up by six."

He grunts. "You can never be up by too much."

"I think I'm going to take him for a little walk. You want to come?" I should get that run in, but I doubt Puck's up for that. Getting my dad to exercise a bit would be worth taking the day off.

"Nah, I gotta watch till the end."

"Come on, Dad. The doctor said you need to get regular exercise."

"I was up and around all day, in and out of the van, climbing stairs. Speaking of which, I went over some things with the bookkeeper today. She said you haven't cashed any of your checks."

I put Puck down and straighten the leash. I've been avoiding this discussion. "Dad, I'm just helping out."

"But you're missing work while you're here, right?"

I don't want my dad to worry about me, but it's embarrassing to talk about the kind of money I make modeling. Plus, I am working at the theater. My weekly salary there wouldn't cover a dinner out in Los Angeles, but he doesn't need to know that. "I got a subletter for my place out west, and I have savings. You don't charge me rent, so I don't feel comfortable taking money from the shop. Can we just call it even?"

He frowns. "Well, that brings up another thing I wanted to ask you about. Barney upstairs was asking how much longer you're staying in the garage apartment. He needs to store some stuff."

My dad is essentially recovered, so I don't really need to stay. My agent would be happy if I got on a plane the minute *Romeo and Juliet* closes at the end of the month. I'm not quite ready to go, but I don't want to screw things up for my dad's paying tenant. "Well, I haven't decided. I don't have to be back until November, so I was hoping to stay a bit longer. But I guess if Barney needs—"

He waves a hand in the air. "Nah, it's fine. I'll tell him to put his crap in the basement. If you're staying into the fall, we'll have to do something about a heater out there. That's what had me moving the office inside the house in the first place, you know. It's drafty out there in the winter."

I didn't know. I never asked why my dad had moved his desk into my old bedroom and my stuff out to the garage apartment. I just enjoyed having my own space when I came home from college for holidays. What a self-centered little asshole I am. "Okay. I'll look into it."

"I can get a deal on some insulation we can put up and maybe some new windows. If you're really staying."

"Yeah, I'm in no hurry to get back."

His scruffy brows rise.

"I mean it, Dad."

"You're sure you're not putting your career on hold because of me? I don't want you to do that. I'm fine."

His grouchy tone is most likely fueled by frustration with his own vulnerability. Which I get. I've been there.

When I was a kid, I wished I was a real member of the Minola family, rather than just an extra at their table. They were a three-ring circus that I wanted to run away with.

But this crotchety old guy would do anything for me. So whether he likes it or not, I'm sticking around until I have to go back. It's not like being away from LA is a sacrifice in any way except financially. The overexposed flash of my life there is colorless in its own fashion.

Then I remember something. "Actually, there's a Shakespeare Boston meeting tomorrow about the next play. I'm thinking about trying out for it, if it's okay with you that I'd stay longer."

"Of course, you're always welcome." He waves me away. "Now get outta here. Gotta watch the end of the game."

"Okay. Good night."

I hadn't planned to audition until the words came out of my mouth, but it's the obvious thing to do. It'll give me a reason to stay and keep an eye on the old man and maybe even figure out a way to make things right with Lucy.

Plus, now I have a dog to take care of.

"Come on, buddy. Let's go for a walk around the block."

I HEAR her before I see her. Her xylophone-like laugh echoes throughout the Pet Palace. Puck seems to recognize it too, since I doubt it's the smell of catnip that has him pulling me toward the feline supply aisle. His feelings for Lucy are a lot less complicated than mine.

Rounding an endcap stacked with toys, we find her. She's got a hand on the upper arm of a good-looking guy, probably in his late thirties. Maybe she offers personal shopper services to all the vet clients. Or maybe she's dating this guy. Heck, maybe she's married to him.

The green-eyed monster raises its ugly head. I inform it that it gave up all claims to Lucy when I walked away from her. As an old family friend, I should be glad to know that she found love and happiness elsewhere.

I just can't seem to muster that feeling. I still want her for my own.

If only I deserved her.

We'd all be better off if I just exit as if pursued by a bear, so I tug on the simple leash the vet's office let me keep. Unfortunately, Puck has his own plan. Three little yaps from him catch Lucy's attention. Her eyes spark with irritation at me, but she squats and holds out her arms to the furry weasel who breaks away to shower her with kisses.

I nod at the other male human, keeping things civilized, but when he squeezes Lucy's shoulder I have to shove my hands in my pockets to keep from batting his hand away from her. His smile is smug as he says, "This must be your client. Thanks for your help, Lucy. I'll tell the girls you say hello."

Lucy waves goodbye as he heads for the front of the store, but Puck's got her attention now. "Hello. How are you, my little man?"

Hands itching to touch her, I step closer. "Guess you guys bonded today."

"Oh, yes we did," she coos. "Over worm medicine and shots and a flea bath. Lots of fun. And lots of treats."

Puck agrees with a sharp bark.

"You were a good boy, weren't you?" She points an index finger in the air. He sits immediately, and she gives him a treat. Then she points at the floor. "Down." He drops, mouth split in a big doggie smile.

"Wow. You taught him that today?"

"He's pretty smart."

"Didn't you used to teach dogs tricks when you pet-sat for them?"

"Yeah, I used to watch a show on PBS about dog behavior, and since we couldn't have a dog, I experimented with the neighbors' pets." She shakes her head, grinning. "Sometimes they were a little too surprised at the results."

Her smile is so addictive that I just keep going, even if a trip down memory lane is dangerous territory. "I remember the... who was it? The Petersons? Didn't you teach their dog to play dead on a cue or something?"

"Oh my gosh, I forgot all about that. After they came home, the kids were playing cops and robbers one day, and thought they'd killed their dog!" If her smile has my heart pounding, her laugh has it bursting from my chest. "The Whitsons, on the other hand, were so happy I got their dog used to the ceiling fan that they paid me an extra fifty bucks. That dog was so afraid of fans that the whole family would just sit and swelter—until I showed up with a solution."

"You should hire yourself out as a trainer."

"Pfft. That was just me as a kid messing around. Plus, I wouldn't even know how to begin running a business like that." Her tone cools, and her expression is back to business. "Anyway, what do you need?"

She's here to help me out with the dog. That's it. No need to make a scene begging for her forgiveness here in the aisles of the Pet Palace. "That's why you're here, remember? I have no idea. I'll put signs up around the neighborhood once I get a chance to develop a picture and go to the copy store, but I'll need stuff to keep him for now."

She levels a look exactly like one her mother would give Tony and me when we were in trouble.

I raise my left hand and place the right one over my heart. "I promise I won't take him to the shelter or abandon him. I wouldn't do that."

Some retort blooms behind her eyes—one I'm sure I deserve—but she presses her plush lips into a hard line and snaps her fingers. "Let's go, Puck. To the dog section. Actually"—she spins toward the front of the store—"let's get a cart. You're going to need it."

As she leads us up and down the aisles, my eyes feast on the Lucy smorgasbord. A scrunchie attempts to contain her wavy, brown hair, but escaped tendrils frame her heart-shaped face like a stylist placed them just so. Her olive-tinted skin glows with a natural flush of pink not even the best makeup artist could achieve. When she catches me staring, her brown eyes flash with temper, so I force my eyes to the cart, which is already filled to the brim with dog stuff.

I'm pretty sure I would've spent far less had I asked a shop employee for help, but I don't care. Time with Lucy is worth any price, though I don't know how much longer I can keep everything I'm feeling reined in. My hand actually shakes as I open my wallet to pull out my credit card.

The cashier studies my card and then peers at me through gravity-defying bangs. "Can I see an ID, please?"

Dammit, not now. Gritting my teeth, I hand over my license.

"Ben Porter?" She flutters her lashes at me after she hands it back. "Are you the Ben Porter that's in the"—I hold my breath and wait for the inevitable—"you know, the ads on the billboards? With you just in"—she lowers her voice to a whisper—"your underwear?"

Lucy barks out a laugh and answers for me. "Are you kidding? Ben's a carpenter from right here in Arlington." She shrugs, shoving toys and brushes and treats in bags. "It's a pretty common name."

The cashier continues to check me out. "I guess." Leaning in, her top falls open to reveal not only her cleavage but her spray-on tan line as she presses the receipt into my palm. "I hope you'll be back soon, Ben Porter. From *Arlington*." She must be a local because she says our town's name like it's missing the *r*.

Lucy swings the cart toward the front door. "Thanks, Chelsea!" I scoop up Puck and follow.

Outside, she stops abruptly. A breath shudders down her torso before she wheels on me. "What the heck? You're an underwear model?"

"Uh, yeah. I was. Well, I guess I am. I'm still under contract. It's not *just* underwear."

She looks me up and down. "Billboards?"

"Yeah. I'm sure you've seen them. They're... around." I wear actual clothes in some of them, but the Callum Keen logo on the waistband of the underwear always manages to peek out. And my chest is always on display.

She narrows her eyes at me. "How long have you been back in Arlington?"

I have to look away to think straight. I flew back mid-June after my dad had the heart attack and it's almost the end of August now. "Uh, a couple months?"

"Two months? And you haven't come by?"

"Honestly, I didn't know you guys still lived in that house. Also, I didn't think…" I can't seem to get the words out. Her brother would be alive if it weren't for me. Why would any of them want to see me?

"What, you're too fancy for us now?"

My eyes fly to meet hers. "No Lucy, that's not it at all." I swallow around the boulder blocking my airway. "This modeling thing is not something I sought out. I went to LA for my last semester of college. I was going to do that even before the accident. Anyway, I was there and… It's a long, boring story, really. I'm so sick of talking about it."

"Hm." She pokes a finger into my sternum and steps in close, her touch boring a hole right through to my heart, even as her blazing eyes sear it. "Maybe we should talk about how you haven't contacted me once in seven years? Would that be more comfortable for you?"

Her chest heaves. Her lips are tantalizingly close. Her heated gaze drops to my lips.

Is there any way in hell that a kiss would be welcome right now?

An excited bark from Puck breaks the moment before I can do or say anything and she bends down to talk to the damn dog. "Good luck, boy. I'm afraid you're going to need it." After one more squinty glare at me, she marches away.

Puck whines.

I want to do more than whine. I want to howl at the moon. Puck woofs out a bark that ends in a little "woo, woo, woo."

"Exactly. She's right, though. I'm an asshole." The dog sighs and looks at me like he's prepared to be disappointed. "I'll try to do better with you, though."

I load the gear from the cart into the van and then open the passenger door for Puck, who jumps in. His paw doesn't seem to be bothering him anymore.

Hopping into my own seat, I start the engine. Puck puts his paws on the dashboard and barks once. As I pull out of the parking space, I allow that it's nice to have somebody riding shotgun again. It isn't my best friend, nor the love of my life, but Puck seems to be happy with me.

And that's something.

I CAN'T HELP IT. *He's my best friend, but he's pushed me one too many times. One step too far. I look over at his face and catch that look—so smug —like he's got your number and he's not gonna let go. I'm so sick of that face. Sick of him bullying other people, bullying me, even bullying his brothers and Lucy. Someone's gotta shut him up for once. So I say it, the thing that will detonate our friendship.*

And it does. Tony's angry voice echoes inside the family station wagon. "What the fuck, man? She's my little fucking sister, and you've been screwing her? What kind of pervert are you? You fucking asshole. I trusted you!"

Then the impact. Screeching. Grinding. Spinning. We fly through the air like it's some kind of insane carnival ride. Weightless. Suspended between the floor and the ceiling of the car as it flips through the air.

Until we're not.

Everything goes black. Am I dead? I can't breathe, I can't see. But it's not like I'm trying to.

There's just nothing.

Nothing.

A sound, then. An awful, rasping, rattling sound. My eyes open. I don't tell them to. It's not dark. I'm not dead. Tony's face. Not yelling. There— right there—he's in my face again. But not. He's not there. Tony is gone.

Something hits me, something wet. It's blood hitting me. Hitting me hard. I'm hitting back. No. I'm pounding on the window. Trying to get out of the car. Trying to get away from Tony/not Tony. Away from the grotesque mask that was my best friend.

WAKING, heart in my throat, Puck whines next to me.

He's licking my face, and I grab him to run my hand through his fur and over his warm skin. "I'm sorry, I'm sorry, buddy," I whisper over and over again.

If only I could apologize to the family I broke.

Just because I lost my temper.

Just once.

But once was enough.

Chapter 4

"Reelin' in the Years" - Steely Dan
Lucy's Catch You on the Flipside Mixtape, Song #10

LUCY

When the door to the lab flies open and Deanna stomps in, I almost drop the slide I'm preparing. We call it a lab, but it's really more of a closet. Stuffed to the gills with a sink, a fridge, stacks of random supplies and a counter crammed with equipment, there's barely room for one person.

She closes the door and leans against it with a groan.

"Need to share?" I can't quite tell if I pipetted enough of the sample onto the slide, so I hold it up to the weak fluorescent light to find the edges. I'll know once I position it, but that's such a pain in the behind with our finicky old microscope.

"Yeah, if you don't mind." She doesn't wait for my permission. "The garage just called. It's gonna cost at least two hundred dollars to fix my car, and that's *if* they can find secondhand parts. I don't have that kind of cash lying around. I just asked Dr. Morrissey for a raise, and she was all, 'I'm so sorry Deanna, our budget is stretched thin, blah, blah, blah. We could maybe give you a bonus at the end of the year, la, la, la. I've been here ten years, I can do everything they can do except perform surgery, and I haven't gotten a raise since I don't know when."

I've seen what I need to on this slide. Eggs galore. This puppy is chock full of worms: roundworms, hookworms and whipworms.

"That sucks." My comment applies to both Deanna and the puppy. "There is a bright side."

"Yeah, what's that?"

I point to the slide. "You could be facing deworming meds and a series of disgusting poops."

She rolls her eyes.

"Sorry. What are you going to do?"

"Well, I have to have a car. The bus takes forever from Medford." She scrubs a hand over her face. "I'm gonna have to beg my cousin Barry to give me a loan and some shifts at his bar to cover it."

"I wish I could help. If I had a car, I'd lend it to you."

She rests her forearms on the counter, dropping her head. "The thing that kills me is that I know Morrissey isn't shitting me. With all the animals they treat for nothing and the people that never pay their bills, the budget *is* stretched thin. At least I don't have student loans to pay off like she does." Pushing away from the counter, she reaches for the door handle. "You're lucky you still live with your parents."

"Yeah, in my nunlike existence."

"Hey, you don't have to have a place of your own to have a little fun. With the money you save on rent you can afford it." She punches me lightly on the arm. "Anytime you want to go out dancing and buy me drinks, you let me know."

I spray disinfectant on the counter and wipe it down. "Last time we went dancing at your cousin's bar, you were the one fending them off with a stick. I was stuck with your other cousin, Gary, who would not take no for an answer."

"Yeah, he's a douche. But I have some other cousins you might be interested in. Larry's not so bad looking. And he's a manager at Friendly's."

"Do they all rhyme?"

"Yeah. My aunt had a thing about it. Or just pick some guy up. We could find you somebody to get your rocks off pretty damn quick."

When I first dropped out of school and went back to work, I went out with Deanna a lot. Did a lot of partying, had a lot of meaningless sex. But it didn't help. It made things worse.

A hand clap from Deanna interrupts my thoughts. "Speaking of sex, I gotta get out there and prep our afternoon spays. Thanks for letting me vent. Last time I went into an exam room angry, a dog took a chunk out of my ass. Not that my ass can't stand to lose a few chunks."

I laugh. "You and me both. Anyway, I hope it works out."

"It will. It always does."

I wish I agreed with her. Sometimes I even wish I could Pollyanna my way through life like I did as a teen. But that girl had no idea what life could serve up.

AFTER I EASE *open the front door, wincing at how its squeak echoes in the crack-of-dawn quiet of the house, I tiptoe to the stairs.*

"Lucy?"

My mother's voice is gentle, but it sends my heart to my throat anyway. Turning around, I make myself face her from the living room doorway. "What are you doing up, Mama?"

She doesn't look like she has the energy to get off the couch, but her eyes are blazing. "Wondering where my daughter is."

I shrug. "I told you I was going out."

She lifts her chin. "If you're going to make a habit of this, you're not"—a sob tries to escape from her throat, but she swallows it back—"you're not welcome to live here anymore."

"You're kicking me out?" I have been kind of wild since moving back home, and my mom would not be happy to hear that I don't even know the name of the guy I screwed and did coke with last night. But I can't believe she'd actually make me leave.

She takes in a deep breath and lets it out, her eyes on her clenched fists in her lap. "I can't take it any longer, Lucy—not knowing where you are, when you're coming home. If I'm going to hear from the police or the hospital that my daughter's been in an accident. That she's dead." She looks up, her eyes brimming with tears. "We can't go through it again."

Part of me wants to roll my eyes and yell. Tell her that it couldn't happen again because I'm the reason it happened in the first place. But I can't. "Does Papa want me out too?"

"I don't want you to leave, Lucy. And no. So far, your father doesn't know that you've been out until the wee hours most nights of the week. He goes to bed early." She shakes her head. "Sometimes he leaves for work before you get home."

The judgement in her voice pisses me off, but before I can come up with another justification for my irresponsible behavior, she cuts me off with a hand in the air.

"I know it's the time of your life where you need to... sow your wild oats. But I can't sit by and watch you risk your life. So it's either stop it, or do it where I can't see it. I'm sorry, I just... can't."

It's not her words that get me. It's the haunted look in her eyes that twists the knife of guilt and shame in my gut. And the fear that she's right. Maybe I'm courting death, hoping that it'll take me away from the pain I've been drowning in since my brother died on the way to pick me up from college.

But she's also right. If I went the same way, it'd kill her.

So I decide to stop.

POUNDING on the door brings me back to the present.

"Lucy, what the fuck?" Cindy's voice comes through the closet door. "Did you not hear the bell? You're up in exam two, and we're crazy busy out here."

Rushing to reel in my emotions as I stow away the time—my past echoing the Steely Dan song—and get out of the lab, my scrub pocket catches on the door handle and rips. "Goddamn it!"

I slap a hand over my mouth. I haven't taken the Lord's name in vain for years. That morning when I crept home smelling like alcohol and cigarettes and sex with some stranger, I vowed never to take that path again. Shaking like a wet dog, I force myself back to the present.

What the fuck, Lucy, is right.

Sorry, God. At least I didn't say it out loud. That's the best I can do today.

Chapter 5

"Every Little Thing She Does is Magic" - The Police
Lucy's Totally Tubular Tuneage, Song #3

BEN

Zoning out in front of the Boston University theater building as I wait for Puck to do his business, I'm startled by a clap on the shoulder and a resonant voice in my ear. "How now, you whoreson peasant! Where have you been these two days loitering?"

Even though I'm usually up this early, my brain's not as quick with the Shakespeare as Will Talbot's. "Loitering" is the only word that sticks in my brain. "Um, am I late? I thought the meeting was at eight."

Will shakes his head. "You answer: 'Marry, sir, I carried Mistress Silvia the dog you bade me.' Or Launce does."

I puff out a laugh. "Not every actor has your freaky ability to recall Shakespeare quotes at the drop of a hat. I'm lucky I can get all of Romeo's lines out every night."

"Ah, nobody listens to you once you take your shirt off, anyway."

"Right, thanks for the reminder."

He opens the front door to the theater building and gestures for us to precede him. "Are you dog sitting or something?"

"Nah, he's just a stray. Showed up at my house yesterday. I have to put up some signs to see if I can find his owner."

"Well, when I walked up, it looked like you were either a crazy person talking to a dog or an actor working on his Launce audition. I'm hoping it was the latter." He gestures to the oversized Army jacket I grabbed on my way out this morning. "You're even dressed for the part."

"Oh, this is my dad's from when he served in Vietnam. I borrowed it so I could sneak Puck into the meeting. Like this." I scoop the dog up and tuck him inside the roomy coat, but he pokes his head back out.

"Nice name." Will scratches underneath the dog's chin. "Are you a 'merry wanderer of the night'?"

"Hobgoblin is more like it."

Our steps echo in the empty hallway. "I'm glad to hear you're auditioning at all. I was worried you were moving back to LA."

Puck wriggles against my chest, and I readjust his position. "I don't know what I'm doing, to be honest, but I'm not quite ready to go back. If I'm in the show, I'll have an excuse to stick around and keep an eye on my dad."

It might also give me a chance to mend fences with Lucy, but I'm not jinxing that by talking about it. "So, who are you auditioning for?"

"I'm just gunning to play Hamlet this winter, so I'll take whatever they give me."

"I guess I'll think about the Launce thing. Though who knows how long I'll have the dog. If I find his owners, I'll have to give him back. Speed would be fun, actually. I always think of Launce as an old guy."

Will opens the stairwell door. "I don't think his age is indicated in the text anywhere."

"Well, you would know." I scratch the stubble I let grow on days we don't have shows. "I can't say I'll be too sad to put Romeo to rest."

I shudder. The moment the costumer suggested taking my shirt off in one of my scenes, I knew it was a bad idea, and oh, had I been right.

Will's grin mocks me. "What, you find girls screaming about your chiseled chest and abs distracting?"

I grunt. "Just a little."

Will punches me on the shoulder. "Come on. Women throwing themselves at you after the show? You gotta love that."

I'm not sure if any of this needling is fueled by resentment. "Not really. And you've seen it. It's actually humiliating. I always thought that it was ridiculous when women complained about getting catcalled. Like they secretly enjoyed the attention? But now I get it. It makes you feel… exposed."

Will sighs dramatically. "It's tough being an Adonis, I guess."

"Yeah, right." I hesitate outside the meeting-room door. "Hey, I'm not sure Puck's allowed in here, so I'm just going to sit in the back and hope nobody notices." At the sound of his name, the dog's nose pokes out again.

Will laughs. "Good luck with that."

I gently ease the curious snout back in. "Stay," I whisper, wishing I was good at making him behave. Maybe I just need to carry treats around like Lucy does. Or is it just her? Lyrics from that Police song filter into my mind. Everything she does certainly does turn me on. To me, *Lucy* is magic.

"Excuse me." A woman—I think she played Helena in the first show of the summer season—is trying to get through the doorway.

"Sorry." I step back to let her enter and then duck in behind her.

She whispers, "Cute dog."

I shake my head and button the jacket up to the top as I ease into a chair along the back wall. Craning my neck, I check out the refreshments table, wondering if I can keep Puck quiet by feeding him snacks.

Deb O'Rourke, Will's housemate and the company costume designer, startles me and gets a yelp out of Puck when she swoops in for a side hug. She shifts away to look me up and down. "You okay?"

"Yeah, I'm just—"

I break off when Puck tries to get comfortable on my lap inside the jacket. Deb makes a face like she's Ripley and I'm Kane and an alien might erupt from my chest at any moment. "That's a pretty interesting jacket you've got there."

"It's a dog," I whisper. "I'm trying to keep him hidden."

"Oh, I want to see." Then she whisper-yells across the room at her girlfriend, another designer. "Pam! Come here!"

"Deb," I moan, crossing my arms over my lap.

She stands in front of me, hands on hips. "Don't worry. It'll just look like I'm interested in your coat. Which I kind of am, actually. Did you hear we're doing a sixties military thing for this show?"

Prying my arms open, she pulls me up, dumping Puck at my feet. "Oh my god. He's adorable!"

Pam's Brooklyn accent cuts through the crowded room. "Yeah, yeah, pretty much everyone in town knows Ben's adorable. I mean, those billboards are everyw—Awww!"

Puck's on his hind legs to greet his new fans. I slump back in my seat, giving up.

Pam picks him up. "Who is this?"

"His name is Puck."

"Puck? How could you name a dog after something that gets hit with a stick? That's awful."

Deb swats her. "No, dummy, like the fairy in *Midsummer*." Deb kisses the dog on the nose. "It fits him."

"Oh, that's better." Pam nods. "Hey, did you bring him for *Two Gents*? I thought we were going with a puppet or, like, one of those leashes where it looks like there's an invisible dog."

Deb looks behind her to the other end of the room, where the director sits. "I don't think it's been decided yet." Deb takes Puck from Pam. "Are you a smart puppy? Are you? Are you gonna be a famous actor?"

After tucking him under her arm, where he pants happily, both designers turn the spotlight on me. Pam cocks her head, looking me up and down. Deb puts Puck on my lap and steps back. They look at each other, back at me and then at each other again.

Deb crosses her arms and nods briskly. "We think you should audition for Launce." She draws a frame in the air around Puck and me. "I like this look. A lot." She points at my two days' worth of beard. "This, too—grow it after *Romeo and Juliet* closes. It'll make you look older as well as… rougher."

Pam nods. "Yup. Let's go tell Nick. We'll make him love it too."

"Wait, I—" Before I can say that I'm not sure I'm confident about auditioning for one of the more difficult clown roles in the canon, the women bookend Nick Dorset, the director of *Two Gents*.

Eyes, framed by glasses so big they're almost comical, study Puck and me while Deb excitedly shares her "design" ideas, which are more than likely also directorial ideas. She's good at getting her way, but Dorset seems like he might be tough to bully. He nods, his wide mouth stretched into a polite smile. When Shakespeare Boston's artistic director calls the meeting to order, Nick raises a brow at me before giving her his full attention. Thankfully, no one seems to mind Puck's presence.

As the meeting drags on, the few bits of Launce's dialogue I know play through my mind. It would be a challenge. It's been a long time since I've felt funny. I was pretty good at getting laughs in high school and college shows. That goofy guy hardly feels like me anymore, while Romeo's tragic tale seems to fit me like a second skin.

I wasn't confident about acting at all when rehearsals started, but my rusty acting skills came back quicker than expected. Maybe it'd be the same with clowning.

Puck has settled down now that he's not trapped in my coat. He drops his chin on my knee and huffs out a soft sigh.

And then it hits me.

If Puck were to play Launce's dog Crab in the show—which is a possibility, even if I play a different character—he'd need some train-ing. I just happen to know someone who is very good at training dogs. As Puck's current caretaker, that would mean Lucy and I would have to spend time together.

These thoughts lead to other thoughts. Memories of Lucy. Memories which have me shifting Puck onto the chair next to me and crossing my legs to ease the tightness in my groin.

"BEN! Hi! Want to see pictures of the baby animals I bottle-fed this summer?"

Lucy skips down the back steps of the Minolas' house, boobs bouncing under a thin tank. Tony and I are leaning against the old trampoline in the backyard, trying to work up the energy to ride our bikes to the community pool.

I swear that when Lucy left to go away for the summer, she'd been more... spherical. Adorable, but still the little kid that was part of the neighborhood gang, the little pest that followed her big brother everywhere.

Now? She turned fifteen while she was at her cousins' up in Vermont, but really, it's like she skipped teenager and went straight to totally hot babe. The sight of her has my dick throbbing in my shorts. Part of me's praying she'll clamber up and jump on the trampoline so I can feast on the sight of her shapely thighs and ass and those boobs—

A sharp elbow catches me in the ribcage. "Ow! What the fuck, Tony?"

His eyes shoot lasers at mine.

Yeah, I'm probably drooling as well as staring at Lucy, but I'm only human.

When she tugs on my hand to pull me closer, Tony practically growls in my ear. She's saying something about lambs and kids and calves. Reminding myself that my eighteen is really a lot older than her fifteen, I try to sound normal as she snuggles in next to me to flip through Polaroids.

"Oh yeah, they are cute!" Focus on the baby animals, dickweed, not the smokin' heat of your best friend's little sister. "Wicked cute!"

She sighs, and my head bobs, following the swell of her chest.

"It was so fun taking care of them. And it was so hard to leave. I'll miss them." Her lush lower lip juts out in a pout. All I can think about is kissing

that pout away. She arches her back to tuck the photos in her shorts pocket, and I think I might die, her breasts are so perfect. Before I know it, she's squeezing me in a side hug and I'm sucking in my belly, suddenly self-conscious at how soft it is. "I'm gonna go show these to Marianne. See you later!"

As she disappears around the side of the house, I hang onto the trampoline to keep myself from following her. "Man, when did Lucy get hot?"

Before I even clock that I said the words out loud, Tony's got me by the front of my shirt.

"Don't ever say anything like that again. She's my little sister, you asshole." He pushes me away and stalks off. Before disappearing into the house, he points at me. "Don't even think it."

A HAND CLAP from the production manager signals the meeting's end and drops me back to the present, my heart thumping heavily in my chest. Puck whines, and I pat his head absently.

The tall blonde plops down next to us. "Hello, little dog." Puck immediately abandons me for a new audience. She scratches behind his ears with one hand and holds out the other to shake mine. "Hi, I'm Isabelle—Bella—York."

"Right. You were Helena in *All's Well*. You were great. I'm Ben."

"Thanks. Yeah, and you too—nice work with Romeo. I guess you're new to the company too?"

"Yep, *R&J* is my first."

She nods and looks around. "Are you hanging around now, or…?"

I check my watch. "No, I actually have to get to work."

"Great, I'll walk out with you."

Man, I hope she isn't going to hit on me. That would be so awkward.

At the door to the stairwell, Bella takes in a big breath. "So, I have a proposition for you." At what is likely a very clear look of panic on my face, she laughs and holds up a hand. "Not that kind of proposition, don't worry. I'm a single mom with no interest in—or time for —dating."

I shake my head, my face heating. "Sorry, I'm an asshole to even assume—"

"No problem—believe me, I know how it is."

I let her precede me down the stairs. "So, what's your proposition?"

"Well, I couldn't help but overhear Deb and Pam talking to you about auditioning for Launce, and—"

"That's their idea, not mine." Puck's scrambling down the steps, straining against the leash. Maybe he's finally decided that he needs to pee. "As you can see, this guy is not a trained actor dog or anything, and I haven't played a clown role in Shakespeare since Francis Flute in high school."

"I played Snug the Joiner in high school!"

"That's funny; we had a girl Snug, too."

"Well, hear me out. I was thinking of auditioning for Speed, myself. It's tough being the new girl on the roster in a Shakespeare company, or any girl for that matter. And I'm getting old." She catches my eye after I make a *pfft* sound. "Actor old. I'm thirty-two."

"You look way younger than that. Anyway, I'm twenty-eight."

"Yeah, but you're a guy. It's different for guys."

I almost argue that it isn't for models, but I don't want to go down that rabbit hole. It's weird, but being so far away from that world, I don't even feel like that's my job anymore.

Bella opens the stairwell door, and we both match Puck's brisk pace toward the exit. "Anyway, I can't play the young girls for much longer, but I'm not a matron yet. Helena was a lucky exception. It's hard to get directors to look at me for male roles, but I think Speed is possible. And I think we'd both have a better chance of convincing them to think outside the box if we come in prepared."

When I open the heavy doors to the outside, Puck makes a beeline for a patch of grass. "Sorry, nature's calling." I look over my shoulder at her. "So, you want to work up a scene for our audition and, what, do it together?"

"Yeah." She catches up to us. "All three of us. What do you think?"

"I guess it can't hurt."

We spend the next few minutes figuring out a time to meet, which isn't easy. She works for her mom, like I work for my dad, plus she has her kid's schedule and I'm still performing half the week. After exchanging phone numbers, I head toward the van, thinking again about asking Lucy if she'd train Puck.

Tony's words echo in my mind. *She's my little sister, you asshole.*

I ignored Tony's wishes in the past with disastrous results.

Maybe this is my second chance. A chance to make things better instead of worse.

FRIDAY MORNING, I'm on the stage of Shakespeare Boston's new winter home—a beautiful stone building that used to be a church— waiting for the signal to begin. For this callback audition, the lights in the audience are dimmed, but not completely dark. *Two Gents'* director whispers to the stage manager. A handful of others cluster near them in folding chairs, including Deb. She gives Bella and me a big thumbs-up.

We spent a couple hours rehearsing this scene, using the ping-pong technique I learned in a clowning class in college. Each of our lines is punctuated by a crisp head turn either to the other actor, Puck or the audience. It's like throwing a ball back and forth. I hope I remember the choreography because if we hit it right, I think it'll prove that we have what it takes to play this iconic pair of fools. All Puck has to do is sit still. Hopefully, that won't be too much to ask.

Glancing down at the dog in question, who for now sits calmly to my left, and over at Bella, who's bouncing on her toes to my right, I grip the walking stick I snagged from my dad's closet, an important prop. I'm wearing the Marine jacket and baggy cargo pants. Bella's convincingly boyish in wide trousers and a boxy top with her hair in a low ponytail, a black cap on her head, and no makeup on her face. Puck looks like himself.

"Right. Sorry for the delay." Nick Dorset's Northern Irish lilt fills the hall. "Let's see what you two—uh, three—have worked up."

Puck yawns loudly, which gets him a laugh from our small audience. Good way to start. I raise an eyebrow at Bella, and she nods. I exit stage left with Puck and re-enter to start the scene.

From the moment Bella/Speed greets me/Launce with "'Launce! By mine honesty, welcome to Milan,'" everything rolls along just as planned. We get laughs left and right.

When I say, "'Ask my dog: if he say ay, it will! if he say no, it will; if he shake his tail and say nothing, it will,'" Bella and I snap to Puck, who stoically ignores us. In perfect sync Bella and I look at each other, back at Puck, then back at each other. Bim, bam, boom. Finally, Bella looks straight at Nick to announce, "'The conclusion is then, that it will,'" earning a loud cackle from the director.

I'm riding the high only attained by making an audience laugh when disaster strikes. Just before the end of the scene, someone drops something backstage. Puck jumps up, lunges toward the wings and lets out a series of loud yaps. I get him back under control while staying mostly in character. We finish gamely, but I fear that all our hard work might have been undermined by the one canine flap.

"It went great," Bella whispers after we exit.

"Sorry about that," someone mumbles from the darkness.

"It's okay," I answer. To Bella I mutter, "If he's going to be an actor, he's got to learn to stay focused."

"I think we've seen what we need to, thank you both," the assistant stage manager calls out, dismissing us.

"Okay, thanks." Bella sticks her head around the curtain and waves as another pair of actors heads up to do their bit. I don't know them, but they look more the part. I'm not sure if having been in one show with the company helps us or not.

Back out in the hallway, I whisper an apology to Bella. "I'm sorry. I hope Puck didn't screw that up for you."

"Are you kidding? That was so fun. And I'm sure they get that he's a dog."

I set him on the floor, and he immediately flops onto one side and yawns. I wish I was so nonchalant about auditioning. "Well, yeah, but obviously something like that would be a problem in a performance."

Bella squats to pet him. "Yeah, but you haven't really trained him yet, right? How long could that take?"

"Honestly, I have no idea. I guess if I get the role, I can always have the empty leash as a backup, like they originally wanted. He's been so good, so far. I was getting excited about the idea of working with him. That's weird, huh?"

"No, not at all. He's a funny little guy. I mean, look at this face." After one last pat, she stands and squeezes my upper arm. "Listen, I've got to go. I have to change into girly clothes and doll up this face before I go read for Julia."

"Wow. I didn't realize you were called back for both roles. Good luck."

"Thanks. I've got some stiff competition in that fresh-out-of-college new girl, but hey, you never know." She smirks and trots down the hall.

I look down at Puck. "What happened back there, boy?" He just wags his tail. "Not sure if I should be talking to you or not. If I'm an actor preparing for a role, it's not as crazy." He almost looks as if he's considering an answer before he drops his head back to the floor. "Yeah, I wish we could just lie around until tonight's show, but it's back to work for us. We've got to get to the shop."

After a couple hours of heavy lifting and battling Boston traffic, I pull into the driveway back at home. As I climb the stairs to my apartment to grab some dinner before heading to the outdoor theater, the lively click of nails keeps pace with my heavier tread, a comforting sound I'm getting used to.

"Arf!" A week ago all his barks sounded the same, but I've learned that this one means he's more than ready for his dinner.

On the way to the kitchen, I notice the blinking light on the answering machine. Adrenaline has my heart racing and my gut dropping. It's always nerve-racking waiting to hear about an audition, but since I put up "Lost Dog" signs around the neighborhood,

I'm equally anxious that it might be Puck's owner calling to claim him.

Funny. Lucy worried I'd abandon this dog. Now, I don't want to let him go. I put off listening to the message, filling the bowl with kibble and giving him fresh water.

"Guess we have to bite the bullet, buddy. Fingers crossed for good news." He has no response, so I just push the button.

"Hullo, Ben. It's Nick. We'd like to offer you the role of Launce. Congratulations. Deb is pushing hard for Puck as well, but I'm not so certain that it will work. If you have a trainer who can assure me that he won't be out of control during a performance, I'll consider it. We don't have a budget to pay one, but we can offer a half page of advertising in the program. Let me know, but in any case, we're looking forward to having you and Bella as our clowns. Becky will be in touch with details. Cheers."

I release the breath I've been holding and laugh out loud. Not only am I over the moon to play Launce, but now I have an excuse to call Lucy. I have no idea what to do about the untold truths that still loom between us and I know it's selfish, but I want to see her again.

She might tell me to shove the idea of training my dog where the sun don't shine.

But that's a risk I'm willing to take.

Chapter 6

"Good Girls Don't" - The Knack
Lucy's Copacetic Shagadelic Mixtape, Song #6

LUCY

Saturday morning, it's hot and sticky for August. By the time I get to church, every crease of my dress is damp and my stocking-encased legs feel like sausages, so the cool and dark of the confessional is welcome. I kneel and make the sign of the cross just as the screen slides open and Father Signorelli says the usual greeting—in Latin, even though he's supposed to have switched to the post-Vatican II form. I'm glad our church does things the traditional way. When I went to the Newman Center the few months I was at UMass, getting general absolution didn't feel like enough, but the alternative they offered—sitting face to face to confess to a priest—was too embarrassing.

I dab my brow with a tissue before beginning. "Bless me father, for I have sinned. It's been two weeks since my last confession. These are my sins. I snapped at a coworker because she asked me some irritating questions, and I yelled at my brothers for leaving their dishes in the sink. I have been uncharitable toward an old, um… friend because I'm still angry at him for things he did a long time ago. I talked him into buying things he didn't need to because… because I wanted him to suffer."

"Hmm. Those are unbecoming behaviors in a young woman."

"Yes, Father. For these and any other sins that I cannot remember, I humbly ask pardon of God and penance and absolution of thee, Father."

"Do your rosary and say five Our Fathers for your penance."

I bow my head, say the Act of Contrition and do my best to focus as Father prays for my forgiveness.

When I step out of the box and into the incense-laden air, the weight of my sins doesn't lift from my shoulders like it usually does, probably because I neglected to confess the many, many lustful thoughts that've set up camp in my nether regions.

I guess you could argue that I'm preventing harm by omitting those sins because if Father Signorelli heard what I've been up to alone in my bed at night, he'd surely have a stroke.

WHEN I RETURN from my lunch break on Monday, I'm greeted by Cindy in full-on puppy mode.

"Oh my god, that Ben Porter left you a message, Lucy!"

Stowing my purse in my locker, I spend more time than necessary changing back into my scrub top. I spent the break running errands—picking up a prescription for my dad and stocking up on toiletries for the family while I was at the pharmacy. I might've also picked up a few magazines which might just happen to contain a few revealing photos of Ben. It isn't a sin to just look, right?

When I close my locker door, Cindy's right there on the other side. "Isn't that exciting?"

"Yes?" A balloon of hope floats up. I haul it back down to earth. No need to get all excited. He probably just has another question about the dog. I scan the corkboard where notes are usually pinned up. "Where's the message?"

She finally stops bouncing up and down. "He didn't call. He came in while you were out and I got to talk to him." She whispers this like it's the most exciting thing to have happened in weeks. Maybe it is. Although watching a dog yak up an entire package of tube socks last week was pretty entertaining.

"Oh. Okay." I keep my tone cool, with some effort. "What was the message?"

"He asked me to ask you if you'd train his dog so it can be in a play! I wish I knew about animal training! How did you learn?" She grabs my forearm. "Do you need an assistant?"

Not sure where to start, I just nod. And then shake my head no. By the time my head's circling, I realize something. "Did he leave a number?"

Cindy narrows her eyes. "Don't you have his number?"

I don't want to think about all this right now, so I exit the break-room. "I guess I can get it from his chart if it's not the same."

She's at my heels, nipping away with her questions. "Same what?"

"Um. Same everything. Number, house. Because he's like... famous now?"

"Are you sure you really grew up with him?"

"Yep. I'm sure I did."

Her smooth brow crinkles. "No offense, but you seem a lot older than him."

"He's three years older than me, Cindy."

"So, he's like mid-thirties?"

I stifle a sigh. Cindy's only eighteen, so everyone is old to her. "Just FYI, Cindy, I'm twenty-five."

"Not even! I thought you were way older than that."

My brows go up as I stare her down.

"I mean, like, in a good way. Like you majorly have your shit together."

"Uh-huh."

Three bells sound, indicating that an owner is in for a pickup. I'll take any excuse to escape from the interrogation, so I press the button indicating that I'll grab the post-surgical cat. "I'm not sure I'll have time, anyway."

She follows me. "But you were saying you were trying to save money for that certification course. If he's a rich model, charge him extra."

She's driving me crazy, but she has a point. How much money would it be worth to risk further stirring up the grief I thought I'd buried years ago?

Opening the cage to ease out a still groggy but now stitched-up and gonad-free cat, I whisper, "Hey, buddy, time to go home."

Cindy, still at my elbow, closes the cage. "When was the last time you saw him anyway? I mean, before now."

"Seven years ago." Until last week, the last time I saw him was at my brother's wake. But she doesn't need to know that. "Things... ended badly."

Talk about understatement of the year.

"Seven years! Lucy, jeez. Seven years ago, I was in elementary school! That's forever ago. Forgive and forget already." A single bell sounds, letting us know that a new client needs to be moved to an exam room. "Do you still want the cat discharge, or whatever's behind door number one?"

I hand over the cat. "I'll take the new patient." I don't have any ex-boyfriends left to surprise me, so I walk briskly to the waiting room, eager for a distraction. Whether it's an engorged tick to be removed or a puppy needing its shots or a busted-up tomcat, taking care of an animal is always preferable to listening to my inner monologue.

Deciding what to do about Ben will have to wait.

LATER THAT AFTERNOON while filling a prescription, I have to blow out a breath and force myself back to the present moment. Memories of Ben will not stop invading my thoughts. Even over the weekend, before Cindy dropped the "Ben wants you to train his dog" bomb, while I was nagging Sal into working on his college application essay instead of making yet another mixtape for his current girlfriend, songs from the many mixtapes I made for Ben played through my head.

Like the obvious mix of sex-themed songs I put in his boombox the day I made it clear that while good girls didn't, I would. I wanted to lose my virginity. With him. And do a bunch of other naughty things.

When I said: *"I just want to know what real sex feels like, how it works. I trust you, Ben."*

He asked: *"Don't you want to be in love?"*

Clearly meaning: "I'm not in love with you."

But did I care? No, I just barreled on. From Tony's warnings, I knew that once a guy gets going, he can't stop, so I took off my shirt to show off the lacy bra I'd spent a stupid amount of money on. From that point on, it was pretty clear he was into my body. But the only other thing I remember him saying was, *"Tony will kill me."*

Tony was his friend before he was mine. They spent way more time together.

I didn't listen. I just tried to remember everything I'd read and… brazenly seduced him. I didn't think about any consequences beyond getting pregnant—which I took care of by going with my friend Marianne to Planned Parenthood—because his touch was a match to my gasoline-soaked body. I couldn't get enough.

When it was all over, he was obviously distressed. All I could think about was doing it again.

He drops his forehead on a sigh. It rests briefly on my sternum, but then he's up and pulling on his boxers. He picks up my clothes and hands them to me. "You should probably get dressed too. My dad'll be home soon."

He paces in a circle, hands on top of his head. "I already feel guilty. Your mom—your parents—trust me."

"Ben, stop." I make him face me. "I wanted this. I trusted you. Plus, it feels so good. How can it be wrong?"

Oh, young Lucy. How can it be wrong to only think of yourself and your own pleasure? Let me count the ways.

Grrrr. I've lost count of the pills I'm dispensing. Again. After pouring them all back into the bulk container, I count out loud this time, write out the instructions and slap the label on the bottle. Slamming the meds cabinet closed, I head back into the exam room to give the owner of the energetic shepherd mix with a ripped-off dew claw instructions for keeping the bandage clean and teach the anxious woman how to give him the antibiotics. Luckily, this dog doesn't have a yellow or red sticker on his chart, so I don't have to worry about trying to sneak meds down the throat of a dog that'll rip me to pieces.

Then, making sure that my radiation monitoring badge is pinned to the lead vest, I'm off to take and develop X-rays for the Jack Russell terrier who jumped out of a moving car. I give him an injection to ease the pain, but we can't sedate him because he's looking shocky. I can't use sandbags to keep him still because the weight could exacerbate his injuries. Trying to keep him in place with the lead gloves on is like trying to sew on a button with oven mitts, so I finally just take off the left glove and run the x-ray without it. Who needs two hands, anyway?

Once I get him stabilized, I grab a SlimFast to get me through the rest of the day, since I did errands instead of eating on my lunchbreak. Before I can take more than a couple sips, a Persian loses his lunch all over my scrubs. Which does a good job of suppressing my appetite.

What won't go away? The jumble of feelings in my gut. There's no phone number anywhere on Puck's chart, so I'll have to go over to his old house to find out how to get in touch with him. So I can call him to tell him that I can't train Puck.

Or that I will.

I can't decide.

I could use the money for all kinds of things, like a certification course or even first month's rent for my own apartment. Or a down payment on a car. I just don't know if it's worth the price. I'm completely frazzled just knowing he's in town. Actually spending time with him could send me over the edge.

If I just blew him off completely, it'd serve him right, but he's a client of this practice and I'm a professional so I will stop by on my way home tonight and tell him… whatever I decide.

Chapter 7

"It's All I Can Do" - The Cars
Lucy's Totally Tubular Tuneage, Song #5

BEN

Monday evening, I'm holed up in my apartment studying commentary on Launce's speeches when I hear an unfamiliar knock.

My dad's polite double rap was always accompanied by "Dinner!" or "Ben? Phone call." But my dad hasn't tried to get up the stairs to my place since his heart attack. This person is aggressively pounding away, so I slump into the couch and peer over the top to see if anyone's peeking through the window.

Finally, the knocker gives up, and I flop onto my back. I just don't feel like dealing with a Jehovah's Witness or a kid pounding the streets for MASSPIRG. Puck seems to have other ideas, however, because he sails off the couch and skids to the door. When a musical "Hello, Puck!" penetrates the door, he barks excitedly.

Lucy.

Why is she here? Did I miss a message from her? Then I remember that I didn't leave my number. I wasn't sure giving it to the redhead at the vet was a good idea. She knew a little too much about me. My phone number is unlisted for a reason.

"Do you want me to train this dog or not, Ben?" Lucy calls through the door. Before I have time to talk myself out of it—or she alerts the entire town to my presence—I launch myself over the back of the couch and swing open my front door.

"Hey! Sorry, I was…" I look around my mess of an apartment, searching for the end of my sentence.

"Whatever." She charges in, and I shut the door behind her. "What do you need this sweet boy to do and when and what are you paying?"

Puck's attention ping-pongs back and forth like in the scene from *Two Gents* until she scoops him up. Fierce as ever—dog on one hip, hand on the other—she lifts her chin as if she's defying me to actually try and do this with her. "Ben?"

"Sorry. I… sorry. What were your questions again?"

"What do you need him to know how to do?" She spaces the words out like she's talking to an idiot, which I deserve.

"Right, so, I'm going to play this character that has a dog and talks to it in a bunch of scenes. I auditioned with him, and he was great, except when someone moved around backstage. Then he went crazy barking. Obviously, that would be a problem in a performance. So, I'd need him to… I guess, sit and stay and only pay attention to me? Is that possible?" She frowns and puts Puck on the ground. He sits and stares at her lovingly. "I'll pay you whatever your rate is, plus the theater can give you a big ad in the program, so that might help build your business. If that's something you want to do."

"When?"

"When what?

"When would we do the training, when is the play, when would you pay me?"

I raise my hands, palms facing her. "Listen, just so you know, I did call a couple of other people I found in the Yellow Pages. I figured you might not want to work with me. The only one who returned my call just went on about crystals and past lives. You're kind of my only hope." *And I'm prepared to beg if that's what it takes.* "I'll work around your schedule as much as I can. I have performances of *Romeo and Juliet* Thursdays through Sundays for the next couple weekends. Other days, I'm doing my old delivery route for my dad and—"

Her head shakes once. "Why?"

"Why what?"

"Why are you working for your dad? Aren't you like a millionaire or something now?"

"Uh. No. I'm not. I mean, the thing is—"

Before I can go on, she scrubs a hand in the air between us like she's erasing my words. "You know what? I don't want to know." Puck stands on his hind legs to nose at her hand. She makes him sit before petting him. "What kind of a deadline are we talking about?"

"Let me check to make sure I don't get it wrong." I jog to the coffee table to get my Filofax, relieved to have an excuse to get some distance between us. Lucy's scent—a delicate citrusy something—is bringing up some intense memories. Memories of things that happened right here in this very room.

I glance up at her after counting weeks on the calendar. "He'd need to be ready to perform in about a month." I trace a finger over the pages when I can't get a read on her expression. "We start rehearsal a week from tomorrow, September 6th. We open October 7th but techs are the weekend before that, so he should be ready to go by then. Is that doable?"

She paces the room. Puck's eyes track her, already as keyed in to her as I am. On the edge of an emotional cliff, part of me wants her to say, *No. I can't do that. I don't ever want to see you again.* But most of me—not just the baser parts—needs to take this leap.

She stops suddenly and faces me. "I can't guarantee anything. So you're going to need a Plan B if he doesn't pick up the training quickly."

"We will. We can just use an empty leash if we have to. It just won't be as good."

She squats and snaps her fingers. Puck trots over to sit in front of her, making it look easy. "This is going to take some time. Not just me with him, but you and me with him." She stands to point at me, a no-nonsense expression on her face. "You need as much training as he does, if not more. You'll have homework. Things you'll have to practice many, many times a day." She gives me a look I've seen before, only last time she was straddling me on the couch I'm currently gripping to keep my hands off of her. "And it's not going to be cheap."

My heart thumps in time with Puck's tail. "That's fine. Sure. When do you want to start?"

She checks her watch. "I've got to go home right now and make dinner. Lucky for you, I only work till three on Tuesdays and Wednesdays, so I can meet you tomorrow at four." She pulls a folded piece of paper out of her back pocket. "Here are my rates and a little description of the training process. If you want to do it, I'll need a check tomorrow."

Whatever it costs, I'll pay it. It's all I can do. I get it now. I've been waiting for her for seven years. I'm not giving her up this time around.

"Guess you and I are going back to school, buddy." I meet her fierce gaze. "See you tomorrow, Lucy."

A breathy little sound escapes her lips before she nods curtly, spins on her heel and bangs out my front door.

AT THE SOUND of the purposeful knock on my front door promptly at four the next day, Puck leaps off the couch and barks excitedly. I follow, wishing I could do the same. As I've been unable to settle on any task, the past hour has been an unproductive one. The past twenty-four hours, I've spent way too much time obsessing over memories.

Memories that I need to lock away pronto. She's doing me a favor. Yeah, I'm paying her, but she's not just making time for us in her busy schedule. She's choosing to rise above the store of resentment she must harbor toward me. I owe it to her to keep things professional. So, dialing my expression to a pleasant smile, I pick up Puck and open the door.

Before I can say a word, she sweeps past me. "One of the first things we'll need to work on is the *quiet* command. We'll start inside this afternoon, and you should also practice without distractions until you've got the *sit, stay, down* and *heel* commands, but—"

She breaks off, her eyes locked on the wall behind me. After she left last night, I unpacked a box I'd had sent when I decided to stay all summer, and put up a framed photo of Tony and me at age twelve, grinning proudly at the camera as we hold up a Little League trophy. And one of Lucy. It's kind of an arty shot, one I took of her sleeping. Her face is hidden under her hair, but her shoulders and neck are visible and it's obvious that she's naked under the tangled sheets. Only the two of us know that it's her.

She coughs once but doesn't say anything about the pictures. Instead she tosses her bag onto a chair and focuses on Puck. "Let's see what you know, little man."

She takes him through a series of commands. He responds to each without hesitation. Either someone taught him these things already, or she's a genius. I figure it's a bit of both.

Lips pursed, she looks me in the eye for the first time since her arrival. Pulling a Ziploc bag from a pocket, she tosses it to me. "It looks like you're definitely the one who needs the training."

I fumble the catch but manage to grab it before Puck does.

"This is to get you started, but you'll need to pick up more treats that size. We'll try to get to the point where he's cued either by a hand signal or maybe something in your dialogue onstage, but you should tell them you'll need a pocket in your costume for treats, just in case."

I grab the notebook I started for the show, which is already stuffed with images I xeroxed at the library, as well as other research. I flip open to a new page and write "CRAB"—the name Shakespeare gave Launce's dog—and then make a note about pockets. I show

Lucy a photocopy of an old Marine uniform. "I think I'll be wearing something like this, but I'll talk to the designer to make sure."

For the next hour, Lucy's in the bossy mode that Tony used to tease her about as she runs me through my paces. I'm a bit concerned about how she wants me talk to him: gruff and low for commands, high-pitched for praise. Both sound ridiculous. She assures me that once Puck and I establish a strong connection, I'll be able to drop the verbal cues.

Then she lays out my homework: practicing everything in no fewer than ten short sessions every day. "Normally, I'd say five is enough, but you've got a tight schedule and we need to get these solid so you can move on to hand signals as well as walking at heel. We'll also need to introduce distractions." She blows a sigh past her lips as she looks out the window.

All I can think about is kissing those lips. She kept such a quick pace during the lesson that I was mostly able to keep desire at bay. Before I can ask if she wants to hang out for a bit, she showers Puck with kisses, grabs her bag and practically runs out the door.

Shaking myself out of a lust-induced haze, I notice the check sitting on the kitchen counter. From my porch I yell, "Lucy! You forgot your check!"

"Whoops." She slaps her forehead, laughing, but by the time we're within touching distance, her guard's back up.

Willing myself to be patient with her, I hand over an envelope containing the check and two tickets to *Romeo and Juliet*. "Thanks, Lucy. I mean it." Our eyes lock briefly, then she turns toward the corner of the garage and walks down the old path cutting through the neighbor's backyard to her old house.

Either she still lives with her family, or she's stopping by to say hello. I keep her in sight as I climb the stairs back up to my place, but she doesn't turn back around. Not once.

"BEN! LOOK WHAT I'VE GOT," *Lucy calls, waving something over her head. Problem is, from up on my apartment porch, I've got such a good view of her bouncing cleavage as she jogs down the path that I can't look anywhere else.*

Once she skips up the steps, I can't get her inside fast enough, but before I can get my hands on her, she dodges away.

"Hang on, mister." She dangles a cassette in front of my nose. "I stayed up half the night making this mixtape to get us in the mood."

"You know just seeing you gets me in the mood. Just thinking about you."

"Well, maybe it's for me," she says over her shoulder with a flirty smile. After sliding the tape into my boombox, hips swaying in anticipation, she pushes play and slowly turns to face me as "Do Your Thing" by Isaac Hayes starts up.

Then she begins do her thing.

My dick was hard before—but her grooving with the sensual music as she slowly peels away her clothes... I think I might explode. I hang on, though, because I know if I do, I'll make her scream my name when I do my thing.

With her. Over and over again. All night long.

Chapter 8

"He's So Shy" - The Pointer Sisters
Lucy's Keep on Truckin' Mixtape, Song #4

LUCY

Back home after my first lesson with Ben, I sneak up the back stairs, avoiding my family. Without turning on any lights, I peer out my bedroom window and lean left until I can see the back of Ben's apartment. In the early dark, with his lights on, I can see him moving around inside.

How is it that he's been here half the summer, less than a hundred yards away, and I never noticed? I roll my forehead against the cool glass. How many times did I press my face to this very spot the summer I was eighteen, waiting for his lights to flick on and off, the signal that he was back in his apartment?

My fingertips go to my lips, a memory of the very last kiss we shared so present that I can't believe I thought I'd erased it. He held me tight in the shadow of his garage, my lips desperate to hang onto the feel of him, and I couldn't tell where he ended and I began. Then, like always, we had to break apart to pretend that we were just friends so he could walk me back down the well-worn path from his house to mine—the path originally created by Ben coming to our house to see Tony. I can still hear the creak of our back gate signaling Ben's imminent arrival. A sound that disappeared after the accident, when Tony—when the two of them…

Squeezing my eyes shut, pressing my lips together, I refuse to give in to tears.

Despite these efforts, the ache of missing Ben is joined by the ache of missing my big brother. The unfairness of it all. Tony didn't get to serve his country or even be a grownup before he was killed by that drunk driver. My mom and dad still keep track of that guy, but I don't like to think about him. I don't want to imagine him still alive, whether he's in prison or not. If I let those thoughts in, I'll drown— not just in sorrow, in rage. For all the losses that crash caused: my brother, my first love, even my parents, since they both disappeared, my mom into volunteering for Mothers Against Drunk Driving and my dad into work.

I eventually learned that the only way to keep my head above it all is to stay busy, keep my to-do lists full. There's the everyday stuff of shopping and laundry and cooking. Tonight, I should get on Sal to write his college application essay and make sure Vinnie's doing okay with his courses at the community college.

Which I'll do as soon as I can disconnect from this windowpane. I just can't seem to do that. Or let go of memories of life before the accident. Just seven years ago. I don't even feel like the same person anymore. Ben's different, too. Quieter, more subdued. He was always shy, but now he's… weighed down.

Cindy's tales about his life in California strain believability. He goes to Los Angeles and gets famous, then suddenly comes back to work for his dad? What could've happened to make that happen? I'm pretty sure I know what made him leave Arlington originally, although it's a bit egotistical to assume that he left just to get away from me.

I eventually manage to push away from the window and pull the curtains closed, but instead of going in search of my brothers, I turn on a lamp, grab my bag and pull out the magazines I bought. Flopping onto my bed, I flip through *Rolling Stone* until I find a photo of Ben. Tanned, taut muscles glisten above tight, low-slung white briefs. It looks like Ben and… not. It isn't just the extra abdominal ridges or bulked-up biceps. His jaw's harder, his eyes hooded. No goofy smile. This Ben is untouchable. Unapproachable.

Tossing *Rolling Stone* aside, I pick up *Us*. In the celebrity news, there's a picture of Ben in a tux on the arm of some actress. He's smiling at the woman, but again, it isn't the Ben I knew. It's like Ben playing a role.

Maybe this is who he is now, though. Hard to tell from the handful of interactions we've had, during which, if I'm being honest, I've been so angry I can't be sure I really saw him. Pretty sure I've been hanging on to my idea of the jerk who left me when I needed him most.

Do I still need him? My body screams that it *wants* him every time I get within arm's length. My eyes back on the magazine pages, I wonder if the sweet, funny boy I knew even exists anymore.

Enough mooning, Lucy. This is ridiculous. Chucking the magazine across the room, I can't believe I agreed to train his dog. Even charging him more than I thought he'd ever pay, it isn't worth having to spend time with him. I'll either find out that he has indeed become a self-involved jerk or that he is the same guy but isn't mine anymore.

Plus, if he wanted to see me, wouldn't he have contacted me when he moved back to town?

Somehow, I'm back at the window. His lights are off. He's probably out partying with whatever gorgeous model types live in Boston.

After spending fifteen minutes nagging my brothers, I return to my room and reach under the bed to pull out a box of stuff from high school. Digging through it, I unearth a photo. Me and Ben in his bed. He'd held the camera at arm's length to capture our smiles as we snuggled together. It's just as sexy as the one I saw hanging in his apartment, but in a different way. He gave it to me right before I left for my freshman year at UMass.

I'll always be here for you, no matter what, he said.

Only a couple of months later, he broke that promise.

I grab the *Rolling Stone* again and look back and forth between the pictures, unsure which image, which words, I want to believe.

THE NEXT MORNING, restocking supplies with Cindy before we open for the day, I can't seem to stop yawning. I haven't slept well lately.

"So, tell me what you know about Ben Porter," I say as casually as I can.

She spins to face me, hugging a box of gauze to her chest. "Why?"

I shrug. "Just curious. I can't believe that this guy I grew up with is famous."

She narrows her eyes at me. "Have you seen him again? Has he been back here? Was it on my day off? Why didn't you tell me?" She closes her eyes and squeals. "Oh my god, if I were in an exam room alone with him, I would not be responsible for what happened."

I'm not sure if I should tell her that I'm working with Ben. It might be something he wants to keep on the down low. But the theater did offer an ad in the program to give me credit for training Puck, so it's probably okay. "Yeah, he hired me to help out with training the dog he brought in."

"Oh my god! You are so lucky!" She grabs my forearm. "Do you need an assistant?"

I hate to disappoint her, but I don't need help and I'm not sharing. Not very Christian of me, but it's the truth. "Sorry, I don't think that would work."

She makes a pouty face and rips open another box. "I can't believe somebody famous could be from Arlington either—that's where you live, right? Or is it Medford?"

"Arlington," I say. "But why is he so famous? Is it just the ads?"

"Well, he was part of this group of models that Callum Keen, like, adopted. Or kept, almost like pets."

"What do you mean?"

"I forget how it all started, but he cast this group of men and women for this one campaign and put them all up in his compound up in the hills in Hollywood. The photos for the campaign were like, arty. Some famous guy took them." She groans. "So sexy. Like nothing anyone had ever seen before in a fashion ad. There was this one where there were two guys and a girl, mostly naked, in bed with the sheets all rumpled. I had that one up on my wall for the longest time. Ben was one of those guys. Oh, that chest." A shiver runs through her from head to toe. "Makes me feel all... *you know* inside."

"Wow." I ease a box of hypodermic needles out of her hands so she doesn't accidentally stab herself. "I'm not sure if I want to see that picture."

"You'd never look at him the same way again."

I wonder about that. Just being within five feet of him makes *me* feel all *you know* inside. Seeing him in bed with another guy and a girl would probably drive me to violence. Or at least to ripping up the photo. "So. it was just that they were in these famous photos?"

"Well, yeah, and they lived this really... what's the word where you, like, indulge in, like, pleasurable stuff all the time?"

"Hedonistic?" I suggest, all too aware of that kind of lifestyle myself.

"Yeah, that's it. So it was like orgies all the time. There were also reports that they were starving themselves to stay thin. And taking drugs." She holds out a hand and I feed her boxes of cotton padding as she continues. "There was a lot of drama. They all dated famous people, like actors and actresses in big movies and stuff. Ben is always in those red-carpet pictures at awards ceremonies. He looks just as good in a tux as he does in his underwear. I probably still have some of those magazines in my room somewhere. I can bring some in to show you if you want. There's one where this sheet is draped and you can see almost everything." She sighs. "Those pecs, those abs..."

"Uhhh..." It's a little weird to parse Ben's parts with Cindy, especially since I've seen Ben without any clothing more times than I can count. Of course, back then he wasn't all muscle. "Too skinny,"

Mama always said, heaping pasta on his plate. Of course, she said it when he was a pudgy twelve-year-old and when he'd grown like a weed to become a string bean.

"It must be kind of boring for him to live here with all the regular people," Cindy continues. "No big movie openings or anything."

I still can't picture Ben on a red carpet. "It's a different life here, for sure."

"He'll probably go back. I mean, the stuff I've read said that he's taking a break for 'family reasons.'" She closes a cabinet. "What do you know about that?"

I bend over, pretending to look through a big box of odds and ends. "I don't know. We don't really talk about anything except the dog. We're not close anymore, obviously."

I shrug and close the box, folding the flaps over each other carefully. It isn't easy to hide my feelings or what I know about Ben's life now. Which, admittedly, isn't much. He's doing plays, he's staying with his dad. Driving the delivery truck like he did in high school and college.

It's almost like he's hiding. But from what?

"Well, you tell him if he's bored and he wants a fun night out, I know all the good clubs. I'd show him a good time," she says, waggling her eyebrows up and down.

"I'll let him know." I do a final check of the cabinets. "Looks like everything's ready to go."

"Time to make the donuts." Cindy mimics the sing-song voice of the Dunkin' Donuts ad.

"Yep. I'll check the kennel this morning if you'll make sure the exam rooms are ready to go."

"Sounds good. And hey, you gotta get me some gossip on Ben. Find out if he was serious with any of those actresses. Or if he's"—she sighs—"available."

"I'll see," I throw over my shoulder.

Now I'm even more confused. I can't reconcile the Ben I knew with the guy Cindy just described.

As I dispense morning meds to the animals recovering from

surgery and check their suture sites for signs of infection, I remind myself that I'm training Puck for the money, and to challenge myself. As a trainer. That is all.

Static hisses over the intercom. "Lucy? Can you bring Ribsy to exam four?"

I push the talkback button. "Got it. On the way."

Grabbing a leash, I locate the patient—a scruffy mutt obviously named after the dog in the Beverly Cleary books, one of my favorites as a kid.

He limps a little as we walk to the front. "That's a good boy," I coo. When we reach the exam room and I open the door, Ribsy whines excitedly and his entire rear end wags. The waiting woman holds out her arms, her smile wide with joy.

Probably just what my face looked like when Ben would drive up seven years ago.

I CAN'T HELP MYSELF. *I wait by the window every afternoon like one of our patients waiting for its owner. When Ben pulls up in front of the animal hospital, I'm out the door, and hauling ass down the walk faster than you can say Jack Robinson and yelling "See ya tomorrow" over my shoulder to the receptionist.*

"Hey, gorgeous" is the greeting I get along with a tantalizing kiss so hot I don't know if I'm gonna make it home without ripping my clothes off. Only the blare of a horn from a car behind us can tear us apart.

And that's only the appetizer. For the full course, we have to get back to Ben's apartment. Thank god they keep me running at the animal hospital, otherwise I'd go crazy waiting until I could get naked with him again.

"You drive; I'll get the party started," I say, breathless from the kiss as much as from my sprint to get to him.

He laughs as he puts the van in gear. Shifting in his seat, he looks pointedly at his lap before pulling out into traffic. "As usual, you started the party the minute you got in the car."

Grinning, I dig in my bag for a mixtape decorated with colorful magic-

marker swirls. "I stayed up late last night to make this." I'm squirming now, remembering how hot the songs made me, even on my own. At least I know I'll have an outlet with my own personal sex god this afternoon. "I think you'll find it inspiring."

I slide the cassette into the stereo and press play. I can't not move to the funky beats of Grace Jones's "Pull Up to the Bumper." It's the only way I can survive the twenty-minute ride to his place. Yeah, I'm going to blow somebody's horn later.

Sometimes I can't believe we're getting away with this. Everyone thinks I'm such a good little Catholic girl teaching a motherless neighborhood boy how to cook.

How to sizzle, maybe. And oh, is he a good student.

My dancing might be a little distracting. We'll be lucky if we don't get into an accident.

Scratch that. We're lucky in every way. But mostly, we're going to get lucky minutes from now.

BY THE TIME I'm walking up the steps to Ben's place for our next session, I've banned all sexy thoughts and have a professional—that is, friendly but distant—smile plastered on my face. I've agreed to do this so I'm going to do the best job I can. One suggestion from Ben, however, and all my good intentions fly out the window.

"What would you think about going to Menotomy Rocks today? I've practiced a ton around here, on the sidewalks and the backyard. The field in the park might be a good place to branch out, don't you think?"

When we were little, my brother Tony and his friends spent just about every day after school playing at Menotomy Rocks Park. I usually tagged along. Sometimes another girl would join us. Sometimes the boys just had to put up with me because I was Tony's little sister.

One day Ben joined us. He was the new kid. Tony pulled him into the group, and he never left. Well, until he left and never came back.

"Lucy?"

"Uh, yeah. Sure. That's a good idea." It's not. It's an insane idea. Too many memories there. But they're fond memories. At least we didn't have sex there like we did in this apartment. "Okay. Let's go."

"We can take the van if you want."

"No." I try to find that smile again. How is it that he's not affected by all this? "My car's out front. I'll drive."

It's a short trip. We used to walk there as kids. I keep the conversation focused on training to keep memories at bay.

"Tell me about the play a little bit more. What sorts of things will you need him to do?"

As Ben describes the various scenes, I keep getting distracted by the sound of his voice. Like so many things about him, it's the same, but different. That summer, he was twenty-one, about to be a senior in college. His voice wasn't exactly pitched higher then, but it wasn't as rich in tone as it is now. Like the rest of him, it was thinner. I never really thought about the sound of his voice before, but in this moment it has me dying to be close to him. To feel its vibrations skin to skin.

He cranes his neck like he's checking to make sure the park isn't too crowded. "So, what's the plan?"

What's the plan? How about you and me making out in the backseat?

Down, girl. Bad Lucy.

"Lucy?"

"Yeah?"

"What should we do?"

He's paying you Lucy, and it's not for sexual favors. "Right." Turning into the parking lot, I get out of the car as fast as I can, needing distance. Striding into the park, assuming he and Puck will follow, I scan the area. I can hear kids' voices up in the hills of the forest, but the big field is free.

At Ben's heel as they enter the park, Puck doesn't strain at the end of the leash. He takes in the surroundings without losing focus on his master.

When they stop five feet from me and Puck sits without being asked, I nod. "Nice work. You've been practicing."

Ben's smile is wide. But it's for the dog. "He's so smart."

"Let's try working off leash. Give him the heel command and challenge him to stay with you by surprising him with turns. If he takes off, say his name sharply followed by the word C-O-M-E."

Ben follows my commands and successful redirects Puck when they flush out a rabbit. Thankfully, it's unlikely there will be any of those onstage.

After that, we hike up into the hills. Pushing away the memories of so many afternoons spent playing capture the flag or cops and robbers or just exploring this magical park, I ask, "Do you have your lines memorized yet?"

"Rehearsal hasn't started, so not really. Just the scene we auditioned with, but that's all dialogue."

Sitting on a rock, I point to another rock with a flat top a few feet away. "What if you guys stand there and you just tell me a story, but like, include the dog? I want to see what happens. If he'll do things that are distracting."

Ben places Puck on the rock and starts to climb up himself.

"Hang on. Let's break this down. I think you're ready to start with non-verbal commands."

It only takes a few tries and a few treats for Puck to get it. The next time Ben hops up onto the rock, he slaps his thigh twice and the dog scrambles up after him. Ben stands tall, slaps his thigh once and Puck sits. When Ben tries to say "good boy" out of the side of his mouth in the high-pitched tone I told him to use for praise, I get the giggles.

"What? You said I have to talk like that."

"I know, but you sound ridiculous."

"Thank you, Ms. Obvious."

"You're welcome." I lean back on my hands. "I guess there's no chance that Shakespeare wrote 'good boy' into any of your speeches?"

"No, mostly Launce is mad at the dog."

"Hm. That means we've got to build up trust between you so he won't be affected by the anger."

"I guess so. I hadn't thought about that."

I look around the park. "Maybe what we need is to get him to follow you while you talk using a big range of feeling." I gesture back in the direction of the parking lot. "We'll run out of light soon, so let's head back. Along the way, just say whatever, but use all the emotions you can."

"Alright, but no laughing at me."

"Aren't you supposed to be funny in this play?"

He narrows his eyes at me for a half a moment before pulling the muscles of his face down, turning his perfectly sculpted features into a goofy mask. Then he drops his hands and shakes his whole body as he makes some very odd noises. In response, Puck drops into a play bow, front legs spread wide, tail in the air. When he barks, Ben stops wiggling and mirrors Puck. Slapping his thigh, man takes off and dog follows.

All the way down the hill, Ben morphs from one extreme to another. It's like watching Looney Tunes.

When I catch up to them, Ben straightens so that he seems even taller than usual and wags a finger at me. "No laughing, missy!" He says this in a falsetto, like a school marm.

My hands go up in the air. "I'm not laughing."

He makes a face at me before stomping away. The madder he gets, the funnier he is. Forgetting all about the job I'm here to perform, I end up in a game of Mother, may I? with him, unsuccessfully stifling my giggles when he catches me moving.

By the time we get back to the car, I'm howling with laughter. Ben drops the character he's been playing, but his smile is golden. "That was the most fun I've had in a long time."

Yeah. Me too.

Back in the car, Ben reaches over to change the station on the radio, leaving NPR behind. When he finds a music station, he turns up the volume. The drive back is short, but he gets me laughing again when he sings along with The Pointer Sisters' "He's So Shy" in a falsetto even higher-pitched than the one he used earlier. Maybe the goofball I knew and loved hasn't completely disappeared.

When I pull up in front of his dad's house and put the car into park, I'm grinning as I shake my head at him. "You're a nut."

He shrugs, like *what can I say?* After collecting Puck from the backseat, he leans back in the window and lets out an enormous sigh. Nodding slowly, he says, "Thank you, Lucy. That was—I needed that."

This time I say it. "Yeah. Me too."

He gives me a little salute, slaps his thigh, and heads up the driveway. Watching him go, I let the music wash over me, something I haven't done in a very long time.

After Ben left for LA, I spiraled out of control for a while. That made things even worse, so I swung to the other extreme. I went back to church and quit all the bad behaviors that got me into trouble in the first place. But I don't remember deciding to stop listening to music. Singing along with a mixtape of my favorites doesn't hurt anybody, as long as I don't sing too loudly.

Plus, I'm a good girl now. I may be fantasizing about Ben, but I'm working hard and taking care of my family. I could probably do more good in the world—join the Peace Corps or something—but I'm doing the best I can.

Instead of turning back to the news, I turn the music up for the short trip home. I would dig out one of my old mixtapes, but I gave all the best ones to Ben.

Chapter 9

"I Want You to Want Me" - Cheap Trick
Lucy's Copacetic Shagadelic Mixtape, Song #5

LUCY

The next morning, I hold out my hand for Mrs. O'Neill as she steps out of the confessional. The elderly woman is a force of nature, running half of the committees at Saint Bonaventure's, but she looks a bit wobbly at the moment. "Thank you, dear. I must have stood up too quickly."

"Do you need me to walk you to your car?"

"Gina's waiting for me. We'll walk home together."

Across the dim chapel, Mrs. Rinaldi waves from near the doorway. Mrs. O'Neill is surefooted as she heads in her direction and other people are waiting, so I step into the box, close the door and open the screen.

"Bless me, Father for I have sinned. It's been one week since my last confession. These are my sins. I yelled at one brother because he left his clean laundry in the middle of the floor and the other brother because he left the paper we'd worked so hard on at home and got his grade docked. I took the Lord's name in vain when I was driving to work and a man cut me off, and I used profanity when a cat scratched me at work."

Silence from the other side of the screen. Instead of the gentle scolding I usually receive, I hear, "Mm."

And more silence.

Words scrabble their way up my throat to fill that silence even as my jaw does its best to hang on to them. "I... I also can't stop... stop feeling anger and other... things."

More silence. I think. My heart's pounding so loud I can barely hear anything else.

"Anger is a powerful agent. It can be a fuel for right action. It can be a cleansing fire that leaves room for growth, if handled skillfully."

My jaw drops. Breaking protocol, I try to see through the screen. "Um, where's Father Signorelli? Is he okay?" Our parish priest is ancient and hasn't been looking healthy lately.

"Father Signorelli is attending to some personal business. I am Father Krausnick. I'm filling in."

"Oh, sorry. Okay."

"Let's unpack your sins. You were angry with your brothers. How old are they?

"Nineteen and seventeen."

"Sometimes when we serve others, we deny them the right to serve themselves."

The way this usually goes? Father Signorelli listens to my sins and tells me to say a bunch of Our Fathers and do something nice for someone, which is why I do my brothers' laundry and help them with their homework in the first place. Taking care of them makes me feel better about myself. "So, are you saying that I should stop doing things for my brothers?"

"Guilt is an indulgence that smothers self-compassion. Shame is a heavy shroud that snuffs out love for the self."

This guy is so far off script that I have no idea what I'm supposed to do or say next. Did he say this kind of stuff to Mrs. O'Brien and Mrs. Rinaldi? Not that I can imagine either of those ladies doing anything sinful beyond coveting someone else's flower garden.

"To live is to sin. To be human is to sin. To deny these truths is hubris. Grace comes when we transcend the mind's limits and accept our faults as opportunities for growth."

As his words filter through my confusion, the hamster wheel that powers my brain hitches to a stop. Some part of me floats up until I can see myself from the outside, see how pissed off I am and how hard I work to hide that anger. How I stuff every hour of every day with dutiful obligations that I tell myself make me good. Deserving of life.

"It's a sin to ignore God's benevolence, the gifts he's blessed us with. It's a sin to forgo the simple joys of life. And it's a sin to deny love. Think on this."

"Um... okay. I mean, yes, Father."

As odd as his suggestions are, something tells me that I need to hang onto this feeling with both hands.

"Give thanks to the Lord, for He is good."

"For His mercy endures forever."

"The Lord has freed you from your sins. Go in peace."

"Thanks be to God."

Gifts, joy, love. Think on them. That's it. No penance.

Father Signorelli's dismissal always leaves me with a dogged sense of purpose. Now, as I step out of the darkened box and into the dusty light of the chapel, I'm weightless. Free, even. Like, any time I need to, I can float up, up and away in a beautiful balloon.

Fueled by hope.

THE MORE BEN and I work together, the more fun I have. I think I'm actually really good at this training thing. Then there's Ben. Somehow we've fallen back into the way things used to be between us. Goofing around, teasing each other. There is an added tension underneath everything, which could be attributed to a whole laundry list of things. Part of me wants to figure out what it's about and part of me wants to stuff it away like I do every uncomfortable feeling.

The final performance of *Romeo and Juliet* is tonight. The tickets Ben gave me have been sitting on my bureau taunting me. I'm not a huge Shakespeare fan, but curiosity, as well as yesterday's confession experience, convince me to check it out. So, after finishing up the dishes from my family's Sunday afternoon dinner, I decide to just go.

A couple of hours later, sitting alone as the stage lights fade to black for the last time, I'm glad I didn't call Cindy or ask my mom if she wanted to come with me. I need to be alone with everything the play has stirred up. Well, alone with a hundred strangers, half of whom are loudly crying along with me.

The tragedy onstage wasn't just about two star-crossed lovers. Ben's pain—the haunted loneliness, the anguished guilt—was all too real. Nobody's that good of an actor.

In the early scenes, Romeo *was* Tony as a teen—a swaggering but lovable horndog. But as the deaths multiplied, Ben seemed to draw on something deep inside himself.

His Romeo does remind me of the ads that I now notice everywhere: on bus stops as well as billboards. I've been wondering why I never recognized him in them before, but now I get it. Model Ben and Romeo Ben are hollowed out by a despair that I never could have imagined in *my* Ben.

Lights rise overhead. Numbly gathering my things, I follow the other audience members shuffling slowly down the aisle and toward the parking lot like cattle in a chute, everyone still caught in the dreamworld of the play. I never thought dusty old Shakespeare could be so relevant, but the director used the play to mirror issues that plague Boston right now: racial divides, drug and alcohol abuse, even the gaps between rich and poor.

I really want to talk about the play with someone, I just don't know who. Not Ben. Our paths have taken us in very different directions.

But just as I'm telling myself yet again that this is a side of Ben I've never seen before, a memory flashes. When he and his dad first moved in, my mom sent Tony and me to bring dinner to welcome them to the neighborhood. His house was unbelievably quiet. We couldn't believe he was home all by himself or that he had to make dinner.

Hamburger Helper. Tony had been jealous. We'd only ever seen it on TV.

The grass is always greener, I guess.

As I sink into the driver's seat of my car, another memory floats up.

I'M KEEPING *busy in the kitchen, loading and reloading platters of food. If I don't, I'll either be sobbing or stuffing my face. I think the loaves and fishes story from the Bible must've had its origins in an Italian funeral. Every day for the past week, no matter how much we eat—me and Sal and Vinnie make a good dent, my parents, not so much—the next day, it's replenished itself. Today, the food just keeps coming. Our house is stuffed to the gills with mourners, the sounds of talking and eating and laughing and drinking and crying rolling in a wave into the kitchen every time the swinging door opens.*

Every time it does, I look for Ben in the sea of faces. Finally, I get glimpse of him. Wait—is he on crutches?

I drop the pan of stuffed shells I'm holding onto the counter and push through the door. There he is. My mom's hugging him. When he looks over her shoulder and catches my eye, his face pales and he pulls away from her. She puts her hands on his cheeks, says something, and he nods. She hugs him one more time, awkwardly, because of the crutches and difference in height between them. She turns to greet yet another mourning neighbor or relative.

And his eyes are back on mine.

I haven't seen Ben since I left to start college two months ago. Or talked to him or even gotten a letter from him, even though I sent him a bunch. That hurt—a lot—but I was dealing. School, new friends, even some fun dates were a good distraction.

This was not how I saw our Thanksgiving reunion going.

I want to talk to him, even though I'm mad at him for his radio silence, but not in front of all these people. I tip my head toward the back of the house and raise my brows at him. He looks at the door and nods.

Pushing through the crowd on my way to the back porch, my grimace-smile made acceptable by the fact that I just lost my big brother, I take in big gulps of the bracing air once I get outside. I have to beat back memories of Tony in this backyard, though: shooting hoops, hurling a baseball into a net, flipping a lacrosse ball in the air over and over again. He was rarely without a ball in his hands. I kinda wished we'd put a bunch in his casket. Just in case.

A sharp click, a scrape and a few thumps sound behind me.

"Lucy." His voice sounds like he's been smoking since he was ten. Or screaming into the wind from the side of the football field.

Or bawling for a week, like me.

I gesture to the cast on his leg. "What happened to you?"

Pain fills his eyes, and his face is white as a sheet. "You don't know?"

"Know what? I haven't seen you since August, you asshole."

He slumps against the door, lets the crutches fall and covers his face with his hands. "Fuck."

"That's all you have to say? I left for school, I hear nothing from you, then my brother dies on the way to pick me up and bring me home for Thanksgiving, and that's all I get?"

He squeezes his head so hard his knuckles go white. After a few beats, a horrible groaning noise grinds in his throat, then he drops his hands so quickly he loses his balance. Instinctively lunging for him, I try to grab him by the forearm, but he grasps my other arm and pulls me in so our foreheads touch.

"I was there too," he grates out. "I was in the car, in the accident."

I jerk back, my heart pounding, and stare at him for what feels like forever.

And then I run.

Watching all these people grieve over the brother that I killed with my selfish demands has my heart in shreds. But the fact that I might've killed Ben, too—I can't face it.

Out into the cold, the wind, I can barely breathe. In my stupid heels and hose and black dress, I stumble around the corner of the house, duck between bushes and pray that Ben doesn't follow.

Unfortunately, that prayer was answered.

A KNOCK on my car has my eyes flying open. The Ben on the other side of the glass is seven years older than the one in my memory. Swallowing the wave of feelings brought up by it and the play, I crank the window down. "Ben! You scared me."

"Sorry, I just saw your car and wanted to see if it was you." He rests both hands on the roof, bending his long torso until we're eye to eye. "I'm so glad you came tonight."

Grabbing a tissue from my purse, I blow my nose. "It wasn't fun to watch, but you were good," I say, glad I have Shakespeare to blame for my tears.

"Ben, are you coming?" a female voice calls across the parking lot.

He waves at her. "Yeah, I'll meet you there," before turning back to me. "We're having a closing party tonight. You should come, meet some of the *Two Gents* cast."

I grip the steering wheel, not sure if I'm ready to spend time with Ben without the structure of dog training to keep me from touching him. Or hitting him.

He grins. "It's a fun crowd ready to blow off steam."

Actually, I am sure. I'm not ready. "Thanks, that would be nice—"

His widening smile stalls my train of thought. How can curving lips bend my will so effortlessly? Forcing myself to look away, I scrabble in my purse again. By the time I find my keys, I'm back under control. Giving all my attention to the ignition switch and tricky clutch in our family station wagon, I say, "But I can't. Work tomorrow, you know."

When his face falls, I press my lips together, not allowing myself to want him to want me or to need him to need me.

"Sure, yeah. Okay, well then, I'll see you tomorrow for our appointment?"

"Yep."

He straightens and steps away as I shift into reverse. "Thanks for coming."

My resolve hanging by a thread, I back out of the parking spot and drive home.

THE NEXT MORNING, my head still clogged with memories, I push open the door to exam room three. "Good morning, how are we do—" My mouth and my body freeze when a snarling chow chow lunges for my jugular.

Thankfully, the owner has a muzzle on the dog and a firm hold on the leash. Despite the fight-or-flight response surging through me, I speak calmly and slowly. "I am so sorry. I didn't realize it was Twinkie in here. I'm going to exit, give her a few minutes to calm down, and we'll try this again."

I catch an irritated nod from the human as well as a growl from the dog as I slowly close the door. Out in the hall, I scan the chart, something I should've done *before* entering.

Deanna raises a brow as she squeezes by with a cat carrier. "Everything okay?"

"Yeah." I hold up the chart, which very clearly indicates an aggressive patient. "I just barged in on a red sticker."

"That doesn't sound like you."

"I know, I'm just…" What I want to say is, *I've just got my head up my ass*, but I don't say those things anymore.

She bends the folder to eye the paperwork. "Oh, Twinkie. Yeah, she'll be cool as long as you are. She's not too smart, so a do-over will probably work."

"That's what I was hoping for."

Deanna gives me an assessing look before lifting the meowing cage. "Gotta go knock this baby down, but if you need to talk…"

"Thanks, I'll let you know."

I'm a pro at dealing with aggressive dogs. Usually. What I'm not so good at is dealing with my own feelings about a guy who I don't want to admit that I've missed like I'd miss a vital organ.

Big breaths. Get your shit—dammit—dang it—act together, Lucy. Twinkie needs her exam, her owner needs reassurance and you need to get your head on straight.

Chapter 10

"Do the Dog" - The Specials
Lucy's Keep on Truckin' Mixtape, Song #7

BEN

The first day of rehearsal for *Two Gents*, I enter the musty basement room where we'll be working, Puck trotting obediently by my side. Lucy's instructions click through my brain, so instead of heading straight for the table in the center of the space, I make an abrupt turn to the right. Puck's shoulder brushes my leg before he adjusts. He matches my pace as we walk the perimeter of the room. When I stop without warning, he stops and sits.

"Good boy!" I say as softly as I can and slip him a treat. I point to the floor, and use a low, firm voice. "Down." Puck grunts but complies. I praise him again, tossing him another treat. Saying, "Let's go," I zig-zag back to the other end of the room, trying to throw him off with random changes of direction. By the time we get to the table, we've attracted some attention. I stop, Puck sits, and our audience bursts into applause. Puck lets out a sharp bark but when I shoot him a look, he grunts and lies down.

Nick leans back in his chair at the head of the table. "Who is responsible for this?"

"An old family friend." Lucy isn't a family friend; she's *my* friend, my ex... what? Girlfriend no one knew about? Secret forbidden lover? My inability to attach a label to the relationship makes me feel a little better about the fib.

"Either the pair of you are either very good students or he's an excellent trainer."

"She—the trainer's a she—it's all on her. And this little guy." I scratch Puck behind the ears. "He's very trainable, she says. I'm the problem student."

I'm not being modest. My initial attempts to replicate Lucy's ease with Puck were a complete failure. The dog just stared at me like I was an idiot.

Nick crosses his arms behind his head. "My imagination is already turning up all sorts of ideas for comic bits. Do you think she'd been able to teach the animal to perform specific actions?"

"We've talked about that. Right now I'm using verbal cues and giving him treats. But she says if I work hard, we can progress to visual cues, or even to habitual training. Like how he sits now when I stop?" I indicate my new shadow. "We could choreograph some of that into the blocking."

Nick nods slowly, obviously mulling over possibilities, before speaking to the stage manager, who gives us a five-minute warning. Actors and designers gathered by the refreshment table begin to find seats at the two long tables set up end to end with packets at each place. I'm not sure what to do with Puck, but when Bella waves me over, she points at a seat next to her.

"Puck gets a chair, too." When he hops into it, she asks, "Is it okay if I pet him?"

"Yeah, Lucy—that's the trainer we're working with—said that he should get lots of experience with everyone in the show. It may be that you'll end up giving him commands too."

As I take my own seat, Bella makes some sort of baby talk nonsense while scratching under Puck's chin.

Reading over the schedule in my packet, I realize I should confirm one more time that I need to be back in Los Angeles for a shoot two days after the show's closing date. *R&J* was extended twice due to its popularity. I can't afford for that to happen this time. Getting up, I tell Puck to stay out of habit.

It's strange to think that just a couple weeks ago, I didn't have him in my life. It feels like he's always been there.

A few minutes later, we go around the table and everyone introduces themselves. Lots of familiar faces. Will and Randall have the male leads Proteus and Valentine. Jessica—my Juliet—plays female lead Sylvia. It's pretty amazing that none of the actors harbor ill will toward me, despite the chaos that my presence caused at first. Once the house manager started making a pre-show announcement warning that disruptive audience members would be removed from their seats, but promising that actors would be available to sign programs after the show, the catcalls fell off. Despite the fact that I was always the one with the longest line for autographs, no one seems to mind. They probably get that the crazy fans are all about my bare chest rather than my acting chops. I rub the two-day-old scruff on my cheeks, hoping that this role will allow me to disappear a bit more.

After the introductions, Nick and the designers talk a bit about the concept. The play will be set in San Diego during the Vietnam War rather than sixteenth-century Milan. Many of the characters will be Naval officers or young recruits. My character, Launce, is a crusty Marine.

As we read through the play, my mind drifts to time spent with Lucy the past two weeks. She has every right to be wary of me. Each day, I dig deep for the courage to tell her all the reasons why I left town without explanation. Selfishly, I want more time with her, even if that time's spent in agony, wanting to touch her, to kiss her, to make love to her again. The likelihood of any of those things happening is very low, whether I tell her the whole truth or not.

Then my mind finds its way back to a day that started horribly but ended as sweet as anything I can imagine.

LOUD BANGING JERKS *me out of a deep sleep. I sit up, disoriented. It's twilight, not the middle of the night. I'm on the couch. Must have fallen asleep.*

The knocking doesn't quit, so I heave myself off the couch and to the front door of my apartment. When I haul it open, Lucy falls into my arms, sobbing.

Now fully awake, I remember the poor dog we saw get hit by a car this morning. My arm around her, I ease her to the couch and let her cry into my shoulder until all that's left are a few hiccups. I grab a napkin off a pizza box and offer it to her.

After noisily blowing her nose, she hiccups again. "I'm sorry." Her voice is hoarse.

I shift away slightly so I can see her face. "I take it that he didn't survive?"

She shakes her head. A sob shudders through her. "How will I ever be able to be a veterinarian? This hurts so much."

I squeeze her shoulders. "Maybe it's something you just get used to? Plus it's not like you're going to witness the accident like we did. I still can't believe that car just kept going." And I'm still pissed I didn't think fast enough to get the license plate.

"I just keep wondering if he would've survived if I'd known what to do right away." The pain in her voice slices through me.

"Did you talk to Dr., uh..." I can't remember the older vet's name, the one that came running out after I dashed in to let them know we had an injured animal in the van.

She shudders out a breath. "Dr. Fields. Yeah. He called me to let me know. He was great. He said you do grieve, but it gets easier. That sometimes the best you can do is give the animal a good exit, which is better than we do for people most of the time."

I rub her thigh. "If we hadn't been there, who knows how long it would've been before someone did something."

She grabs my hand. "I just wish..."

"What?"

Another sob escapes past her lips. "I wish I'd saved him."

I hug her to my side again. Tony would be pissed off if he knew about us, not to mention Mr. Minola and that still bothers me. She's so warm and soft and it feels right to hold her, but maybe this thing with the dog is a sign.

A hand snakes its way around my waist and tunnels under my shirt, making my breath catch.

She hesitates. "Did I hurt you?"

"No, it's just..." I can't tell her the effect she has on me, how she's had a starring role in my fantasies of late, both awake and asleep, so I just say, "That tickles."

Her fingers play over my belly. "Hmmm. How about this?" My abs go rigid.

"Wow. You almost have a six-pack there." Her voice is husky. Sexy, dammit. I hold my breath. Close my eyes. Everything hangs in suspension for half a heartbeat. Before I can do or say anything else, she's straddling me. Her hands cup the sides of my face, her breasts press against my chest and her warm softness squirms over the hardest part of me. Also the neediest.

I attempt to hang onto reason but when her mouth covers mine, I'm lost. In her, with her. Our bodies are a perfect mortise and tenon.

Lucy's no little girl. She's a full-on woman. It's obvious that she wants me. I mean, she said so this morning and now, her pelvis grinds into mine as her hands grip the back of my head with a confidence she's acquired since our first time. Her moans as my hands roam her body tell me she needs this as much as I do. I'm not sure how we got from her using me to lose her virginity to this being a regular thing, but I can't seem to say no to her.

Breaking the kiss, I roll her to her back. Pressing light kisses to her temple, her cheek, her ear, I whisper, "God, I want you Lucy. But—"

"No buts. I want you, Ben." She grins at me, a wicked look in her eyes, which makes her even sexier somehow. I caress her soft curls and draw a finger down her jawline.

Her hands reach around to pull me in. "Listen, Ben. I've been doing some research." A blush blooms on her round cheeks. "I have things I want to try out and... I want to do them with you because I trust you. This doesn't have to be a big thing. We don't have to be like, dating. We'll still be friends like always. Just with... some special sauce."

My heart stutters. She's telling me what she wants. Who am I to say no?

Kissing my way over every curve, I slowly undress her until she's writhing underneath my lips. Shucking my own clothes, I grab a condom.

I pause, unsure again.

Her eyes fly open. "What are you waiting for, mister? Move it along!"

Laughing, I kiss her again, and we move together like our bodies were made for each other. When she does some new thing with her hips, I lose the control I've been hanging onto by a thread. I pound into her, and she meets me thrust for thrust until we explode together, sensation reverberating through both of our bodies.

SHAKESPEARE'S WORDS invade the memory. Swallowing, I check my script to figure out where we are, and I shift in my seat, hoping no one has any idea what's been going on inside my head. Or my body, which is hidden by the table, thank god.

I have a monologue coming up. I have it memorized, but I'm so discombobulated it'll be safest to just read it. When my cue comes, I have to clear my throat a couple of times to get started. "Nay, 'twill be this hour ere I have done weeping," I begin, thankful that I'm supposed to be overwhelmed by emotion for this scene.

My acting teacher's voice echoes in my head. *Use it. Whatever's going on, just put it on the text.*

Chapter 11

"Can't Stand Losing You" - The Police
Lucy's Totally Tubular Tuneage, Song #2

LUCY

Thursday afternoon after doing the early shift at work, I'm at rehearsal for *Two Gentlemen of Verona* for the first time. After I make a few simple suggestions, Nick Dorset leans in close and bumps my shoulder with his. "Lucy, you're brilliant. You're a natural. Are you sure you've never directed a play before?" The director's charm doesn't set my every nerve ending on fire the way just being in the room with Ben does—which is why I'm still doing my best to keep things all business with *him*—but Nick's brogue is adorable and he's obviously very intelligent. I mean, he thinks I'm brilliant.

And I'm pretty sure he's flirting with me. Meanwhile, Ben is giving off all sorts of conflicting signals. One minute he's glowering at me, the next he's solicitously bringing me water, the next he's snapping with impatience.

I wonder if Nick's attention is actually making him jealous. Even though his mood swings make my job more difficult, I kind of want to find out.

Making sure Ben can see us, I scoot closer to Nick. "My only experience with Shakespeare is working backstage on a couple shows in high school—in which Ben appeared, by the way," I add in a stage whisper. Not too soft, though. I want Ben to hear. "He was Brutus in *Julius Caesar*. His death scene was pretty funny. But I don't think it was supposed to be. He also played that character in *Midsummer Night's Dream* that has to dress up as a woman."

"Francis Flute, the bellow's mender." Nick's grin eggs me on.

I glance over at the man we're gossiping about. His smile is definitely forced. He *is* jealous. "That's it. Ben was hilarious. He used this warbly, high voice. All the guys in that troupe would try to make each other crack up onstage, but he was the best at it."

That year, he was eighteen and I was fifteen. I'd had a crush on him for years. Now, I tilt my head to the side as I call out to him. "Do you remember that I was the assistant to the assistant stage manager for that *Midsummer* at Arlington High?"

"What I remember is that you always knew everyone's lines and you'd hiss them at us from stage left if we forgot."

"But you never forgot yours."

He smiles, but it doesn't reach his eyes. "I didn't want you to be mad at me."

Well, you're mad at me *right now.*

Nick claps his hands. "All right. Let's get back to work." He looks to the stage manager. "Janet? What's next?"

She checks her watch and calls to the room, "We're back. Scene four. Launce, Proteus and Julia, are you ready?"

Ben's friend Will—a tall, dark-haired pale-skinned guy—and a petite black actress named Rhonda—who looks like she's barely out of college—move to stand in the area marked as "offstage" by masking tape on the floor.

"Well, then." Nick looks down at the dog. "Puck, are you ready to go at this again?"

Puck barks, and it's like he's actually saying yes. "My word, he is an exceptional animal. You have your work cut out for you, Benjamin."

"Actually, it's Benedick," Ben says, a bit grumpily.

"Like the character in *Much Ado*?"

"It's a family name, but yeah."

Nick nods back. "How unusual. My apologies." He points toward the stage and draws a circle in the air. "So, we'll run Launce's monologue and keep going to the entrance of Proteus and Julia."

As Ben performs at an emotional full tilt, Puck does every single thing we practiced. Everyone watching is laughing. Nick grins broadly and winks at me.

When Will and Rhonda enter, Will/Proteus yells at Ben/Launce, "How now, you whoreson peasant!"

When Ben cowers in fear, Puck charges at Will, straining on the leash and barking ferociously. Will jumps back and Rhonda screams. Obviously thrown, they glance at Nick briefly before continuing with their lines as Ben scrambles to get Puck under control.

Will was pretty aggressive there, so Puck's reaction tells me that he feels he has to protect Ben. At the end of the scene, Ben has to pick up Puck and carry him off.

Nick looks over at me. "Well, that was interesting."

"Sorry about the scream," Rhonda says. "I didn't know that was going to happen. He's such a sweet dog."

Nick hops up to meet them at the edge of the playing area. "In performance, should something happen with the animal that wasn't rehearsed, you must carry on. He will always be in the present moment, and you must react in kind. If you don't, the fourth wall will be broken and you'll lose the audience."

I join them. "I'm sure we can work on this. I think Puck thought Ben was vulnerable because he was crouched low and crying. He thought he had to protect Ben from Will."

This leads to a discussion of how Crab's reactions could add to the story being told. Even though I haven't studied theater like they all have, Nick includes me like he values my creative ideas as well as my skills with Puck.

As rehearsal winds down, I'm just getting started. I can't jot down ideas fast enough. Even though my day started almost twelve hours ago, doing something new and challenging is energizing.

When I go to gather my things, Ben follows me. "Thanks, Lucy. I'm sorry this has taken up your whole evening."

His warm hand on my shoulder awakens a slew of memories, all featuring his work-roughened hands running over my body.

"Hey, it's your dime," I say, waving his apology away as I will the blush heating my cheeks to cool down. "Besides, it's a lot more fun than I thought it would be. It's rewarding to train a dog to behave, but it's pretty darn cool to get him to do things that make people laugh."

I make myself meet his gaze, but the longing in it is harder to face than the jealousy I've been stoking. So I mumble a goodbye and push the heavy church door open. Outside, I have to stop and get my bearings. When I went into the church basement a few hours ago, it was still light out and unseasonably warm. A front must've come through while we were holed up down there. Now, the parking lot's damp and tiny puddles sparkle in the streetlight. It isn't raining at the moment, but the temperature has dropped about twenty degrees. Shivering, I head for my car, but Ben's voice stops me.

"Lucy, wait up." He tries to follow me, but Puck sprints for a patch of grass. "Sorry. Guess he needs to go."

I grab a sweater from my car while Puck does his thing. As soon as Ben gets close, I'm shivering again, and it's not from the cold. While we were surrounded by other people, it was easy to put my confused mass of feelings aside. Now they're bumping around inside like popcorn in hot oil.

We both just stare at each other for a long moment. Finally, he takes in a sharp breath and blurts, "I was just wondering if you want to have dinner? Maybe tomorrow night after rehearsal? I get out early."

"Um, sure," I say, even as I know it's probably not a good idea. "I think my family can spare me for one night. There's a new restaurant in Arlington Center that I've been wanting to check out."

"If it's okay with you, I'd prefer to eat in. I can cook if you want to come over."

"What, you don't want to be seen with a girl who isn't a movie star?" I say, only half joking.

A pained look crosses his face. "No, I just don't want to be seen at all. It's just too much work."

"Yeah, I get it. I guess." Spending time alone with him at his apartment—a place so full of memories of my bad-girl days—is not easy. At least without knowing what's going on between us. Being direct worked in the past, I suppose, so I just spit out the question, even though I'm not sure I'm ready to hear his answer. "What do you want from me, Ben?"

His answer is instantaneous. "Whatever you're willing to give me, Lucy." His eyes are half hidden by a flop of hair, but the loneliness there is clear. "A friend I can just be myself with."

And who is that? I wonder. But what I say, because I'm a sucker for an animal in need, is, "Sure. I'll see you tomorrow, then."

"WHO KNEW *you were so funny, Ben?" Tony asks as he whaps Ben on the back of the head, knocking his baseball cap off. "Catch you two later."*

Ben picks up his hat and then jangles the keys in his pocket. "You don't need a ride home?"

"Nah. Tory 'n me are gonna hang out," he waggles his eyebrows as he says the words. "And then she'll give me a ride home."

He shoves Ben and goes for me, but I duck out of his way. "Tell mom I'll get something for dinner, squirt."

Ben's already halfway to his car, and I have to run to catch up.

"I knew," I say, panting.

"Knew what?" Ben's face is kind of red. Not sure if he's embarrassed or mad. Or happy.

"That you're funny."

He smiles that smile that I feel like is just for me. "Yeah?"

"Yeah." I bump shoulders with him. Or I try. My shoulder hits his elbow

these days. I swear they both grew a foot while I was away at my cousins' farm this summer. "Those faces you make at the dinner table whenever Tony's being a showoff? I have to work really hard to keep from laughing."

He turns to me, his chin drawn down. "What do you mean?" He sounds as droopy as he looks. Then he squeezes his whole face over to one side somehow. It's like he's made of rubber. "What faces?" Lifting his brows and fluttering his lashes he says, "I don't know what you're talking about," in a high, squeaky voice.

I can't help but laugh, and then he attacks me, tickling me, "What are you laughing at? There's no laughing at school."

When I manage to get my fingers under his shirt to tickle him back, he declares, "No tickling! This is a very serious place, young lady!"

By the time we get to his car, we're both breathless, but he manages to beat me to the passenger side and open the door for me with a flourish. "Inside, wench!"

I try to match his English accent. "Call me not wench, peasant."

"Forgive me mistress," he says, bowing low. "I am thy humble servant."

When he offers his hand to help me into the van, I say, "You may kiss my hand, serf."

But when he does, suddenly it's not funny anymore. His gaze holds mine prisoner while his lips whisper a caress over the back of my hand. As a tidal wave of desire swamps me, I jerk my hand away and stumble back, landing on the van seat ass-first. Like a total dork.

After getting my legs inside, I make myself look at him. His face is as red as mine must be. But before I can figure out how to tell him that I like him like him, he slaps his hands to his cheeks and pushes them together to do the old "Lady, can you please open the elevator door?" routine.

Playing along, because I probably misread what happened anyway, I press his nose and he separates his hands slowly, like doors sliding open to say, "Thank you."

BY THE TIME I get home, thoughts about today's rehearsal are all mixed up with memories from high school. Hanging out with Ben in the car on the way home from rehearsals was an unintentional gift from my brother. Then, as now, I'm not only aching to kiss Ben again, I want to laugh with him again.

It occurs to me that doing theater in high school really changed Ben. He stepped out of my brother's shadow for the first time since he'd moved to the neighborhood. When Ben woke up, girls started noticing him. Girls like me. I didn't have the moxie to go after him until a couple of years later, but I'd wanted to. Suddenly, he wasn't just my brother's friend, my goofy almost-brother. Ben was sexy.

He still is. But still, there's something broken inside. And stupid me, I really want to fix it. I just don't know if I can do that without getting into trouble again.

Guess I'll find out tomorrow.

Chapter 12

"Teenage Kicks" - The Undertones
Lucy's May the Force Be With You Mixtape, Song #4

BEN

"Okay. Dinner ingredients are ready to assemble. What else?"

Puck gives me such thoughtful look I wouldn't be surprised if he actually answered me. I always thought people who talked to their pets were crazy. Either I'm crazy, or it's just what happens.

He doesn't answer, but I do remember that I should light the candles I bought, hoping it doesn't look like I'm working too hard to make things romantic. In the living area, I rearrange the video cassettes on the coffee table, going for, *Oh yeah, I just picked these up from Blockbuster to watch over the weekend.* The truth is, I agonized over the choices so long that it threw off my whole dinner prep. I rented *Roxanne*, *Broadcast News* and *The Princess Bride*, hoping one of them would tempt Lucy to sit next to me on the couch for a couple of hours.

Puck barks and a knock sounds, making me fumble the cassettes. She's here. Wiping my suddenly sweaty hands on my khakis, I open the front door.

It's not Lucy, though. It's my dad.

"Dad?" I can't hide the surprise in my voice. This is the first time he's climbed the steps of my place since he got home from the hospital. "Everything okay?"

He glances over his shoulder before shoving his hands into his armpits, his brow furrowing. "Ah, I thought I'd take that dog of yours for a walk. You been bugging me so much, and Mrs. Rosen across the way called and asked if I'd walk with her. I couldn't say no to her, but I thought if I had the dog, it would be less awkward." He shrugs, looking about as nervous as I feel.

I bite back a grin and put on a mask of concern. "Mrs. Rosen's a widow now, huh?"

"Yeah, Myron died a couple years ago. Since then, I go over there and fix things every once in a while, and she cooks for me sometimes. She said she needs to exercise but doesn't want to go by herself, especially now it's getting dark earlier. So I'm helping her out. Anyway, can I have the dog?" He holds out a hand. Puck's already dancing between us like he's all in.

"Sure, I guess. Um, Lucy's coming over for dinner in a little bit."

"Lucy? Lucy Minola?" He smiles, something I haven't seen for a long time. "She cooking?"

"No, I'm cooking. She's been training Puck for the show I'm doing. I'm paying her, but I thought I'd cook her dinner to thank her."

"You're cooking?" He frowns. "Not that healthy crap you tried to get me to eat, I hope."

"Dad, you just have to get used to it."

"All I'm saying is, if you're trying to impress her, that ain't going to do it. I'll keep Puck till you come get him so we don't interrupt… anything."

"It's not like that, Dad. It's Lucy."

"Uh-huh. He can watch the game with me. He likes that."

"Okay. I'll come get him after I walk her home."

"All right. C'mon, Puck." He grabs the leash from a hook by the door, chatting with the dog as they head down the stairs. "Don't know why you're named after a hockey puck. Didn't even know Ben was a Bruins fan."

The kitchen door shuts behind them just as Lucy appears around the corner of the garage.

"Did you think I forgot how to get here?" she asks as she climbs the stairs.

"Oh, no, I was just—my dad came to take Puck for a walk. That's okay, right? I mean, in terms of his training?"

She pauses in the doorway. "Yeah, that's fine. Isn't there a scene where he'll have to be backstage while you're onstage? Someone will have to watch him then."

"That's true. I hadn't thought that far ahead." She's so close. All I want to do is wrap my arms around her and breathe her in. "Well, come on in."

As soon as I close the door behind us, however, I regret letting my father take Puck. I'm not sure how to behave without our furry buffer.

She looks around, inhaling. "Smells… interesting."

Suddenly feeling like a gawky teen again, I give her a wide berth as I head toward the kitchen. "I hope you'll like it. I learned some stuff from the chef at the house where I stayed for a while. I still have to do a couple more shoots to fulfill my contract, so I have to stay in shape, and I found that eating a macrobiotic diet helps."

"Macro… biotic?" She looks as dubious as my dad. "Is that a kind of food?"

"Sort of. It's all about eating real food instead of processed stuff. No refined sugars or flours, no alcohol, no pre-made food. Lots of vegetables. I don't follow it rigidly—where you only eat stuff in season from your locality—and I do eat some lean meats and an occasional glass of wine."

She nods slowly. "That sounds very Californian."

"Let me hang up your coat." She hasn't moved from the doorway. "Do you want something to drink? Wine or…? I don't have any soda or anything. Water with lemon?"

"Plain water's fine." She flashes a smile so tight it's almost a grimace. "I don't really drink."

Of course. "I don't either—it's not part of my diet—but when I was at the store, I just figured…" I'm babbling now, so I shut my mouth and pull a pitcher of cold water from the fridge.

When I turn around, she's managed to find the one spot in the kitchen that's as far away from me as possible. I set her glass on the island, thinking she'll have to move closer to pick it up. She just crosses her arms. This is a disaster. She obviously can't stand to be in the same room with me without Puck here.

I lift my glass, barreling on. "Cheers."

She finally picks hers up, backing up again to down half the glass. "Guess I was thirsty."

I set the pitcher on the counter.

"So." Her eyes dart away from mine to skitter around the kitchen. "I'd ask if I can help, but I don't even recognize what you've got going here."

"Nothing to do, really. It just needs assembling. If you want to grab a couple bowls and plates, we can get started."

I hand her two large spoons and gesture to the small round table by the window. "Go ahead and sit down."

When I set her bowl in front of her, she peers at it suspiciously. "What's this?"

"Miso soup."

Her brows scrunch together.

"It's fermented soybean. It's a yin food."

"Yin food?" She half laughs and there's a flash of something, maybe a smartass comment she'd like to make, but she just stirs her soup. "Interesting."

I lift my bowl. "You can use a spoon, but I like to sip it from the bowl."

"Okay, but don't tell my mom." She takes a tiny sip. "Not what I expected. But it's interesting."

"You keep saying."

She tries it again and then sets it down and studies the bowl like it might jump up and run around the room. "Well, it's different. I'm not sure how to describe it."

Neither of us seems to be able to start an actual conversation, so we finish the soup in silence. When I stand to clear the bowls, she starts to rise, but I stop her. "Let me wait on you. Just relax." I hear a sigh after I set the bowls in the sink.

When I look up from plating the next dish, she's looking out the window. "The leaves are gorgeous this fall."

I used to be able to read each and every expression that crossed that beautiful face, but tonight, she's so guarded I have no idea what she's thinking or feeling.

"You have a nice view here. I forgot that."

"When the leaves are all gone, your bedroom window is visible from there. Assuming that's still your room?"

She nods. "Yep."

"Remember when we used to send each other messages? Flashing lights?"

She nods slowly, her face still a mask. "Yep."

Guess she's not up for a trip down memory lane. I serve the main meal, describing the health benefits of each dish. "This is a particularly high-protein diet. Usually you'd have either tofu or seitan."

When I sit, her eyes meet mine, but they're not happy with me. "Is this some kind of message?"

"What do you mean?"

"That you think I need to lose weight?"

"What? No." I shake my head. "Are you kidding? You look great. Beautiful," I add, then wish I hadn't because she rolls her eyes. "It's just—this is what I'm used to cooking now. My dad won't even try anything I cook, but I wanted to share it with you. Since you taught me how to cook all those Italian dishes. Which I'd love to eat but can't."

Tension flattens her full lips. "Because you have to go back to California."

"Well, yeah. I'm obligated to at least two more shoots. And I have to 'maintain my physique.' It's part of my contract, which I can't afford to break."

She picks up a single piece of tofu. "Really? I thought you'd be rolling in dough."

"I made a good amount of money, and I've saved a lot of it. But CK Enterprises has very good lawyers. It's easier to just bite the bullet and finish up the job. The working out I have to do keeps me sane, anyway."

She's picking through the plate, politely trying everything. I lift a fork heaped with brown rice and steamed broccoli. "I hope you don't hate it."

She finishes chewing and swallows. "Well, it's better than it looks, I'll give you that. I like the vegetables, actually." She forks up a snap pea. "And this sauce is really interes—uh, complex. The tofu is surprisingly good. But that stuff?" She points at the seitan. "Is disgusting. Sorry, but I am not finishing that."

"Yeah, it's an acquired taste." I scoop up a piece. "It's good for you."

"Too bad. I'm not eating it."

"I won't make you."

"As if you could." She huffs out a laugh, and her face relaxes—not completely, but I'll take it. I ask about her work. After a few stories, we're both laughing.

"I'm sorry." She shakes her head. "All my work stories involve barfing or poop, not exactly good dinner conversation."

I sit back and set my napkin on the table. "It's okay. I've lived with a bulimic model or two, so I'm used to the barfing."

"You lived with a model... or two?"

"Oh, yeah." I scoop up the plates and take them to the sink. "A whole bunch of us lived together for a while. It was Keen's way of controlling our image. Supposedly. I think it was also some sort of strange social experiment for him."

"That must have been..."

"Interesting?" I finish for her.

She smirks. "*An orgy* is what I was thinking, actually."

A dry laugh escapes past my lips as I lean back against the counter. "He was probably hoping for that, but it was the opposite. We were all so fucked up it was more like one long group therapy session. But we were close, in the end. At least I thought so." Picturing the stark, modern mansion tucked away in a canyon, I suddenly realize that after everyone moved out, we barely saw each other anymore.

"The end? What happened?"

"He got bored, and the PR people decided it'd run its course." I shrug. "We all got our own places."

When I first came home, after my dad's heart attack, I assumed I'd be back in Los Angeles within a week. But something shifted. I'd just stumbled into modeling, and I didn't plan to ever act again. My agent wanted me to, but I was afraid of it, I guess. Now that I've found my way back to the theater, I don't want to give it up. Disappearing into a role does something for me that modeling can't. I guess posing for the camera is playing a character in a way, but without the words and story it's nowhere near as satisfying.

What I really *don't* miss? Playing a role in my downtime, too. Pretending to date people who just want arm candy. Until I came home and stepped off that treadmill, I didn't realize how draining it was. When I first got back, all I did was visit my dad at the hospital, eat, work out and sleep. When rehearsals started for *Romeo and Juliet*, it was like I woke up again.

Acting energizes me. Modeling drains me.

"Ben?"

I look up from the sink. "What? Sorry, I guess I zoned out there."

Lucy's on the other side of the island, and we're back to square one. "I was saying thanks for the meal. I'm going to head home."

"Are you sure? We could watch a movie. I rented some videos."

She looks at the TV, then back at me before walking to the door, shaking her head. "You're paying me, Ben. We're all good. You don't have to feel sorry for me."

"What?" I rush to catch her. "I don't. Of course I don't."

She whips around, hands spread in the air. "Then what the fuck is this?"

I put on the brakes, mirroring her gesture. "I just—I miss you."

Her hands fist at her hips, and she looks at the ceiling. "So, you think you can leave, disappear completely for seven years, and then come back and I'd be like 'Oh, Ben is paying attention to me again. I'm so lucky'?"

"No, of course not." I'm scrambling to catch up and just blurt out the first thing that comes to mind. "You were my closest friend. You and Tony. And I—"

"You left, Ben. You left, and so did everyone else." Her voice is wobbly, but her gestures are sharp, punctuating her words. "Tony was gone and my whole family disappeared into grief—my dad works all the time, my mom runs around all over raising money for Mothers Against Drunk Driving—and you skipped town just when I really needed somebody. You think you can waltz back now and we'll just start up where we left off?"

"No, I don't." I shake my head slowly. "I know it was awful to leave like that. After I got out of the hospital, I couldn't face you guys. I thought I'd be a horrible reminder of what you'd lost. And I felt so guilty because—"

"You felt guilty? How do you think I felt? Still feel?" She covers her face with her hands and roars into them, her frustration making me feel like the biggest shit ever. When she runs her hands through her hair and pulls hard, I have to stop her.

Easing her hands out of her curls, I whisper, "I'm sorry, Lucy. I'm sorry I left. I'm sorry I hurt you. I felt like... like I shouldn't have survived. I couldn't stand to be with myself, so I thought you wouldn't want to be with me either."

When she finally opens her eyes, they're filled to the brim with tears. The need to kiss them away erases all reason. Stepping in close, I brush my lips across her cheek. When she moans in response, my mouth finds hers and everything I feel for this woman is unleashed. Before I know what's happening, I've pushed her up against the door. Our lips crash together. Her hands grab at my shirt, then circle to my lower back to pull me even closer. Everything ugly between us dissolves. There's only Lucy, me and the love I've never been able to forget.

Until my phone rings.

Panting hard, I squeeze my eyes shut, wishing I could do the same for my ears. The ringing stops, but the answering machine clicks on with a loud beep. A loud voice follows.

"Ben. Pickup."

"Shit. It's my agent." He and I have been playing phone tag for two days. I have to talk to him about a new shoot he signed me up for that would totally screw up the schedule for *Two Gents*.

"Ben, where the fuck are you?" His voice fills the room, chilling it.

Lucy shifts to the side.

"I'm so sorry, Lucy. I have to tell him something." I manage to grab her hand and squeeze it. "I'll make it quick." After one pleading look, I jog across the room to grab the receiver. "I'm here Kirk, don't hang up. Listen, I'm still coming back to LA, but—" The sound of the front door opening arrests my train of thought. "Um, Kirk, hang on a sec." Pressing the phone to my chest, I get as close to the front door as the cord will allow. "Lucy, please—"

Lips that had hummed with passion moments before clamp down in a firm line. "Don't worry about it. I should get home. I'll see you at rehearsal."

Before I can say another word, the door closes between us.

Frustration roars through me, and I hurl the phone in my hand across the room before collapsing against the door.

LUCY

I make it home, wash my face, brush my teeth, say my prayers and get into bed. But no matter what I do or tell myself not to do, that kiss plays over and over like a 3-D movie.

Ben's touch was lighting fires all evening. The brush of his hand when he handed me a glass or a plate... I can't even imagine what would've happened if I'd tried to sit next to him to watch a movie on the very same couch where we'd explored a multitude of positions back when I was a wild and horny teenager determined to get my sexual education requirement completed before heading off to college. I'd even used textbooks and showed up with diagrams. Ben was a very accommodating TA.

Until he wasn't.

I'd thought we were so mature to pause our relationship when we went off to school. Like I was going to go and use everything I'd discovered about my body and sex and intimacy with any old college kid. I tried. I went to parties, I went on dates, I fooled around with some cute boys. But it was all so mechanical and meaningless.

So even though Ben didn't write me, didn't use the long-distance calling card I knew he had to try to call me at my dorm, I had a plan for Thanksgiving break. I was going to seduce him all over again and convince him that we were meant to be together.

And then the accident happened.

And he went away.

Which he will do again as soon as the show is over. I mean, I don't know what I thought. Like he was going to give up a crazy successful career to stay here in Boston and play house with a girl who can't even manage to move out of her childhood bedroom?

The only thing I do know? I wasn't *thinking* anything when he kissed my cheek. My body has no sense of self-preservation when it comes to that man and his mouth. And the rest of him. It's not even about how he looks. Yeah, the muscles are nice. But for me, it's how my body responds to him. It's like he's imprinted on me, and only his touch, his scent, the way he moves inside me—

STOP IT, LUCY.

Punching my pillow as hard as I can, I press my face into it so it will muffle my howl of frustration.

I can't do this to myself.

I can't fall in love with him all over again and have him disappear again.

As if. Stupid girl. You've already done it. You let him in again. So, what are you going to do about it? Shut everything down? Or give him another chance in the hope that things will end differently this time?

Isn't that the definition of madness?

"BLESS ME, Father, for I have sinned. It's been one week since my last confession. These are my si—" Something catches in the back of my throat, and I can't get the word out. Or breathe.

"Are you all right, Lucy?"

Apparently Father Signorelli's back. I made myself get out of bed this morning—after a restless night where my sex-starved imagination took that kiss from Ben and ran with it—thinking that maybe a session with the substitute priest would help me figure things out.

But now that I know that it's Father Signorelli and he knows that I know that he knows it's me, there's no way I can spill my *actual* sins.

"I'm fine, Father," I force out. "Sorry."

"No need to apologize, my dear. Please continue."

But I can't. I can't tell this old man that I've spent the past few weeks lusting after the guy I lost my virginity to back when I was a wild teenager who only cared about satisfying her every selfish wish, whether that was sex, food, music or just running around outside in the rain. He believes the crap I've been selling since then, that I'm a dutiful daughter and model citizen and I always have been.

So I make some stuff up.

"These are my sins. I yelled at my brothers, I took the Lord's name in vain and I—" I scan my brain for something, anything that's true. Best I can come up with: "And I lied."

I'm lying right now, and I lie to Ben every moment I'm with him.

My heart's slamming against the walls of my ribcage, wanting to call bullshit on all of it—even wishing Father would call me out and say, *Lucy, I know you. I know you're a selfish slut, and you'll go to hell for it if you don't truly confess.*

But he doesn't. He just continues with the rest of the rite. "Very well. For your penance, reflect on your sins as you do your rosary this week."

That's it?

Of course that's it. That's all he ever tells me to do.

"Give thanks to the Lord for He is good," he says, sounding a little bored.

"For His mercy endures forever," I say, wondering if I should have told him the truth just to spice up his day.

"The Lord has freed you from your sins. Go in peace." Did he just stifle a yawn?

"Thanks be to God."

At least that's the truth. Thanks be to God for getting me through that.

The window scrapes closed between us. Shakily I stand and exit the box. Last time I left confession with hope in my heart, my anger washed away. This time, I'm more frustrated than ever.

Teenage dreams… they *are* so hard to beat, because all I can think about is kissing Ben Porter again.

Chapter 13

"Give a Little Bit" - Supertramp
Lucy's May the Force Be With You Mixtape, Song #10

BEN

I avoid PR people like the plague since their efforts almost always take me out of my comfort zone—like, for example, setting me on for fake dates with actresses looking for fans and tipping off paparazzi so our pictures would get into *Star* or *Globe* or *US* magazine. So when Bianca Torres, Shakespeare Boston's marketing director, catches me on the phone early the next morning, I can't help but groan.

"I know, I'm sorry, but I just thought I'd check," she begins.

Bianca is the one who turned the CK fans who mobbed *R&J* into an asset rather than a problem, so I should hear her out. "No, I'm sorry; it's a reflexive reaction. What do you need?"

"Well"—she's obviously excited, and I have to suppress another groan—"I got a call from the lifestyle editor at the *Boston Globe* this morning. She wants to do a feature on you. At first she was suggesting something about your shift from modeling to doing Shakespeare at a tiny non-profit back here in Boston—"

"Bianca," I interrupt.

She laughs in response. "I know, I know, you don't want to keep talking about that. So I suggested a different angle. How about you talk about animal rescue? They can feature you and your dog, and they can include stats about abandoned pets or something like that. Then," she continues, gaining momentum, "we can run a fundraising campaign in the lobby for your local shelter or rescue group or whatever you want. What do you think?"

This *is* a creative angle.

And could be the answer to my prayers.

The other day, Lucy mentioned something about how dogs are so often put to sleep because they're considered unadoptable and how it's so sad because many of them just need training to correct bad habits. She's also grumbled more than once about how badly the vet pays. When I asked if she wanted to expand her training business, she sighed and waved that away, saying it would require so much work to get that going and she didn't have the time or knowledge to do the marketing.

A feature in the *Globe* could be the answer to that problem.

"Okay," I say, "I'll do it."

Bianca gasps. "Seriously?"

"Yeah."

"Oh, Ben this is great. We're a bit worried that people just think of us as a summer theater, so getting this exposure will be so helpful."

"I have one condition."

"Sure, whatever you need."

"I want Lucy Minola to be part of the interview."

"Who's Lucy Minola?"

"She's the woman who has been training Puck. And me. She'll be a great resource. She has some great ideas on how training can be a part of the animal rescue solution. There's no way we'd even try to use a real dog in the show without her expertise."

"Okay, sounds good. I'm sure the paper will be glad that we have an expert on hand. Do you want to call Lucy to get her availability?"

I hesitate. If I ask her, maybe it'll earn me some brownie points.

On the other hand, if the offer comes from Bianca, it might seem more legit.

"I think it'll be simpler if you work it out with her directly."

I give Bianca Lucy's number, and we go over possible times and dates. She thanks me so many times and so effusively that it gets awkward. Celebrity is so weird. Any other actor in the show would probably love to have their picture splashed across the local paper. For me, it just creates problems.

When I hang up, Puck jumps off the couch with a yip and runs to the door. I follow, grabbing his leash. If dealing with PR helps Lucy and dogs like mine, it's all worth it.

I scratch under his chin before heading outside for a walk. "That's right. You're my dog."

LUCY

After I set the phone in the cradle on the kitchen wall, I just stand there staring at it, the conversation with Bianca Torres playing over in my mind. The theater company wants me to do an interview with the *Boston Globe*—the *Boston Globe!*—about training Puck.

She said I can also talk about animal rescue and training and how the two intersect. People give up animals all the time because of fixable problems—like that woman who came into the hospital today. Her cocker spaniel was having accidents all over the house whenever he was left alone, and her husband wanted to get rid of the dog. I gave the woman a list of strategies culled from journal articles I've read and other owners' experiences—like crate training and walking the dog regularly—and some practices designed to desensitize him to her departures.

Ideas flip through my mind. I should figure out which rescue program could benefit most from the fundraiser the marketing person wants to use the interview to announce. I need to find statistics on the number of unadoptable pets that are put to sleep in Boston every year as well as what made those pets unadoptable and which of those behaviors could be managed with training.

I need to get these down before I forget them, so I hop up to scrabble through the junk drawer. I swear I saw a little notebook in there. Hopefully, there's a pen that works too.

"What are you looking for, sweetie?" my dad asks from the kitchen doorway, his suitcoat over his arm, his tie already loosened. Home from another long day of selling restaurant supplies.

"Oh, just a notebook." A spiral at the back of the drawer catches my eye. "Found one!"

I plop down at the kitchen table, find a blank page and start to write. The interview's happening in just a day or two because they have a last-minute opening, so I have to get this research done yesterday. I'll make a few calls after dinner to people who run rescue groups in town. I can contact the city shelter on a break tomorrow. Dr. Morrissey'll probably have ideas too.

The chair next to me scrapes and my dad sits down.

I look up. "Don't worry, dinner's in the oven."

He just smiles at me.

"What?" I rub my nose. "Do I have something on my face?"

"No." He pats my arm. "It's just good to see you happy. That's all."

Stupidly, this has me blinking away tears. I swallow them down. "I love you, Papa."

"I love you too, sweetheart. And I'm grateful for you. Every day." With a nod, he stands, squeezes my shoulder, and walks out the door. Moments later, the television clicks on and the sounds of the nightly news drift down the hall.

The kitchen timer dings. I hop up to check the pasta fagioli. It isn't quite bubbly enough, so I set the timer for ten more minutes and get back to spilling my ideas onto the page.

BEN

Saturday morning, Lucy, Puck and I meet Marcia Landon at the *Globe's* offices. After a quick round of introductions, the reporter launches into her questions.

"I'd like to just address the elephant in the room. Readers—at least the readers in my section—want gossipy tidbits from your time in LA, Ben. Dirt on actresses you spent time with, inside intel on the CK Empire, that sort of thing. Why shouldn't I do my job and try to squeeze you dry?"

My mouth drops open, and I just gape at the sweet, grandmotherly-looking woman sitting across from me. Before I can snap, *Because I'm not interested in talking about that crap and it's not what I agreed to*, Lucy leans in.

"Marcia, anybody can get that kind of gossip. Or make it up. Don't you think a more nuanced portrait would be more provocative? I mean, the *Globe's* not a tabloid." She shoves me on the shoulder. "This guy? He's not just a pretty face. If you saw him play Romeo, you know he's the real deal. He's an actor who can bring hundreds of people to tears. But what nobody knows—yet—is what a goofball he is."

She sits back and snaps her fingers. Puck sits up and rests his chin on her knee. "And the world might never have known if not for *this* little guy."

The reporter leans in, entranced, as Lucy weaves the tale of Puck showing up at my house and how because I didn't just drop him at a shelter for someone else to deal with, I not only ended up with a new best friend, I got the idea to audition for a role that will reveal a whole different side of me.

I finally find my voice. "I can't play the young lover forever."

Marcia gives me the once over. "I don't think you should be retiring that chest next week, young man."

I cough out a laugh. "Well, I'm not. I still have a contract to fulfill."

"Thing is, he's a clown at heart," Lucy says. When our eyes meet, my heart stops at the expression on her face. All I want is for her to look at me like this for the rest of my days. "I've known him since he was a pudgy ten-year-old—"

"Nine," I correct her.

She tips her head to the side. "Really?"

"Yeah, I was nine when we moved to—" I have to stop myself. I'm not telling this reporter where we live. "The neighborhood."

Lucy nods slowly, and a cloud crosses her face. "Oh, right. I guess Tony was ten."

I don't want to get into Tony's story, so I turn the spotlight on Lucy. Her work is the reason why we're here.

"The thing is, though, Lucy—and the training she's done with Puck and me—is making it possible for me to stretch and do this role. Launce is a tough character to play. Having a dog I can play off of, trusting that he's going to remain calm and focused on me in front of an audience, none of it would be happening without her." Now it's my turn to lean forward. "Another thing I learned from Lucy? Hundreds of dogs are dropped off at shelters every year because owners can't deal with problem behaviors like nonstop barking or destructive chewing, most of which could be solved by working with a trainer. It takes some effort, and I'll attest to the fact that Lucy is a very demanding teacher—"

"Hey!"

"Well, you are."

"Only when a student is extremely dense."

I roll my eyes and grin. "So you can train anybody if you can train me?"

She shrugs. "You said it, not me."

I look over at Marcia. She's scribbling notes, but there's a glint in her eye that tells me she's not blind to the chemistry between Lucy and me. That is not something I want out in the open, so I dial back on the teasing. "The point is—well, look at Puck right now."

The dog of the moment is lying calmly at my feet. When I say his name, his eyebrows go up and his tail wags briefly. "He's not whining or begging." I point to the spread of snacks laid out on the coffee table between us. "I can take him anywhere now. But when I first got him, he'd bark at anything and everything. Now, he knows I'm in charge."

At that, he rolls onto his side with a little moan.

Marcia laughs. "He may disagree with you on that."

"Well, that's true. Lucy's the one in charge."

Now that we've steered her down the path, Marcia takes the reins and gets more facts and figures from Lucy. All I can do is watch. The passion in Lucy's voice, in her face—I wish she'd turn it my way again. Maybe she will. Maybe I can get her to forgive me.

Then again, maybe I don't deserve it.

All I know is I want her to be happy. If this interview is the start of something great for her, that's a good thing.

I may have to be satisfied with that. I've been living in a fantasy for years; I guess I'll have to stay there.

Chapter 14

"Pump it Up" - Elvis Costello & The Attractions
Lucy's Right On Rock On Mixtape, Song #8

LUCY

I haven't been needed at rehearsal for the first few days of the week after the interview. I find myself driving down Ben's street on the way home from work, telling myself I'm just going to check in. I actually do have a couple of new ideas for the play. Maybe we can work them out and show them to Nick.

Sure, I could call to discuss it, but it's just as easy to stop by.

Who am I kidding? As confusing and provoking as sharing air with him is, it's an itch I can't help scratching.

After parking in front of the house, I head up the driveway. As I climb the stairs to his place, I hear a clanking sound coming from the garage. I sit down on the step and peer through the filmy glass of the window. Ben's in there working out, just like Tony used to do in our garage. He was always out there, even in winter, playing music and lifting. He had to maintain his "guns," as he lovingly called them. He always had some other guy there to insult and screw around with.

He tried to get Ben to work out with him, but Ben never lasted long, claiming he hated it.

Looks like things have changed. Ben has music going—it sounds like Armored Saint. Deanna's a huge fan, but I wouldn't have associated that kind of heavy metal with Ben. The band's name fits what I'm looking at right now, though. That angelic face is marred by a grimace as he presses a barbell toward the ceiling over and over again. After an insane number of repetitions, his muscles obviously straining, he sets the weight back in its cradle. Barely taking a breath, he rolls off the bench, grabs a jump rope and hops tightly and relentlessly. With no wasted motion, he sets the rope down and drops to the floor to do a bazillion pushups. Then he's back at the weights.

I'm rooted to the spot, watching Ben punish himself with this workout.

It's intoxicating. Maybe this is why he's so successful as a model. He's not only sculpted his body to perfection, but there's something in his pain that's mesmerizing.

Why is he doing this? What exactly is he punishing himself for? And what is wrong with me that I'm turned on by it?

This time when he finishes a round with the weights, he turns toward the window. Panicked, I shrink back onto the steps, and before I know it, I'm halfway down the driveway, my face hot with shame.

THE NEXT NIGHT, it's way past my bedtime by the time I pull into my driveway. Play rehearsals go until ten, but afterward Ben walked me to my car, asking questions about training that I know he knows the answer to. But that was it. No attempt to kiss me again. Things are just awkward between us.

He's a lonely guy and needs a friend.

I wish I were strong enough to be his friend without wanting to be skin to skin with him. To hang onto this good girl armor I've welded around myself.

It probably doesn't help that I spend every night staring at pictures of him while my fingers find their way to places previously so neglected there were likely cobwebs in the corners... which gives me about thirty seconds of pleasure followed by a few hours of guilt.

After I lock the back door, I check the state of the kitchen. Looks like my brothers and my dad put their dishes in the dishwasher, but they left a pot soaking in the sink and random items on the counter. Do they not see them, or do they think it makes me feel needed to have something to clean when I get home? I take care of it all and put plastic wrap over the leftovers they just shoved into the fridge.

Maybe they're right, whether it's intentional or not. Maybe if I spend enough time cleaning, I'll be so tired when I go to bed that I'll be able to stay away from the magazines. I start the dishwasher, set up the coffeemaker for the morning and wipe down the counters, adding items to the grocery list as I go. I move a load from the washing machine to the dryer and straighten up the mud room.

Finally, a yawn hits. I head for the stairs, but a light in the den catches my eye. When I reach in to turn it off, I have to suppress a scream. It takes a moment for me to recognize my mother sprawled on the couch. I've never seen her so... horizontal. Slumped back into the cushions, stockinged feet up on the coffee table, her forearm over her eyes—she doesn't look like herself.

"Mama, are you okay?" I whisper.

She lifts her arm to squint at me. "Oh, Lucy. I didn't hear you come in."

Not only does her voice sound like she swallowed a handful of gravel, she didn't answer my question. I hover in the doorway, not sure if I should join her or leave her in peace. "You're back early from Texas."

Her travel schedule has been brutal lately. She sits up, moving a bit stiffly, but she smiles. "I was able to catch an earlier flight."

"You should go to bed. You look tired."

"I should." She nods but remains seated, her hands spread wide on the cushions.

"Do you want some tea?"

"No, I'm fine." She pats the couch next to her. "Come sit with me. I want to hear about you. What's new in your world?"

I'm not ready to share what's going on in my Ben's-back-in-town-and-I'm-a-mess world, but I kick off my shoes and flop onto the couch. I sit facing my mom, a knee bent and my palm keeping my head aloft. Turning my focus on her is much easier than talking about myself, and maybe I can learn something from her that will help me deal with what Ben is stirring up. She mobilized her grief by helping to create Project Red Ribbon for MADD. They encourage drivers to tie a red ribbon on their vehicles from Thanksgiving to New Year's Eve as a pledge to always use what they're calling a *designated driver*, basically a person in each crowd who doesn't drink so his friends can.

"Is everything in place for the campaign?" I ask before she can start in on me.

"Yes. It goes almost like clockwork now. And with Wyoming raising their drinking age in March, we finally have every state in line—no teenager can drink legally anywhere in the country. We can now start collecting data, and I know the results will prove that it makes a difference." She leans back into the couch cushion, eyes on the ceiling. "But the families of victims from that horrible crash in Kentucky spoke at our meeting—the one where twenty-seven people were killed on a school bus? Seems like every time we have a win, we get clobbered again."

I scoot over to lean against her shoulder, snaking an arm around her narrowing waist. "You're doing good work, Mama. You're saving lives. Tony would be proud."

Her ribcage expands as she takes in a breath. She holds it for a bit before the air whooshes out again. "I hope so," she finally says.

We snuggle together in silence, and I just melt into my mom's warmth. I can't remember the last time we were this close—that I've been this close to anyone who wasn't covered in fur.

"So, are you still seeing Ben?"

I choke out a cough. Even when she's rarely home, my mom always knows what's going on. "Uh, yeah? He's paying me to train his dog for a Shakespeare play. It's been kind of fun, actually. The director likes what we're doing."

Giddiness swirls in my belly, and it's not just about Ben. "They're going to put an ad for me in the program, and I might be in the paper Sunday."

Her head snaps in my direction. "The paper? What for?"

She looks like she used to when we'd chat after school. The glow of her attention feeds me in a way I've forgotten to hunger for. "Well, the PR lady from the theater got the *Globe* to do an article on the dog in the play and the training process. We also talked about animal rescue. It was pretty cool."

"It sounds very cool. I can't wait to read it."

"They took a lot of pictures too. Probably they'll just use ones of Ben and the dog because the dog's adorable and Ben, you know, because he's famous."

Elbow on the back of the couch, head resting on a hand, she asks, "And how is Ben?"

I sit up and pretend that I suddenly need to take off my shoes. "He's okay, I guess. He's more... subdued."

She gives me an assessing look before leaning back into the cushions again. "He was always a good boy, a sweet boy. We should invite him for dinner. Maybe I'll even cook."

A short laugh barks out of me.

She slaps a hand my way. "Hey, I still cook."

"I'm not laughing at that. It's Ben. He eats this horrible diet now. Macro-bio-something. He cooked me dinner, and it was terrible. It's no wonder he doesn't have an ounce of fat on him."

A sly smile takes over my mom's face. "And how do you know that?"

Heat creeps up my neck to my cheeks, but my voice rises above it. "I've seen the pictures. They're, like, everywhere."

My mom nods slowly. "Mm-hm. Well, still, I'd like to invite him over, even if he won't eat my cooking."

"Maybe he could starve himself for a day or two first." I twist a chunk of hair that's escaped from my scrunchie. "I'm glad you want to. I was worried that you'd be… upset that I was spending time with him."

"Why?"

I shrug. "Because of Tony."

My mom props her forearms behind her head and stares at the ceiling. "Some days, every little thing reminds me of Tony and I get overwhelmed with missing him. Other days, I'm just glad I had him as long as I did. No one can take that away from me." She reaches out and puts a warm hand on my knee. "But we all have to keep living. I know Tony would've wanted you to be happy. And Ben. He loved you both."

Her gaze is still off somewhere, and I'm not sure what's behind her words. Is it possible she knows that Ben and I were more than friends that summer? We were pretty careful, but like I said, she's the kind of mom who knows what's going on.

"I love you, Luciana Maria." She squeezes my knee, then releases it. "And I think we both need to get some sleep."

I swallow a surprise tide of tears. "I love you too, Mama."

She lurches to her feet with a groan and holds out a hand. "Come on, baby girl."

I let her haul me up to standing and hold her hand all the way up the stairs. When we part, she kisses my damp cheek and then wipes it with her thumb. "Good night, Lucy."

"Good night, Mama."

All the way through getting ready for bed, her words echo in my head. *Tony would've wanted you to be happy.* By the time I've crawled under my covers, my body's doing a pretty good job of imagining what short-term happiness would look like—me, naked, in bed with Ben. Or anywhere. It wouldn't have to be a bed. His couch and counters and even the van all served in the past.

However, that brand of happiness has proven fleeting and dangerous. I've got to find something to make me happy that I can control, which probably means it should have nothing to do with Ben Porter.

The substitute priest said I should use my gifts. Not sure what

God thinks about dog trainers, but I don't think it's prideful to admit that I'm good at working with animals. Not sure whether it's a career, but maybe if I keep my eyes and heart open, it might bring joy not only to me but to some pet owners as well.

Once I'm under the covers, though, I keep going over and over all the reasons why I should or shouldn't sleep with Ben again. When I finally manage to mentally shove the list into a drawer chock-full of guilt and I'm about to drift off to sleep, a memory wiggles its way out of the folds of my brain.

LYING *next to Ben on a lazy Saturday afternoon is heaven. But I'm greedy. I want to be able to be next to him outside of this room, too. "What if we just told everybody we're dating?"*

"By everybody, you mean...?"

I snuggle further into his side, needing to be as close as possible. "Everybody. My family. My friends. Your dad. I mean, why can't we just date?"

Ben slides his arm out from under me and sits up, looking across the room. The inches between us feel like a chasm.

Pulling up the sheet to cover my nakedness, I ask, "Would you be embarrassed to be seen with me?"

He reaches out to grab my arm and squeeze. "No."

I sit up too, hugging my knees, wishing he'd look at me. "Then what's the problem?"

His head drops, and then he scrubs his hands over his face before speaking into them. "What isn't the problem?" He sighs and then gestures between us. "We shouldn't be doing this, Lucy. If Tony—"

"Tony is thousands of miles away from here," I yell. "Why are you still so afraid of him?"

Well, that got him to look at me, but I regret saying them because now he's pissed. "I'm not afraid of Tony. But he's my friend. And your mom is like my mom. The mom I never had. Every time we have sex, I have to push them out of my mind because I know they'd say this is wrong. You're too young—"

I open my mouth to argue, but he holds up a hand to stop me. "We're too young. Plus, I know you don't go to church anymore, but I can't completely let go of twelve years of Sunday school. Your family is important to me, and I know that they think having sex outside of marriage is wrong." He covers his face again. "A lot of times I feel like it's wrong too. Like I shouldn't be doing this with you if I'm not ready to be married to you. To be responsible for you." He drops his hands, and the look on his face is tortured. "I mean, what if you got pregnant? Your dreams of being a vet, mine of being an actor—they'd be gone. I'd have to go to work for my dad; you'd be a housewife. You'd hate me."

I can't take it. I grab his hand with both of mine. "Okay. I'm sorry."

He eases his hand out of mine, gets out of bed and starts putting his clothes on.

"Do you want to stop this?" I whisper, afraid of his answer.

He pauses, one leg in his shorts, head hanging. When he finally looks up, his lips are pressed together in a grimace. He swallows, then forces words past his tight jaw. "I should want to. If I were a better person, I'd say yes, let's date and pretend we never did this and give it up until we're older and ready to get married." He shakes his head. "But I can't give you up, Lucy. I'm addicted to you, and I'm not strong enough to give you up."

Chapter 15

"Sunday Papers" - Joe Jackson
Lucy's Keep on Truckin' Mixtape, Song #2

BEN

Since our interrupted kiss, it feels like Lucy's been avoiding me. At rehearsal, every time I get within a few feet of her, she suddenly needs to ask Nick a question or tell the stage manager something or go to the bathroom. I even followed her out to her car last night, asking stupid questions she knows I know the answer to, dying to kiss her again, but she's obviously relegated our relationship to strictly teacher-student.

I hate it.

I've been trying to talk myself into just hanging on until Nick decides that we don't need her anymore. We'll still be neighbors, I might run into her around town or when I take Puck to the vet, but I won't be driven insane by the desire to feel her lips on mine again, to hear her sigh my name.

Problem is that kiss is all I can think about, even as it unearthed memories I'd rather keep buried, along with ones that keep me in the shower longer than necessary. I'm tortured by them both.

I have an idea of what I need to do to put Tony to rest, but it's risky. If I tell her the whole truth, she might never forgive me.

Janet calls for a work-through of the next scene, which includes my first monologue. "Puck, are you and your master ready?"

His answering bark gets me off my ass.

Despite my inability to cope with the past, once we're up on stage, it all falls away. Puck's so completely in the moment he forces me to be present and just play. I haven't had this much fun on stage—felt so free to take risks—in I don't know how long. Maybe never. Bella and I feed off each other's goofiness, and Will and Randall are excellent straight men. If I have to be tortured by Lucy's presence, at least I'm getting laughs for my pain.

However, this monologue still has a few sticky spots. On Janet's cue, I enter with Puck and tell the story, laying out my shoes, staff and hat to represent my family members. When I get to the point where I say, "'I am the dog: no, the dog is himself, and I am the dog—Oh! the dog is me, and I am myself; ay, so, so,'" I break character to say, "I'm as confused as Launce here. Maybe I need another prop or something."

Lucy sits up suddenly. "Oh! What if you take the end of the rope you use as a leash and tie it around your neck when you say, 'I am the dog'?"

Nick leans forward. "Right—then could we get Puck to bite the leash when Launce says, 'Oh! The dog is me'?" Nick choreographs movement with his hands as he continues. "You can try to stand when you say 'and I am myself' and then pretend to get strangled on 'ay, so,' wrestle with it a bit, and end up on the floor as if the rope is attacking you until you finally release yourself on the second 'so.' And then take a moment to recover before moving on to the next beat?"

"I think I'm going to need a longer rope, but yeah, I think I get what you're saying."

Janet nods to her assistant, and Becky runs off to look for a different rope while Lucy and I work on teaching Puck to grab the one I've got on cue. She suggests that I growl when I hand Puck the rope, and he quickly picks up that I want to do a tug of war, which totally makes sense for the back and forth where Launce can't figure out who is the dog and who is himself.

Then Becky gets back with a long rope, and Will steps in to supervise. He's the fight choreographer, so he has to make sure that I'm choking myself safely. When all is said and done, we've spent an hour on twenty words, but when I perform it in a run-through later, the reaction from the other cast members makes it all worthwhile. My writhing on the floor as if I'm choking while Puck growls and seems to drag me across the stage has everyone in hysterics.

When we break, I look around for Lucy to thank her for the idea, but she's nowhere to be found. Becky tells me Lucy had to leave. "Oh, and Nick said he doesn't want you to add anymore new business—or props"—she says with a wink—"after the designer run-through this weekend. So we won't need Lucy after that."

I nod, doing my best to hide my disappointment. And panic. What will I do when I don't have an excuse to see her again? "Am I done for the day too?"

Becky looks over the schedule. "I think Nick wants you to stay, but you can take a break. It'll be at least another forty-five minutes until we need you."

Out in the parking lot, I button up my coat as I take in the crisp autumn air, catching the scent of wood smoke. Somebody has a fire going. An image of myself cozied up in front of a hearth with Lucy is quickly replaced by one of a car engulfed in flames. Shaking them both off, I tug on Puck's leash. "Let's go, boy."

As soon as we're no longer performing, life comes crashing back in. I'm going to have to face Lucy with the full truth. If I don't, it'll never let me go.

LUCY

Just as I'm turning the bacon Saturday morning, there's a soft knock at the back door. Weird. When I peer through the curtains, there's a sweaty Ben on the stoop.

I open the door, and he holds up a newspaper. "This was in the driveway when I got back from my run, and I wanted to make sure you saw the article."

The scent of smoking bacon drags my attention away from the sight of his chest in a super tight tee shirt. Not an easy task. "Hang on, I'm burning breakfast."

Scooting over to the stove, I use the few minutes it takes to rescue the bacon and butter some toast to rein in my libido. He doesn't move from the doorstep. "You can come in. Nobody else is up."

He wipes his feet carefully and steps just inside the door. "It's not that I don't want to see your family. It's just weird." He looks around the room. "Your kitchen looks exactly the same."

"Yeah, redecorating's not a big priority around here. Breakfast, on the other hand, is at the top of everybody's list." I swoop the plate of bacon under Ben's nose. "Don't you wish you could have some?"

He groans. "Stop. You're killing me. I miss bacon so much."

I waggle a piece in front of his nose. "Come on. Just have one. All the kids are doing it."

He slaps his hands to his face and squirms. "Peer pressure doesn't work on me. I watched all the after-school specials."

I hold up the bacon and point at his midsection with the spatula. Using a deep, announcer-like voice, I say, "This is your belly." I point at my stomach. "This is your belly on bacon."

Ben shakes his head but he's laughing. "You oughtta take that act on the road."

"Maybe I will."

I do miss this goofy guy. I miss our shared weird jokes. I miss a lot of things. However, kidding around is one thing, but the other stuff we shared? He was right when he argued that it was wrong the first time around. Steering my naughty body away from him, I grab a bowl and start cracking eggs into it. "Read me the article so I can keep cooking. Two large, half-grown males will be here any minute demanding to be fed."

"Okay, but you have to see this first."

Is he going to take off his shirt so I can see those muscles up close and personal? *Oh, Lucy, you need to go back to confession.* I turn, only the teeniest bit hopeful that's what he wants to show me. Sadly, he holds up the front page of the Living section. A large picture of Ben, Puck and me fills the space above the fold.

"Yuck. That's a terrible picture of me."

"No, it's not. You look great." He turns it around. "I really look different with a beard, huh?"

"*You* look great. I look"—I shudder—"I just don't like seeing myself like that." I shake my head and get back to the eggs.

"You get used to it."

I catch his eye and can't help but mirror his grin. "Right. Those agents are gonna be knocking down my door begging me to sign a modeling contract."

He shrugs. "You never know. It wasn't something I ever thought would happen to me. Anyway, I don't think you'll mind what Marcia wrote. I had my doubts that she'd focus on the rescue angle, but she covered everything you talked about."

With a quick glance over at him, I pull out another frying pan. Is he angry that I got all the focus? It's hard to tell because he switches to an actor voice to read the article, which is so long I've finished scrambling the eggs, slicing fruit and pouring orange juice by the time he's done.

I pop plates into the oven to keep things warm and hold up the carafe of coffee. "You sure you don't want anything? Coffee? Water?"

"I'd take a glass of ice water."

It's weird asking him these things. When we were kids, he just grabbed what he wanted like the rest of us did. I fill a glass for him, and he leans against the counter to drink it. After refilling my coffee, I stand next to him to look over the article. My nerve endings are abuzz, and I don't think it's just the caffeine. "This is great. She pretty much wrote everything I said."

He sets down his empty glass. "Not so much about the play, though."

"Will Bianca be upset?"

"It's probably fine. She thought this might reach a different audience. They'll review the play when it opens."

I pull the paper closer to me and trace Puck's cute little face. I bump Ben's shoulder with mine, savoring this closeness. "If Puck's appearance in the show means that more people keep their pets, it'll be worth it. At least to me."

When he meets my gaze, everything melts. All my reasoning, all my defenses, all my willpower just puddle on the floor. I'd do anything for this man. Even at the risk of my status with the man upstairs.

Then a door slams upstairs, and he flinches away from me like I'm as dangerous as bacon. After setting his empty glass on the counter, he heads for the door. "I have to get going. We have rehearsal all day." He takes another look around the kitchen again, a hand on the doorknob. "I guess we won't see you for a bit since Nick cut you off."

I make air quotes as I say, "No more new bits."

"No more new bits," Ben echoes. Unlike me, he does a good imitation of Nick's accent. "He's right, though. We have to perfect what we've got. But you're coming to the opening, right?"

"Opening?"

"A week from Friday? There's a party afterwards. Lots of donors will be there so lots of potential clients." At the sound of big feet clomping down the stairs, his face drains of color and he practically runs out the door. "I'll see you then," he calls over his shoulder.

"Okay then," I mutter as I stick his glass in the dishwasher.

Picking up the paper, I study the front-page photo. I don't look that bad. The grin on my face is real, anyway.

The one on Ben's is too—so different from how he looks in the magazines.

Before I can get lost in a fantasy world, reality crashes into the kitchen in the form of my two brothers. My two loud, ravenous, very much alive little brothers.

BEN

"Ben, what the fuck?" Kirk Vancouver's voice grabs me by the collar and shakes me as if he's across the room rather than across the country.

"What did I do now?" I knew I shouldn't have answered the phone, but I didn't think my agent would call me on a Sunday night. I've been dodging his messages for a few days now. You just never know which Kirk you're going to get: supportive counselor or cutting bully. Thus, the avoidance. Plus, my gut says he has news I don't want to hear.

"What's with the huge photo of you with the mutt and the fat girl in the *Boston Globe*? And what the hell is that beard about? You're as scruffy as the damn dog."

"That *gorgeous* woman just happens to be the love of my life." As soon as the words cross my lips, I regret them. Kirk will somehow leverage this knowledge and probably not in ways I'll be happy with.

He groans. "Oh my god. It's worse than I thought. First you're wasting your time with some two-bit theater, and now you're in love with some girl you just met? Jesus. You need to get back here."

I drop into a chair. Kirk's an asshole, but he isn't a complete dick, especially as agents go. When I needed to get back here for my dad, he moved heaven and earth so I could make a clean exit from work obligations. He gets that family is a priority. I guess it isn't his fault that he grew up in Hollywood and has absolutely no idea that a world exists outside of it.

I take a deep breath so I can speak to him in a calm but forceful voice, like he's just a big, naughty puppy. "Listen Kirk, this is a girl I've known since I was nine years old. I've always loved her. It's a long story, but I am happy here. I'm happy to spend time with her while doing challenging and rewarding work, even if it is on a small professional theatre contract."

He snorts. "What's that, a theater for small professionals?" He laughs at his own lame joke. "Come on, Ben. You've got a career here. You just said it. You're a real actor. I've been trying to get you to see that for years. Now is your time. You can transition from modeling to movies while the iron's hot. Serious movies, not just any old crap. We're talking Oscar-worthy movies. Maybe even a Broadway play. You need to get back here and get your head on straight. Bring the girl if you have to. She'll love it."

His rapid-fire attack has me up and pacing. "I get what you're saying—"

"Great. So when are you coming back?"

"I told you I'd be back for the shoot on November eighth."

"The shoot's that day."

"I know. I already have a flight booked on the sixth, which is closing night. I'll go straight to the airport after the last performance."

"You seriously have to stay till then?"

"Yes, I do." Like a little kid, Kirk thinks that if he asks me to do something enough times, I'll just give in. Sometimes it works, but not this time. "I believe I've stated very clearly that I'm not leaving the show. There are no understudies."

"Jesus. What kind of a rinky-dink joint is this?"

"Kirk, enough."

"All right, all right, but you're mine as soon as you get back. You need to get a pager so I can get through to you. I'm going to line up a couple meetings that week."

I take a deep breath and blow it out again. Kirk took me under his wing when I was a scrawny kid with a busted leg. After I graduated and my internship was done, he hired me. I owe my entire career to him, so it's hard for me to stand my ground. "Kirk, listen, I'm not sure what my plans are after this. So please don't make any commitments beyond my current obligations to CK."

Deafening silence echoes from his end of the line, a rarity with Kirk. Maybe he has another call coming in. "Ben. I think you're making a mistake here." I can hear the strain in his voice. "When you get back, we'll sit down and talk. Just you and me. Meanwhile, no more photo shoots that I don't know about. I haven't heard from the CK people, but this is technically in violation of your contract."

"I didn't get paid for it. It was a PR thing for the theater."

"It doesn't matter. They have control of your image. The beard might actually work for you in this case. You're almost unrecognizable. Hopefully, no one will see it."

I stifle a grunt. "No one" to Kirk means no one in LA or New York. The half a million people who live in Boston don't count. "Okay, Kirk."

"I mean it. No more pictures."

"I heard you."

"And get a pager."

Biting back a groan, I cave. "I will get a pager if you will only use it when it's really necessary."

"Sure, no problem. Get the number to my girl. Gotta jump. Another call coming in. Catch you in a couple weeks."

"Will do."

And he's gone. I can breathe again. Until it hits me. The clock is ticking down. Everything in me wants to use the time I have left to convince Lucy that we should be together. I'm just not sure it's the right thing to do.

For her or for me.

What if dragging up the past just makes her hate me—or herself— all over again?

LUCY

When I walk into the staff room Monday morning, Deanna slaps a stack of *While You Were Out* slips onto the table. "Messages. For you." She points to more pinned on the corkboard. "Jesus, Lucy. You're gonna have to get a service."

Giving my locker the usual shove to get it to close all the way, I give the papers a wide berth as I fill my pockets with treats and clean instruments.

Deanna looks like she's about to explode. "Aren't you at least curious?"

"I guess?" I leaf through the thick pink pile. They're all names I don't recognize, and they all want me to call them back. "Who are these people?"

"All these people left messages on the machine. Sorry, but I gave up writing down the particulars. It took me forever as it was." She jabs a finger at the pile. "Every single one of 'em saw you in the paper and wants you to fix their pets." She barks out a single laugh. "Good luck with that. And you're up in exam four," she calls from the hallway.

"Okay, thanks," I mumble as I shuffle through them.

What am I going to do with all this? On the one hand, the idea of all these potential clients is exciting. A dream come true, even. But how will I find the time? My family depends on me to keep the household running smoothly, not to mention my full-time job. Or the fact that I don't really know what I'm doing.

"Lucy. Exam four." Deanna's back in the doorway. "And there's a waiting room full of patients, so move it."

The rest of the day flies by in a blur.

I spend my lunch hour calling back about half the people, scheduling appointments with some and politely declining others. I'm halfway confident in my dog-training abilities, but I truly haven't a clue how to train a ferret. Or a parrot. So far, I'm meeting the owners of four dogs after work this week. Maybe if I'm efficient and only take clients I know I can help, I can make this work. Knowing I'll be making a difference in the lives of these pets will give me the extra energy I need to make it through longer days.

Good thing Ben doesn't need me anymore.

Because I have to be good and that has to be enough.

Chapter 16

"You're My Best Friend" - Queen
Lucy's May the Force Be With You Mixtape, Song #1

BEN

"Hullo, stranger."

Mira Chakrabarti's smooth voice never fails to calm me. Born in London but raised in the Boston suburbs, her chameleon-like accent's dialed to posh Brit at the moment. That usually happens when she's in director mode. I love her, but that doesn't mean I won't give her shit. "Stranger? Who's the stranger here? You talked me into staying in town, and then you disappeared."

My best friend from college is the reason I'm working at Shakespeare Boston. The week before *Romeo and Juliet* rehearsals began this summer, Mira asked me to step in to play Romeo after the actor she'd originally cast broke his leg. I'd only been in town for a week and Kirk was already bugging me to come back to LA. My dad was on the mend, but I was still worried about him. Plus, I was terrified to return to the stage.

But she bullied me into doing it, and now she's off directing something somewhere in the Midwest. "Where are you, anyway?"

"Indianapolis, for now. We open here in ten days. Then I'm off to Syracuse to direct a holiday show. How are you, darling? I miss you. I'm a bit miffed that I had to find out from Janet that you're doing another show. Launce, eh? That's quite a leap from Romeo. And you're using a real dog? Whose is it?"

"His name is Puck, and he's mine, I guess. He just showed up at my house and no one has claimed him and he ended up in the show."

"A live dog. I'm surprised that fuddy-duddy Nicholas was willing to take a risk." There's a competitive edge to her voice making me wonder if there's a story there that I somehow don't know about, but before I can ask, Puck—who has joined me on the couch and is enjoying a belly rub while I talk—groans with pleasure.

Mira laughs. "That good, eh?"

"Uh, that was Puck. The dog. He's a bit of a hedonist."

"Hmm. Sounds like he's a good influence."

I ignore that and skip back to one of her earlier questions. "Anyway, I think it's going well. We're about to head into tech. It's been a good challenge, and I kind of can't wait for an audience at this point."

"But...?"

Mira can always hear subtext. It's one of the reasons she's such a good director. I just don't know if I'm ready to talk about whatever it is that's happening—or not happening—between me and Lucy. Mira is pretty much the only person who knows everything that happened my senior year of college, but we haven't talked about it for years. "Um."

"Oh my god, you're in love. Who is it? I know it's not Jessica. You two didn't have any real chemistry offstage. Is it that lovely Bella? She's very talented."

"No. I mean, yes. I'm in love. But it's not Bella. She's great, but... Ugh. I'm so confused."

"All right, lay it out for me. You know you want to," she singsongs.

My heart's suddenly slamming against my ribcage, but maybe it'll help to talk it through with someone I trust but who isn't in the thick of this mess. "You remember Lucy?"

"The girl you ran away from?"

"Well, to be fair, I wasn't just running away from her."

"Mm-hmm, you tell yourself that all you want. What's happening?"

"Well, I ran into her again because of Puck, and we've been seeing each other—not *seeing* each other seeing each other, although a big part of me would like that. In fact, we did kiss, but it got interrupted. But the point is, she's the dog trainer we used for Crab."

"You've got yourself tied up in quite a knot over this girl, darling."

"You could say that. But that's not the only problem." I hesitate, wondering if I want to hear Mira's career advice. This is the one thing she might judge me for.

She clears her throat. "The only problem? I don't have all day here, Benedick." Mira uses my given name when she's revving up to boss me around.

"I had a talk with Kirk."

"Ah, the hardworking Kirk Vancouver."

"He wants me to start going out for film. He thinks I'm ready."

"Well, of course you're ready, my sweet. You're an amazing actor. In fact, I hope I can scoot back home for this show. I'm so proud of you for taking that risk."

"He doesn't give a shit about acting chops. Well, he does. But he means timing-wise. He thinks modeling has peaked for me, so making that leap needs to happen soon."

She takes a sip of something. With her, it's either a shot of vodka or an espresso. She's intense about everything. "That makes sense. What's the problem?"

I let out a frustrated breath and get up to pace, the telephone cord tethering me. "I just... I don't know if I want to go back."

"To...?" she prompts when I don't continue.

"To Los Angeles. To *Hollywood*, to that whole... thing. I mean, yeah, some of it was fun. Plus, I worked hard to get where I am. It feels dumb to throw that all away."

"For a tiny Shakespeare company in the provinces?"

"Well, yeah."

Mira hums. She does that when she's thinking. She's likely on her feet too, flitting around her apartment or hotel room or wherever they've put her up. She has a suitcase she hauls along when she works out of town just for household stuff: colorful pillows and scarves and candles that she scatters around her new space, even her favorite spices and knives so she can cook. She brings home with her wherever she goes.

Something clunks down on a countertop on the other end of the line. "Right," Mira says in her let's-get-this-shit-figured-out voice. "What do you lose if you don't go back?"

I look around my own little apartment. The photo of Lucy catches my eye, but I need to focus on the career question first. "Well, the seven years I spent building a career there. That's wasted."

"You've saved money, though, right?"

"Yeah, it's not about that. I mean, that savings won't last me forever, but I could figure some way to make money here."

"So what is wasted?"

I stalk back and forth, swinging the cord behind me. "I have opportunities that most actors would kill for. Kirk, and my current window of fame, can get me into a lot of rooms right now."

The sound of liquid sloshing into a cup comes over the line, and Mira swallows a few sips before continuing. "Alright. Those are reasonable arguments. What do you lose if you go back to LA? Working in front of a live audience that actually appreciates the classics? Or is it about Lucy?"

"I don't know. It's not like I even *have* Lucy." Puck paws at my leg. I point to the floor, and when he lies down, I toss him a treat. "She's still angry at me on some level, though we've had a few moments where... The thing is, I still haven't told her about *everything* that happened when her brother died."

"Because?"

"Because I'm afraid of what she'll think. That she'll hate me. Duh."

"No duh." The old retort sounds ridiculous coming from her. "Ben. Not telling her is bad, and the longer you wait, the worse it will get. She'll be hurt and angry that you didn't trust her."

"I guess, but—"

She overrides my objections before I can make them. "You need to get things straight with her on that front before you decide anything else. Meanwhile, stay in the moment with *Two Gents* and learn what you can from the show. Take each step as it comes. Don't overthink it. Lots of actors are bicoastal, LA for pilot season and Boston for summer… Shakespeare and who knows what in between. There are dogs to be trained all over the world. Who wouldn't want the wife of a famous actor to teach their dog to roll over and shake paws?"

I start to protest that it's not that simple, but she cuts me off again.

"Damn, I have to go. I can't quite seem to adjust to Central time. We're up next week too, so I'll be buried. Tech, dress rehearsal, opening night, tra-la-la! But I love you, darling. Be present for your life!"

And she's gone.

I have to admit, I'd hoped Mira would have a simple solution for me. Though she's given me marching orders, they aren't exactly simple. Being present is fucking hard.

Puck whines. I get up to put the phone back in the cradle and sit down on the floor beside my little Zen master.

As I scratch the spot between his tufted eyebrows, Mira's words echo in my head. *Tech, dress rehearsal, opening night.* Rehearsals always build toward an intense final week. In tech, you work out the set and lighting; in dress, you add the costumes and a few people to watch. On opening, the paying audience shows up.

Maybe that's what I need to do with the story I need to tell Lucy. Rehearse what I'm going to say, then try it out with a few trusted people to work out the kinks, all in service of getting it ready to present to the only audience that truly matters.

The last seven years have proven that I can live without the love of my life.

I just don't want to.

WHEN I OPEN the door late Wednesday night, I'm surprised to find a soaking wet Lucy on my front porch. From the look on her face, it's not just rain dampening her cheeks. Dread ticks away in my brain. Worry turns to panic when she covers her face and moans.

"I'm sorry," she sobs. "I left the house, and somehow I ended up here."

I'm not sure how long we stand there just staring at each other but before I can move or say anything, she drops her hands, her eyes avoid mine and her tone flattens as she says, "You know what, I'll be fine. I'm sorry I bothered you. I can't believe I came over here to cry at you like I used to. I'm sure I was enough of a bother when I was twelve."

My stalled brain finally clicks into gear. "Wait—Lucy, don't leave." I manage to catch her hand, but she shakes her head, eyes on the ground. I give her hand a gentle squeeze. "Come in. Please? You weren't a bother then and you aren't now."

After a long moment, she allows me to pull her inside.

"What happened?"

She shrugs up a shoulder to wipe her nose. "Ugh. Do you have a tissue? And maybe a towel?"

"Of course. Hang on." I jog to the bathroom, and grab a couple towels, start to pull off some toilet paper, then just grab the whole roll. I hand everything over to her and steer her toward the living room area. "Sit down for a minute, okay? I'll get you some water."

When I return, she's perched on one end of the couch with a towel around her shoulders. Even though I hate that she's upset, I'm glad she's here. That despite everything, she still trusts me.

Setting the glass on the coffee table, I sit on the couch, not too close. "Is everyone okay?"

Finally, she looks me in the eyes. "Oh, yeah, I'm sorry. No one's hurt or anything. It's not that kind of thing." Her breath hitches as if the tears want to start up again. "It's"—she blows out a controlled breath—"Thanksgiving."

Guilt closes around my throat like a too-tight collar. I don't know what I could say that would be of comfort, even if I could speak.

"Sal and Vinnie ambushed me when I got home tonight. They're both dating girls now. Pretty serious, I guess." She shakes her head. "I don't know how I didn't notice. It's been over a year for both of them."

"Jesus. Aren't they like twelve?"

She chokes out a laugh. "We don't keep them in a deep freeze. Vinnie's nineteen, Sal is seventeen."

"Wow. All grown up."

"Yeah, a little too grown up."

Her lips press together, but a tear stubbornly rolls down her cheek. I'm aching to pull her onto my lap and kiss it away.

She grabs more toilet paper.

I sit on my hands.

She blows her nose. "They've been invited to go away with their girlfriends' families—one to Vermont, the other out to the Berkshires—for the Thanksgiving holiday." She tosses the wad of toilet paper onto the coffee table. "You know, the kind where people actually celebrate what they're thankful for and drink and play football and go for romantic walks in the snow?"

"Yeah, I think that only happens in movies."

"Well, they want to enjoy it like the rest of America instead of eating pasta and trying not to cry, which is my family's tradition." She grabs another wad of toilet paper and starts to shred it. "The thing is, I don't blame them. I'd leave too, but—" The pain in her voice has that dagger slicing from my heart down to my gut. "But I'm worried about my parents. It's the worst day of the year for them. They need us around them. But we have to move on someday, right? I just don't know... I don't know how."

I can't just sit here and watch her cry, so I scoot a hair closer and open my arms wide. She hesitates for what feels like a century before falling sideways into my embrace. Her shoulders shake. I rest my cheek on the top of her head. I don't know what to say, but I can hold her.

Eventually the sobs ebb, and she slumps into me. She mumbles something into my sweater. I don't want to let go, so I whisper into her hair. "Did you say something?"

She rubs her forehead against my chest and speaks just loud enough that I get it this time. "We just threw it all away."

"What?" I shift and nestle her into my side but keep my voice low. "What did you throw away?"

"Thanksgiving." Her breath hitches and she rolls her head to look at the ceiling. "The food. Pies my mom baked that day. Sweet potatoes she whipped for the casserole, beans she steamed, bread she cubed for stuffing. A whole half-cooked turkey. We just threw it all in the garbage. She's never made any of those things again. I don't blame her, but it's so hard this time of year. Turkeys go on sale and recipes are in the paper and it all just screams, 'Your brother died, and it's all your fault!'"

"What?" My heart splinters. "Lucy, it wasn't your fault. If anything, it—"

She drops her face onto her palms again, and her fingers dig into the curls framing her forehead. "I know, everybody says that," she growls. "Tony *offered* to drive out to pick me up in Amherst." The self-loathing in her voice is killing me. "Not that he had much of a choice after I moaned and whined about having to take the smelly bus."

When her eyes meet mine, all I want is to take that pain away. "Lucy, I was there, and Tony did want—"

"Wait." She puts the glass back down so quickly that it sloshes over. "I have been wondering this for years. Why were you in the car, anyway?"

My heart races. I pull off some toilet paper to wipe up the spill. "I..." I have to force the words past strangled vocal cords. "I wanted to see you."

Her eyebrows come together in a frown. "But we'd broken up."

I nod. "We had."

"I wrote you, and you never wrote back."

My head's heavier than a bowling ball, but I hold it up anyway and force myself to look her in the eye. "I did answer." Before she can protest, I add, "I never sent it. Them."

I grab her hand, thankful that she doesn't jerk it away. "I was an idiot, but the truth is that by Thanksgiving, I couldn't wait to see you again. So when Tony came by the house to say hello and then asked if I wanted to ride with him, I said hell yeah."

The spark in her eye gives me the courage to tell her the rest. "I'm sorry, Lucy. I'm sorry I wasn't there for you. I'm sorry because—"

"Ben, it's okay. You were in the hospital." She squeezes my hand, then lets go to get up and pace. "I'm sure the day was scary for Sal and Vinnie. The police came to get my parents, and the boys ended up with neighbors, not knowing what was going on. The holiday turned into a funeral and a wake. Every year since, we've all just tiptoed around each other, pretending that Thanksgiving doesn't exist, pretending it's just any other day so we don't have to be reminded."

I haven't told her everything, but this isn't the right time. This needs to be about her, about helping her deal with this Thanksgiving. Me relieving myself of my own guilt is not going to help her with that.

She's staring out the window, where drops of rain run down the pane. At least tears aren't still running down her face. The hiss of the heater is the only sound in the room until Puck hops up onto the couch with a doggy grunt.

I pull him onto my lap, needing to hold onto someone. "You know, my house growing up was a little like that. My grandma was good to me, but she and my dad never ever talked about my mom. I guess they were trying to spare me pain. But it was like there was this gaping hole in the house that we pretended wasn't there but had to step around. Like if we fell in, we'd never make it out again."

Out the rain-smeared window, light shines through the curtains on the second floor of my dad's house. "When Grandma died and me and my dad moved here, it was even worse. It's why I spent so much time at your place. Without you guys, I might've never known what a happy family was like."

She looks back at me. "I'm sorry, Ben. I guess I always thought—"

I put a hand up. "All I'm saying is that it could be a good thing for Sal and Vinnie to seek that out, even if they have to go elsewhere. To heal. It's healthy to leave home, Lucy."

She leans back against the window, eyes on the ceiling. "So what does that mean for you and me?"

My heart goes into overdrive, but my brain stalls. *You and me?* Is she talking about us as a couple? "Me and you...?"

She shoves off the wall to pace again, but with less energy than before. "Well, we haven't left home." She gestures around the apartment. "Though I guess you did. You're just back." She makes an odd sound. "Temporarily."

Watching her hands flap at her sides, I say, "I have no idea what I'm doing, so maybe I'm not the best source of advice." Forcing my hands to stay clasped together on my lap, I continue. "But I do know that papering over the problem doesn't solve it. At least it didn't for me. Maybe Sal and Vinnie changing things up will help all of you move through the pain."

She blows out a breath and looks out the window again. "Maybe."

With that exhale, she releases a bit of pain. Her heart needs to heal. That's what's important, not my need to expunge my guilt. Not my need to strip her naked and make her moan with pleasure. "And what about you? That's what you can do something about. What are you ready for?"

She meets my gaze with a shaky smile. "I guess that's what I have to figure out."

Before I can get up to give her the hug I need as much as I think she does, Puck jumps off the couch and sits at her feet. She squats to give him a thorough head rub and he rewards her with kisses.

The rat bastard.

Then she straightens, and her face is a bit more relaxed. "Thank you." She nods slowly. "Thank you for being my friend."

I missed my chance, but I nod anyway, accepting the role in which she's cast me.

"Always, Lucy. Always."

THE EXPLOSION OF METAL, *screeching, grinding, spinning. A hot moan of agony. A cold knife of pain. No breath. Tony's face—draining of life. But somehow still screaming at me.*

"What the fuck, man? She's my little fucking sister, and you've been screwing her?"

*In the back seat—*this is new, some part of me notes*—Lucy sits. Ripping letters into tiny pieces and pulling the tape out of a cassette.*

The impact again. So dark. Tony's face, no longer yelling at me. Dead. Gone. Pain. So much pain. And then... nothing.

My ears buzzing, eyes blinking. I can't see.

Pounding in my head. Pounding on the window. Trying to get out of the car. Trying to get away from Tony.

What was Tony.

Isn't now.

My best friend.

Gone.

I WAKE, panting and drenched in sweat, Puck barking from the end of the bed.

Grabbing my pillow, I heave it across the room.

A COUPLE DAYS later we're into the long tech weekend, which means way too much time to stew in my thoughts. No acting is required, we just have to hit our marks so the designers can do their work. And then sit around and wait.

When I check my watch, I can't believe it's only four thirty in the afternoon. It feels like midnight. We've been at the theater since ten this morning. There's still an hour and a half till the dinner break, after which we'll be here until ten p.m. Puck yawns, and I join him. It's a long day for man or beast.

It doesn't help that I can't stop thinking about Lucy. The only time I've spent with her this past week was in her kitchen Sunday—a surreal step back in time—and when she came over in tears the other night. Both times I ached to kiss her again, but both times it felt wrong. At her house I felt like I was a teenager again. At my place, she really just needed my friendship. And it doesn't feel right to pursue anything else with her until I tell her the whole truth.

I've got a monkey brain right now and I'm antsy as hell. I wish I could sneak away for another run, but Launce's scenes are sprinkled throughout the show and because of the stopping and starting tech rehearsals require, there's no telling when I'll be needed next.

I look up when the door leading to the performance space creaks open, thinking it might be Becky looking for me, but it's Bella. She squats down next to me, and Puck wiggles over my lap to get to her.

She scratches under his chin. "Hello, buddy."

I stretch up to my feet, yawning again. "Where are we?"

She crosses her long legs and leans back against the wall. "It's the beginning of Act Three. They're dealing with the ladder and Valentine's cloak, so it'll probably be a while."

I jump up and down, trying to get my blood moving. "I need a run. Muscle cells are dying."

"We can't have that. Girls all over the country will have to go into mourning."

"Hilarious." I shove her lightly, and she goes with it, rolling onto her side. Puck takes it as an invitation to play, jumping on top of her. Laughing and fake growling, she mock-wrestles with him until he starts barking. Then she turns her mom voice on him. "Shhh, puppy. You'll get us in trouble."

I have to defend my dog. "You started it."

"*You* started it."

"Did not."

"Did too."

We keep this up until Puck starts barking again and we have to call a truce. I check my watch. Four thirty-seven.

Bella nudges me with her toe. "Why don't you run at the beginning of the dinner break? I'll watch the pup."

"Really? That would be great."

"Yeah, Mom's bringing my daughter to have dinner with me. Delilah's been begging for a pet so she'd probably love to play with him."

"That'd be great." I shake out my arms. "I just need to move."

"Do you want to run lines?"

"Not really."

"Yeah, me neither. I'm just bored."

"That's tech rehearsal for you."

"Yup." She leans over to grab her purse and paws through it until she finds a tube of lip balm.

Puck has nestled in next to her, so I take a walk around the lobby, or what passes for a lobby. It's just an open room with a few cafe tables near the area where they'll sell refreshments at intermission. After I do a half-hearted series of calisthenics, I flop back down next to Puck and Bella.

She closes the magazine she'd been flipping through. "So, what's going on with you and Lucy?"

"What do you mean?"

"Ben. You're obviously gaga for her."

"It's that obvious?"

"Uh, yeah. You look at her like I look at chocolate, which is about as exciting as things get for me these days. So, what's the deal? Are you guys dating? Fuck buddies? What?"

"You talk that way around your kid?"

"Nah, I manage to curb my sailor talk when I'm with her." She holds up a finger. "Except when I'm driving. She knows she's not allowed to use that language until she's old enough to drive and has to deal with Boston traffic."

I laugh. "Yeah, good luck with that."

Bella seems to have a few secrets of her own—I mean, I've never heard her talk about a husband or boyfriend, but Delilah must've come from somewhere. At the same time, she's open-minded. She might be the perfect person to do a dry run with.

It's not like we have anything else to do.

Not sure I can look at her while I tell this story, I prop my elbows on my knees and my forehead on my hands. "Lucy and I have a history and I need to tell her something, but I'm worried if I don't do it right, she'll never forgive me."

Puck squirms out from between us to go sniffing around.

I peek at her. "Can I tell you? Like as practice? No judgement?"

She sits up, hands in the air. "As you can imagine, my life has not been sin-free. I am in no position to judge anyone."

"I don't know about that."

She drops her habitually cheeky grin. "You can tell me anything. Seriously." She points to her face. "Unshockable."

I move so I'm sitting cross-legged facing her, determined to just spit it out. "Lucy and I had a thing the summer before she went to college. We kept it a secret from her whole family. They were like *my* family; her big brother was my best friend, and I knew they wouldn't approve."

She nods, and I let my gaze follow Puck's progress around the perimeter of the lobby as I continue.

"We didn't break up exactly, but we decided that we'd give each other the freedom to date other people when we went to school. I didn't *want* to see other people, but in August it seemed like the best thing to do. By Thanksgiving, I was missing her like an amputated limb. So when her brother Tony came by and asked if I wanted to ride with him to Amherst to pick her up, I jumped at the chance. He'd been on a ship for months—he'd just enlisted in the Navy." My jaw tightens, picturing him with his super short hair. "I'm sure in his mind, it was a chance for us to catch up."

I can still hear the razzing that started up the minute my butt hit the passenger seat. He'd bulked up big time and grown a few inches. I was a scrawny twig in comparison. "Tony was giving me all kinds of shit about all kinds of things. The usual guy stuff, but mostly about how skinny I was."

"What? You haven't always had the body of an Adonis?" When I give her a look, she slaps a hand over her mouth. "Sorry," she says through her fingers. "You're just so easy to tease."

"You're telling me." I blow a breath through my lips. *Just get this over with, Ben.* "Anyway, I wasn't exactly working out back then. I was studying acting and I'd stopped working for my dad, so I wasn't lifting stacks of lumber or cabinets anymore."

Bella squints as if she's trying to picture a different version of me.

"The thing is, he was my best friend growing up, but it was always his way or the highway. I always put up with it. But that day he went too far. He called me a fag, and it lit me up. I mean, I actually had gay friends at school, and I knew the word was hurtful to them. Suddenly I was telling him I was pretty sure I wasn't gay because I'd been fucking his sister all summer."

I squeeze my eyes shut, but that makes it worse. The awful images that haunt my dreams are right there in technicolor. "The next thing I knew, we were in a ditch, the car was upside down, and Tony was suspended over me making this awful wheezing sound. I managed to crawl out of the wreck, but I couldn't get him out. I wasn't strong enough." I shake my head, the irony killing me. "All I remember after that is waking up in the hospital, my leg in a cast and my dad telling me Tony was dead."

"Wait, what?" Bella hugs her knees to her chest, her eyes wide. "What the fuck happened?"

"While Tony and I were yelling at each other, a drunk driver ran a light going eighty miles an hour and slammed into the driver's side. We spun, clipped a light pole and flipped into the ditch."

Both hands cover her mouth. The playfulness in her eyes is wiped away. "Oh my god."

I lift a finger in the air. "And it gets worse. When I got out of the hospital, I went to Tony's wake, but I could barely look at Lucy, let alone talk to her, because I felt so guilty. And then I ran." My tone slips from self-mockery to disgust as I remember telling myself it would be better for everyone if I just disappeared. "All the way to California. I did my last semester of school there, but really, I ran away. I couldn't face them. I never told any of them what happened."

She doesn't say anything for a few beats. When I make myself look at her, her brow is furrowed.

"Well, they know what happened," she finally says. "You were hit by a drunk driver."

"They don't know about the fight. They don't know I didn't save him."

She drops her chin. "Ben, come on. You truly think you could've saved him?"

"If I'd been lifting like he'd always bugged me to, I might've had a chance."

She covers her whole face, takes in a huge breath and lets it out, but she doesn't say anything.

"What?"

She drops her hands and clasps them tight in her lap. "Why does his family need to know about the fight?"

I can't believe she doesn't get this. "If we hadn't been fighting, Tony might've seen the guy coming. He could have stopped in time."

Sitting up straight, she shakes her head definitively. "No way. If he was going that fast, nobody could've reacted in time." She reaches over and places a hand on my knee, gripping it firmly. "Ben. This accident was not your fault." She jiggles my knee until I meet her gaze, which is kind but firm, probably one she aims at her kid. "If you really think you need to tell Lucy, you could soften things. I mean, like maybe say you were trying to tell him about your relationship, and the discussion got heated—"

"But that's not what happened." I tick off the course of events on my fingers. "I was defensive, I overreacted, I pushed his buttons and he lost it."

Bella shakes her head slowly. "I get that you feel horrible about all this—to be fighting with your best friend and then suddenly he's dead. That's… that's beyond awful."

There's a surge of emotion in her voice, and she sniffs and swipes a hand over her face. "I get having regrets. I've done things that have made life pretty crappy for other people—people I care about." A sob hitches out. She takes in a ragged breath and pushes through whatever's upsetting her. "But I have learned that punishing myself doesn't help those people. In fact, I have to forgive myself so I can support them. Everybody fucks up, does stupid shit. But nobody is omnipotent.

"Especially not you. You. Did. Not. Cause. That. Accident." She knocks her knuckles on my knee with each word. "Honestly, I don't think hearing about it will help anyone, especially not Lucy. But *if* you tell her, I think you first need to deal with your own pain. It totally sucks that you were fighting with Tony just before he died. It sucks you're not the Incredible Hulk, who *maybe* could've pulled him from the car, but who knows what would've happened then? What I do know? You didn't kill him." By the time she's finished this monologue, her voice has dropped to a fierce growl.

Puck whines, startling me. Realizing that my fingers are gripping the fur at the nape of his neck, I relax them to smooth the spot. "Sorry, buddy."

I don't know what to think about what she just said. My heart's pounding so loudly in my ears that it's hard to think.

But I did it. I told her. "Thanks. Thanks for listening. And not judging."

"Anytime." She nods slowly before standing and stretching into a yawn. "Yeah. I need some chocolate."

She manages to smack me on the side of the head before jogging away.

Chapter 17

"Feels Like the First Time" - Foreigner
Lucy's Right On Rock On Mixtape, Song # 9

LUCY

"How are things going with the play practices, Lucy?"

I'm inhaling my lunch—a mushroom calzone left over from last night's dinner—while Cindy picks at her healthy-looking salad. No wonder she looks like a bird. She eats like one.

I put down my fork to take a breath and answer her. "Oh, I'm finished with those. They don't need me anymore."

What I'm not about to admit, even to myself? That I miss seeing Ben and bossing him around every day. Not that I have an extra second in my schedule. Since the article in the paper landed, I've raced out of here at the end of every shift to drive around the city and train dogs and their people. Then I slog back home through rush-hour traffic to make dinner, clean up and nag my brothers about homework before collapsing into bed. Then I wake at the crack of dawn to do it all over again.

So I've been busy, but the time in the car is primetime for obsessing over Ben. It's not just the billboards. I've been listening to an unapologetically sexy mixtape that I made for us way back when, making me wonder if it would really be so bad to resurrect that part of me—that naughty girl.

"Are you going to the play?" Cindy asks.

Suddenly, my appetite's gone. I wrap up the remains of the calzone and chuck it in the trash. "I probably should. Opening night's tomorrow with a party afterward." Just the thought of having to watch Ben surrounded by gorgeous women at a party turns my stomach. "I'm not sure if I want to go."

Cindy drops her fork and her jaw. "Why the hell not?"

I go the sink to wash my greasy hands and get away from her scrutiny. "I don't have anything to wear. And I have to work the next day."

"Who gives a shit? You have a chance to dress up and hang out with a bunch of hot actors, including *Ben Porter*, and you're not going because you don't have anything to wear?"

I try to pull a paper towel from the dispenser, but it's jammed again, so I have to pry one out. And that's why my voice is strained, not because I'm conflicted about Ben. "Cindy, I don't really know those people. Plus, it's Shakespeare. I mean, the dog scenes are pretty funny, but the rest is probably boring."

She hustles over to get in my face. "Are you insane?" she asks, like I just picked up a bunch of sharps from the hazardous waste box and started juggling them.

Ignoring her, I use the paper towel I worked so hard for to wipe down the counter around the sink. "Cindy, I have to do the early shift here the next morning. Just the thought of it makes me tired."

Cindy plants her palms on the countertop, drops her head and takes a deep breath before standing as tall as her five-foot frame allows. "It is time for an intervention. You, Luciana Maria Minola, have officially become an old woman at the ripe old age of… how old did you say you were again? Thirty?"

Why does she keep saying that? "I'm twenty-five."

"Well, you act like you're fifty-five." Sharp elbows make pointy triangles at her sides. "You're coming with me."

"But I—"

Before I can list the things I need to do, she's dragged me outside. Cindy is surprisingly strong. "No buts, no excuses, no questions. We're outta here."

Moments later, we're screeching down the back streets of Somerville in a little car that only someone as tiny as Cindy would drive. On our way out, she told Deanna we had a wardrobe emergency and we'd be taking a long lunch. Deanna hadn't blinked, just waved us on. We did have a surgery cancel this afternoon, so I feel slightly less guilty about bugging out in the middle of a workday.

Is Cindy right? Have I become an old cat lady without the cats?

I can't remember the last time I did anything just for fun or anything even a little bit naughty. If you don't include kissing Ben Porter.

How long will it be before I've done enough penance to atone for my selfishness the day Tony died?

How will I know?

Cindy knocks on the car window, startling me. "Lucy!" She opens my door and flaps her hand. "We're here. C'mon."

"Okay, okay. Hold your horses."

The second I'm out of the car, she slams the door shut and pushes me toward a gnarly-looking building.

Eyeing the heavily graffitied door and rusty metal stairway, I ask, "What is this place?"

Cindy clasps her hands to her heart like we've reached the end of the rainbow. "Heaven. It just looks like hell back here. This isn't the customer entrance, but Roxy doesn't mind if I park back here." She giggles as she skips up the stairs and wrenches the creaky door open. "I'm a regular."

Once we're inside she bellows, "Roxy, I've got a fashion emergency! Do you still have that red dress?"

I follow her down a narrow hallway lined with racks of plastic-sheathed clothing and neatly stacked boxes. The heavy scent of incense doesn't quite cover the mustiness I usually associate with a thrift store. I'm not a fan of shopping of any kind—except for groceries—but the idea of wearing something that's been between the folds of someone else's skin creeps me out big time.

Once we enter the actual shop, I have to admit that the place is kind of magical. Soft lighting, lush maroon drapes, and pale pink walls make it cozy. Mannequins, posed like they're dancing, pop with color. It's the polar opposite of the bright white and stainless steel of our clinic.

"Honey, I told you, that dress ain't never gonna fit you. It's not made for your Twiggy body," a deep, raspy voice drawls from somewhere.

"It's not for me." Cindy pulls me around a row of clothing racks topped by hats and presents me to a vision of glamour that belongs to the smoky voice. Tall and broad shouldered, her dark-skin gleaming in the low light, she looks like *she's* ready for an opening night gala. A long, sparkly silver-and-blue dress swishes as she gracefully walks around a counter to greet us.

Cindy flutters at my side. "It's for my friend Lucy here. Lucy, Roxy. Roxy, Lucy."

I wave uncertainly, and Roxy gives me a regal nod.

Cindy bounces up and down. "Wouldn't that dress look great on Lucy?"

I cross my arms over my ample chest. "What is it? A circus tent?"

Cindy rounds on me, her expression fierce. "Lucy. Just because you spend all day every day in scrubs doesn't mean you can't dress up nice. I'd kill for your boobs. Wouldn't you, Roxy?"

Roxy looks me up and down. "If they're real, sure thing, honey." One side of her full mouth quirks up. "Hell, even if they're not. You're like a Sophia Loren crossed with Marilyn Monroe."

Roxy twirls a finger in the air in front of me, and I obey the order to turn in a circle. My face probably matches this famous red dress.

"Mm-hmm, that frock would be perfect with your figure." She taps purple-tinted lips with a matching manicured nail. "I may even have something that will make it just divine."

Before I can argue, I'm strapped in what Roxy calls a "foundation garment." I think it's really just girdle. After she floats the dress over my head, she zips me in, fluffs, poufs and tugs, holds my hand as I step into some very high heels, and then parades me out so Cindy can see what she's done to me.

I can't quite gauge her reaction. Her hands cover her mouth, and her pale blue eyes are wide.

Roxy steers me over to a three-way mirror. When I work up the courage to look at my reflection, I can't quite believe my eyes. I'd gasp, but I can't get that much air in. There was so much going on in the dressing room, I hadn't quite clocked that Roxy had twisted my hair up on top of my head and draped pearls around my neck, though I did notice when she swiped a dash of red across my lips.

The whole effect? She's turned this lumpy vet tech into a va-va-voom starlet.

Cindy's hand perches on my shoulder as she catches my eye in the mirror. "After work tomorrow I'm coming over to do your hair and makeup, and then I'll strap you into this baby." Her whisper's a blend of reverence and a not-to-be-trifled-with demand. "You're going to that party, and you're gonna rule the room."

I open my mouth to protest but she silences me with the nasal sound we all make when a puppy's about to pee on the floor. "Anh, anh, anh. I'm not taking no for an answer." She raises a finger and her chin high. "I'm even going to take your shift Saturday morning. So, you better have a good time 'cause you're gonna pay me with two Saturday a.m. shifts whenever I want 'em."

I take a long look at myself in the mirror again. It sure isn't the Lucy I'm used to. This woman is much closer to the confident eighteen-year-old girl that propositioned young Ben Porter so many years ago. Maybe it is time to stop hiding her light under a bushel.

I meet my friend's eyes in the mirror. "All right, Cindy. You're on."

I END up rescheduling my Friday afternoon training appointments because I have no idea how long it's going to take Cindy to truss me up and fix my face and hair. I wouldn't have been able to be present for my clients, anyway. I've been useless at work all day as it is. Veering between excitement and anxiety in anticipation of the night ahead, I can't stop wondering what will happen if I unleash my passions on the world again.

Weeks ago, that substitute priest's words put cracks in my determination to cage the Lucy that led Ben down the path to ruin seven years ago. Yes, I was a selfish brat to whine about riding the bus home from school. Yes, I put my mom through hell when I was running around town partying. But who did I really hurt by having sex with Ben?

Things started off awkward when I propositioned him the first time. For about two minutes. Once we were skin to skin, all the ways we knew each other—every secret, shared smile, every moment I felt like Ben just got me like no one else ever would—translated to trust. And pure lust. His touch goes past my skin, past my nerve endings and wakes up every good feeling that lives in me. Better than the best lasagna, the best antipasti, the best cannoli I've ever had.

And dammit, I miss it.

Maybe I was right the first time around. Maybe something that feels so good can't be wrong. And maybe it won't hurt to just try again. If we don't sneak around, if we're honest, if we act like the adults we are, perhaps we can have a healthy sexual relationship and nobody will get hurt.

BEN

As I scrub the last of the pancake makeup off my face, I'm thankful the CK makeup artists can't see me now. They'd be horrified I had this thick, pasty stuff on my face in the first place, let alone that I'm using a chemical-filled wipe to remove it.

But right now I don't give a shit. I'm riding the high that only comes from making an entire theater full of people laugh. We could do no wrong tonight. People were laughing so much they were bent over in their seats. They leapt to their feet when the lights went up for the curtain call.

Puck barks sharply and scratches on the dressing room door. "I guess you need a walk before the party, huh?"

After buttoning my shirt, I throw on a sport coat—a freebie from some designer—thinking that it is nice to wear something other than Launce's jacket for a change. Puck barks again, so I grab his leash as we escape out the back door so he can do his business.

Someone steps out of the shadows, and it takes a moment to recognize my fellow actor. "Whoa, Randall, you startled me."

Dark skin glows briefly in the light of a match. He draws deeply on a cigarette before speaking. "Sorry about that." He holds up a package of Marlboros. "You want?"

"Nah. Thanks, though." Plenty of models smoke as a way to keep their weight down, but I'd never taken to it. "I've got enough bad habits."

Randall grunts. "Not that I've noticed."

"I guess I keep them well hidden." I walk along the edge of the grass, letting Puck sniff his way down the row of bushes. "Good show tonight, man."

Randall plays Valentine, the male hero in the show, the one I'd originally planned to audition for. He manages a combination of wide-eyed innocence and lusty horndog in the role. "Thanks. You and the mutt are stealing the show, though."

I don't hear any resentment in his tone, but his face is hard to read in the dim light. "Sorry, I guess?"

He waves the apology down. "Pfft, it's fine. The whole thing is working. We're taking the people on a journey in there, and they leave a little lighter when it's over. It's like church, only better."

"Huh. I never thought about it that way." It's been years since I went to church. My dad and I had been regulars growing up. I'd even been an altar boy.

"Yeah, you know, everybody feeling together, breathing together, it's the best. The best of sex and church all rolled into one." Randall takes a final, long drag before grinding the butt out on the pavement.

I laugh, picturing the priest I'd served growing up if he heard that.

But I get what he's saying. After all, when someone laughs, their body moves pretty close to how it does when they orgasm.

Which brings my thoughts around to Lucy. I wonder if she used the ticket I left for her and if she's staying for the party along with the other VIPs. I look down at Puck. "Ready to meet your fans, little guy?"

"Hopefully, he'll leave some for the rest of us." Randall opens the door wide. "After you."

Moments later, the heart-stopping vision that is Lucy in a curve-hugging red dress glides toward us, heels clicking on the tiled floor of the rehearsal room, which the set and light crew have transformed into a softly lit party room.

"Congratulations! They loved you guys!" she says before throwing her arms around me.

"We couldn't have done it without you," I murmur into her ear, hanging on probably just a little too long.

She squeezes me again and steps away, shoving me with sisterly affection. "Nah, you guys would've figured it out. He's a smart boy."

He answers with an enthusiastic bark, and she bends over to scratch behind his ears, exactly the way he likes it.

Maybe Puck has the right idea with a direct demand for attention. Post-show adrenaline buzzing through my veins, I open my mouth to make one of my own, but before I can find the right words, Bianca steps between us.

"Sorry to interrupt, but Lucy, one of our board members would love to meet you. She has a dog with separation anxiety."

"Sure, no problem." She holds out a hand for Puck's leash. "I think I'll take our little friend along, if that's okay?"

"Yeah, sure. I think he misses you."

As do I is on the tip of my tongue, but before I can say it, they trot away from me.

LUCY

I glance back over my shoulder as the bubbly PR manager steers me across the rehearsal hall. Ben looks forlorn. Maybe I shouldn't have taken his dog away. But I have a job to do too, starting with giving credit where it's due. "Bianca, I've been meaning to thank you for including me in that feature for the *Globe*. My phone's been ringing off the hook with people who need help with their dogs."

She hooks her arm in mine and gives it a squeeze. "I should be thanking you." She looks down at Puck. "And this little guy. We had an incredible spike in ticket sales right after that article. The whole run is almost sold out!"

"Well, it was a very smart marketing ploy on your part."

"I wish I could take credit, but it was Ben's idea."

I'm not sure if I'm more perturbed by her dreamy sigh as she says Ben's name or the fact that Ben wanted to do an interview. "Really? I thought he was avoiding the media."

"Oh, he is. But I'm shameless, so I do my best to pimp him out." She leans in and drops her volume. "I mean, like, a picture in the paper of his bitchin' bod gets butts in our seats. But the only way he'd do an interview was if you were involved. He didn't want his modeling to be in the spotlight like it was for *R&J*. Which I get, but can we just be real here for a second? The man has got some *talent*, if you know what I mean."

She makes a little sound that's half moan, half groan. "I can't believe he's hiding it behind that horrible beard and baggy clothes these days. Although he looks pretty hot tonight. I wouldn't kick him out of bed for eating crackers."

As Bianca looks over her shoulder in his direction, I sort through her rapid-fire spew of words. The only ones that stick are "I wouldn't kick him out of bed." Of course, women everywhere—and hey, probably a few men—drool over Ben on a regular basis.

She winces slightly. "To be honest, I wasn't totally confident that featuring the dog training in the article would sell tickets, but this pup's picture got us a lot of attention, too. Didn't you, boy?" She leans down and he gives her a polite kiss. "Anyway, it all worked out for the best."

She gestures to the huddle of board members by the bar. "Shall we?"

When I nod, her face breaks into a saleswoman's easy smile. "Mrs. Wiseman! As promised, I present Ms. Lucy Minola, dog trainer extraordinaire, with the extra bonus of Shakespeare Boston's newest star, Puck."

The elegant woman laughs and claps her hands together. "May I give him a pat?"

I look down at Puck, whose butt wiggles in anticipation. Not sure if it's the additional attention or the cheese and cracker on her napkin. "Of course. He's very friendly."

As Mrs. Wiseman coos at Puck, Bianca murmurs in my ear. "I'm just going to make sure Ben has everything he needs, if you know what I mean."

As she sashays back toward Ben, her butt wiggles in anticipation, too.

The wave of jealousy rolling over me makes it clear: I want more than Ben's friendship. I have to force my attention back to the board member, already moaning about how her Weimaraner chews the furniture every time he's left alone.

Once my work is done here, though, I'm going to make sure Ben shares a bed with me tonight. I did it once, I can do it again.

BEN

Lucy's perfect no matter what she wears.

But that dress.

It makes everything else fade to black and white. The red fabric hugs her the way I want to. She's been passed from guest to guest—all potential clients, I suppose—all night long. I'm doing my best to be in the moment and enjoy the celebration. When Nick clinks on his glass to quiet the room for a toast, I pick up a glass of champagne. After a few sips, though, I switch it out for club soda. Obviously, drinking and driving isn't something I ever do. Tonight, I want my head clear for other reasons. My senses are already on overload. Every cell in my body aches to touch the skin that dress reveals as well as every bit of Lucy hidden beneath it.

I shouldn't.

Not before I tell her everything.

We may have successfully opened *Two Gents*, but I barely got through a first rehearsal of my story.

"Dance with me, Ben!" Without waiting for an answer, Bella drags me to the makeshift dance floor. As the night goes on and board members exit the party, the music gets louder and the crowd more raucous. Losing myself in the music, in the relief and exhilaration of a successful opening, I let the happy smiles surrounding me boost my mood.

When the music shifts suddenly to a slower tune, I go in search of another club soda. A couple of sips in, my eyes zero in on Lucy. She's dancing with Nick. As I watch, his hand slides down her spine, way too close to her backside.

It's time to make a move.

Chapter 18

"What I Like About You" - The Romantics
Lucy's Copacetic Shagadelic Mixtape, Song #4

LUCY

"May I cut in?"

The sound of Ben's voice has me stiffening in Nick's embrace. The director has been showering me with compliments. In fact, my ears are full of praise from every person I've chatted with this evening, but my radar's been tuned to one channel. The one guy in the room who's avoided me all night.

Until now.

Nick, polite as ever, bows and turns me over to Ben before I can say a word. My body instantly responds, melting into his touch. I think I hear my privates moan in anticipation.

I do not allow my mouth to chime in, however. I want to know up front that he's all in if we're going down this path again. "I was enjoying dancing with Nick. He appreciates all the work I've done on the show, as did every board member I talked to and your fellow actors. Even your dog gave me some love before he was swept away by his fans."

Ben leans in close, his mouth millimeters from my ear. "I've been trying to keep myself away from you all night, trying to give you the moment in the spotlight that you deserve. But I can't do it anymore."

"Pfft." Pretending that his words don't send shivers down my spine isn't easy. "I guess Cindy was right about this dress."

"The only thing I can tell you about the dress is that I didn't like seeing Nick's hands on it."

His voice dips into a register I've never heard before. The vibrations rumble directly from his chest to mine—even breaching the girdle. Struggling to squelch the desire fizzing through me faster than the bubbles in the champagne I've been drinking all night, I force words out of my mouth. "Is that all this"—I look pointedly between our bodies—"is about? Jealousy?'

He presses his forehead to mine with a groan. "No. It's just the straw that broke the camel's back. I've been trying to stay away from you for seven years. But I can't do it anymore."

Separating my chest from his with difficulty, as my breasts enjoy being nestled into his pectorals—not to mention other soft places of mine that ache to press against other rock hard places of his—I look him in the eye.

What I see there erases any lingering worries. Raw need. For me.

Suddenly I can't remember what the problem is.

Cindy's right about more than one thing, darn it—*damn it*. I deserve to have a little fun and it's time to step out of my goody-two-shoes. If being together is something that we both want equally, if it can salve some of the loneliness in his eyes, then I'm ready and willing.

Big breath in. Big breath out. Look him in the eye again. "Okay, then. Let's go."

The need in his eyes turns to shock. "Uh, just like that?"

"What? You want to work a little harder?"

"No. No. I'm good. Let's… go." He grabs my hand, pulls me off the dance floor, then turns around so fast I almost run into him. "Uh, meet you at my place?"

I shake my head firmly. "Nuh-uh. I didn't drive. I wanted to be able to enjoy the champagne, so I took a cab. If you haven't been drinking, you get to drive me home instead."

"I had one sip of bubbly and then switched to soda."

"Well, let's do it then." It's my turn to tug him toward the door. His roughened palm in mine is warm, strong. Familiar. I squeeze it once before stopping to say, "But this time, no secrets. No hiding." A shadow crosses his face. "Okay?"

His head drops like a puppeteer cut a marionette string, but he raises it again just as suddenly, his eyes lit with determination. "No secrets."

As we exit the party room, doubt and desire chase each other around my belly. It's been seven years since he saw this body naked. Will he be disappointed?

Batting those thoughts aside, I remind myself that sex between us was fun. That's the point, if I remember anything from all the books I read when I was eighteen.

However, I am having a hard time keeping up with Ben's long strides in my heels. "Slow down, mister. I'm not used to these shoes."

"Sorry." His grin is not the least sorry. That devilish look sends shivers of anticipation running through me and has me bouncing on my toes while he reaches inside his dressing room to grab his backpack.

As he closes the door, I realize someone's missing. "What about Puck?"

"Oh." He tips his head back toward the party. "He's having a sleep-over with Deb and Pam's dog Rufus and going to a dog birthday party tomorrow. We don't have a show until the evening. That's okay, right?"

He looks so worried I have to laugh. "I'm sure he can handle himself at a dog birthday party. Hopefully, they won't stuff him so full of treats that he barfs onstage, though."

He nods sharply. "I'll call them tomorrow and warn them about that. But right now, all I'm thinking about is taking you home and making love to you all night long."

He gets us out the door and to his car without letting go of my hand. Once I'm tucked inside, he runs around to the driver's side as if he's afraid I'll disappear if he loses contact for too long.

He starts the engine, but before putting the car in gear, he takes my hand again. This time he kisses it, his eyes full of questions that I have answers for—starting with bringing my lips to his for a long kiss full of promises.

Good-Girl Lucy has ruled for long enough. Maybe I can just be a girl for a change. Not Good-Girl Lucy or Bad-Girl Lucy. Just a girl who wants to kiss a boy.

And do a few other things with too.

BEN

I'm doing my best to drive carefully, but the prospect of seeing Lucy naked again has my foot heavier on the gas than usual. When taking a corner has her grabbing the door handle, I ease up. "Sorry, I'm a little impatient to get there."

"I'm with you on that, but I would like to arrive in one piece." She shifts in her seat as we close in on Arlington. "I guess I should stop at home to let my parents know I'm okay. And maybe change clothes."

"No." The word comes out more of an order than a request. "I mean, please don't." Stopping at a red light allows me to take her hand and tug on it until she meets my gaze. "I want to be the one to take that dress off of you."

"Alrighty then." A wicked grin I've missed more than butter lifts one side of her mouth. "I would like to pick up some clothes so I don't have to do the walk of shame."

"No problem." I make the turn that'll take us to her street. "Should I come in? Talk to your parents?" I don't relish the prospect of facing her parents for the first time in years when I'm about to do things to their daughter they don't want to know about, but I will if that's what she wants.

"I think it'll be better if it's just me."

We pull up in front of her house, and I grab her hand before she can get out. "We're both adults now, so—"

"I know." She squeezes my hand. "No secrets this time, right?" She looks over her shoulder at the house. "But it's late. They're probably in bed, so I'll just leave a note."

She opens the passenger door before I can get out to do it for her or even gather my thoughts. "Be right back."

I bump my forehead on the steering wheel a few times. Is this a mistake? I've missed her for so long. I *should* lay all my cards on the table before laying her across my bed. I wish I felt as ready for one as I am for the other.

LUCY

I'm breathless, and not just because of the strictures of this damn foundation garment. Neither the door I'm pressed up against nor Ben's chest yields an inch, but it's the ferocity in his eyes that has sucked all the oxygen from the room.

The tease of feathery kisses along my jaw, behind my ear and down my neck has me gasping, too. Who says air is essential, anyway? The need to be breached is more immediate, even if it's just his tongue or his lips, so I pull his mouth to mine. That crush satisfies for only a moment. I want to be skin to skin sooner rather than later, so I push him backward.

Horizontal. Naked. Now.

Either I said that out loud or he read my mind because he spins us so that he's in the lead, and we stumble toward his room, lips locked. When I bump into the bed, he turns me around and kisses down the back of my neck. I grind my armored butt into his pelvis. I can't feel a thing back there, but since he groans in response, I must've hit my target.

He unzips the dress so slowly I'm like a horse in a starting gate, dancing with anticipation. Cool air and hot kisses on my upper back fire me up further.

Until he hits the girdle. After a pause, the zipper whips south and the dress follows. His grip is the only thing keeping me upright as I step out of the pool of red on the floor.

The moment I'm steady on my own two feet, he turns me to face him again. I resist the urge to look down or cover myself. "It's a vintage dress, so it required vintage support."

"I see that." He bites his bottom lip, stepping back when I try to touch it.

"I'm torn," he says, shaking his head slowly as he explores the edges of the garment. Trailing just the tip of a finger under its bottom edge, sweeping under the garter and sliding to the top of a stocking, his caresses have me barely holding on to my sanity.

How have I lived without this man for so long?

Suddenly, his other hand grips my hip roughly, hauling me in close to whisper, "I've been wanting to see you naked for so long, but now"—he shakes his head and steps back again, his gaze roving from the spill of my breasts to the heels keeping me on my toes—"you're like a pin-up girl, Lucy."

He's laughing, whooping even as he sweeps me up into his arms and tosses me onto the bed like I weigh nothing. "Can you breathe in that thing?"

I nod, giggling, my brain a hormone scramble. "Mostly."

"It's just too sexy to get rid of."

The look on his face makes me feel like a box of chocolates. "There is… access." I spread my legs a bit wider.

Eyes on the prize, he strips off his coat, tie and shirt. Enjoying the show, I stretch my arms over my head. "Make me come, please."

"As many times as possible." After shucking his trousers and boxers in record time, he jumps on the bed, making me bounce.

Before I can move, his hands are everywhere, exploring the contours of the stiff garment and teasing exposed skin. When my gasps push my breasts past their confines, his mouth instantly covers them with greedy kisses.

I'm lost in sensation, and a loud moan escapes when his fingers sneak under the lower ridges of the girdle to find the spot that's as ready for him as it ever was. "I want you inside me," I gasp.

He's got other plans, however. "I don't think my mouth can get to you at the moment. But there are other ways to make you happy."

His waggling eyebrows make me laugh again. Somehow, goofy Ben is even sexier than the broody Ben of the magazine photos. Maybe because I know this Ben is all mine.

Giggles evolve into moans again as he expertly fulfills his promise. It's not long before I'm on the precipice, teetering for a deliciously long time until he drives me over the edge. Quake after quake roils until I'm nothing but a puddle of melted flesh and aftershocks.

Drunk with pleasure, I rock my head back and forth on the pillow with a long sigh. "Let's do that again," I say, sliding a hand down ridged abs to find an even harder muscle. "But this time, this guy gets to play."

He rolls to his back. "I'm ready whenever you are."

Straddling him, I let all my soft parts nestle between us as my thighs squeeze a groan of pleasure from him. When he looks over at his bedside table, however, he frowns. "Shit. I'm not prepared for this."

Turning his chin back to face me, I whisper, "Lucky for you, I am."

He laughs, smacking my thighs lightly. "You little minx. You knew you were going to get laid."

Rising slowly so that his hands drag deliciously over my heated skin, I shake my head. "It's not like I *bought* condoms." One at a time, I snug his palms around the part of him I'm more than ready for. "Hang onto this for me, will you?"

As quick as I can, I swing off the bed, kick off my heels and run to the front door, where I'm pretty sure I dropped my handbag. Seconds later, I'm astride him again, opening the purse's clasp and pulling a string of condoms from a pocket in the silky, red lining.

Holding it up, I say, "They came with the dress."

Chapter 19

"Got to Get You Into My Life" - The Beatles
Lucy's Right On Rock On Mixtape, Song #4

BEN

"So, what do we do now?" I ask Lucy the next morning. She's tucked into my shoulder and it's so perfect I don't ever want to move from this spot. At the same time, not having to hide our relationship opens up a world of possibilities. "You're not training Puck. I'm not driving you to work in the van. That's pretty much been how we've spent our time together in the past." The hills and valleys of tangled sheets shift as Lucy stretches. "Besides what we've been doing, of course."

She stretches her arms over her head, revealing tempting territory. "Is there really anything else of importance?"

"I suppose you have a point there." As I kiss my way over the silky skin her stretch has exposed, my body clearly agrees. We made love multiple times last night before collapsing into a deep sleep. Suddenly, I'm ready to go again.

She purrs with pleasure, arching into my hands and mouth. "I can probably suffer through another round."

A stomach rumble sounds between us. "Was that you or me?" I look down at my belly.

She pokes my side. "Are you allowed calories?"

"No tickling, missy." I try to sound stern, but laughter overwhelms the attempt.

Dodging away from my hands, she pokes and prods and pinches away. "Where do you put them? In these muscles, I guess."

Unable to capture her busy hands, I slide on top of her, our bodies fitting together with an ease that belies the seven years of distance between us.

Some time later, she collapses on top of me with a final shudder, her body covering mine like the coziest blanket I can imagine.

Until her stomach rumbles. "That's definitely you," I say.

She rolls off of me, laughing. Suddenly energized, I jump up to whip the sheets away, taking a good long moment to admire the sight of her lush body filling my bed before holding out my hand.

"Quick shower and then let's get some food."

"And coffee," she demands with a Boston accent.

"And coffee." I take the "aw" in "coffee" even further.

As I tug her the short distance from bed to bathroom, she says, "Thank god you don't drink that Morning Thunder tea or some other Californian nonsense."

"I'll never not be a Bostonian, no matter how long I live on the West Coast." I reach past her to turn on the shower in the tiny bathroom.

"Live? Not lived?"

"Well, I do still have an apartment there. And some work commitments. But I'm here now," I add when her eyebrows knit together. "Except for the shoot I have right after the show closes."

She nods briefly before whipping her hair up into a messy bun and tipping her head at the compact shower. "Maybe we'd better do this one at a time."

"Sure, whatever you want. I'll get coffee started." Kicking myself for bringing up California, I grab a clean towel from the small dresser outside the bathroom. "This is for you." She's already singing in the shower, her mellow alto filling the space along with the shower's steam. Setting the towel on the sink, I throw on some sweats and put some music on before making coffee. While it brews, I pull breakfast options from the fridge, wishing there was bacon.

How had I lived without this? Giving up bacon was a challenge, of course, but Lucy? There's nothing in the world like Lucy's body. Even now, after I've caressed every inch of her over and over again, all night long, she still shudders with pleasure with each kiss. She creates an urge to give and take pleasure that's as sweet as it is shattering.

I don't think I can pretend that I don't love her anymore.

So what *do* we do now? Despite the ease between us, I'm still in dangerous territory.

"Your turn," Lucy calls breezily from the bedroom. When she emerges seconds later, wearing one of my button-downs and not much else, her smile makes it clear that she's still with me.

Maybe it's as easy that. Maybe we can simply move forward, let go of the past, and find a new future together. "Coffee will be ready in a minute." I kiss her lightly on the nose. "And I am here. Now. With you."

"Me too." She drags a finger along my jaw before returning my kiss. "Get cleaned up, and I'll make some breakfast."

Slapping me on the butt, she dances into the kitchen, moving to the beat of "Just What I Needed" by The Cars, and I have to make myself get into the shower. After fueling up, we have the whole day together.

And if all goes well, we'll have the next and the next and the next.

LUCY

I can't imagine how I'll ever get off this couch. There's a *Star Trek* marathon playing at low volume on the TV, and coffee cups and other dishes are scattered across the low table. My head's on Ben's lap, he's absently playing with my hair and every goddamn inch of me is satisfied.

Yeah, that's what I said. If I can spend a day fulfilling all my desires, I may as well say whatever words I want. At least inside my head.

Thank goodness Cindy took my Saturday shift. Time with Ben is precious if he's going back to California when the play's over.

He draws a finger over my brow, which probably just creased with worry. "Tell me about your job at the vet. Are you happy being a —what's your actual title?"

Instead of answering, I grab a pillow to put under my head. "Your thighs are hard." They may be lovely to look at, but they're not very comfortable to rest on.

"You on the other hand"—he grunts as he hauls me up to sitting so he can lie with his head in my lap—"make an excellent pillow."

"Part of the joys of eating what you want." Flopping back into the comfy, old couch, eyes on the ceiling, I nestle into his embrace. "Though I guess no one would ever hire me to model their clothing."

"I would." He snuggles in under my bra-free breasts, punctuating his words with kisses. "I'd hire you to model naked, in lingerie, anything. I don't get why women want to be so skinny. It does nothing for me."

I pat one of my rounded hips. "Lucky for me."

"Lucky for *me*." He burrows into my side, where he knows I'm ticklish. I squeal and squirm, but he gets me on the other side with his hand.

"Agh! I thought there was no tickling!" I try to pry his naughty hands off me but I'm laughing too hard and he's way too strong.

He stops suddenly. "I won't tickle you if you answer my question."

"What was the question again?"

"Are you happy at your job?"

"Hm." I drop my head back on the cushions again. "I guess. I mean, I don't know. It's a job. The days fly by, and it's rarely boring. I do wish it were a bit more challenging and I wish I made more money, but you don't work at a vet's office to get rich."

"Not even if you were the vet?"

My dream had been to go to vet school—a dream that will never come to fruition since I didn't finish college.

"I don't think so. My boss sure isn't rolling in dough. People just don't understand how much it costs to run a practice. They want to pay twenty bucks and have us just tell them what's wrong. They don't want to spend a hundred bucks for all the diagnostics you sometimes need to figure things out. It's not like the animal can tell us where and when and how much it hurts."

He flips over onto his back and settles into my lap. "I have to admit I was surprised. I mean, my bill when Puck had his shots and everything was way more than I pay when I go to the doctor."

"That's because *you* have health insurance. Puck doesn't have a job that pays for his insurance like you do."

"I guess I need to get him an actual paying gig, the lazy bum."

I trace a finger along his cheek. I love that Romeo's gravity has been banished from this face. I kind of even like the beard, especially how it feels. "Anyway, I'm glad I didn't go to vet school. I'd just have massive student loans and a lot of headaches. With my job, I get to spend my days making animals feel better and then go home and not worry about it."

"Well, good."

"What about you? Are you happy?"

He nods slowly. "Much happier now that I'm home. It's good to be closer to my dad, and I love the theater company. It already feels like another family." The hand he's got tucked around my waist draws circles on my hip as he talks. "I'm glad I have a lot saved from modeling, though. I don't know how any of them live on what they pay at the theater."

His chest lifts and releases in a sigh.

"So you're going to keep doing it? The modeling."

"I don't know. I'm getting a bit old for it." He drags his free hand down his face like he's trying to erase his thoughts. "Plus, I was pretty burned out when I left. But the money is so good. I kind of feel like I have to keep at it as long as I can. You know, ride that wave."

"So you're going back."

"Well, I have to as soon as the show closes. I have a job that's been booked for a long time." He grabs my hand and hugs it to his chest. "But I'm thinking, since I have a reason to now, that I'll go back and forth." He catches my eye, looking like a dog begging for a treat. "Maybe you could join me there sometime? Laze around by a pool while I'm out there slaving away on a set somewhere?"

I squeeze his hand but don't manage to hold his hopeful gaze. I love Ben. I always have. But like he said earlier this morning, we've never really been together. It's like I don't even know Ben the adult. I know his body. Even covered with all the new muscles, he smells the same, moves the same way. But I don't know any of the little day-to-day details or whether we're even compatible as a couple outside of the bedroom.

"I have a thought." I sit up straight and push him up to sitting. Once he's facing me, his expression's dialed to worried, so I don't hesitate to share. "I think we need to go back to the beginning."

"Um. Okay." He looks at me sideways. "What does that mean, exactly?"

"We skipped that part. We were kids. We ran around the neighborhood together. You drove me to work. We had sex a lot. Then you left. And now we've jumped straight to sex again. We've never, like, dated."

"We spent a lot of time together the past month at rehearsals and training Puck."

"Yeah." Jumping to my feet, I pace the perimeter of his tiny living room. "That's not dating. I don't really know a lot about you. What you do in your spare time. If you have spare time. What your bad habits are."

"I know that you used to be able to burp-speak an entire sentence."

"Yeah, I may have lost that skill." I tap my chin. "Although I think I can still do the thing where you make the farting sound in your armpit."

He stands, hands on hips. "No way. I'm the reigning champion at that one."

We face off across the coffee table. "Yes, but now you have underarm hair, which totally muffles the sound."

He shrugs. "I'll shave my pits."

"Wait. Have you ever shaved your body hair?"

An embarrassed-looking smile creeps across his face.

"You have!"

"I haven't *shaved* anything except my face." He scratches the scruffy beard he's grown for the play. "But I have been waxed." He shudders. "Not my favorite part of the job."

I stalk around to his side of the table and try to lift the edge of the button-down he's wearing over a pair of those famous CK briefs. "I guess America has seen pretty much all of you."

He covers his crotch with his hands. "Except the best part."

I cross my arms, tip my head, and look him up and down. "Hm. Not sure what the best part is."

"Oh, really?" He narrows his eyes at me, then after looking around the room briefly, he zips to the TV, turns it off and turns on his stereo. Trailing a finger down a short stack of cassettes, he grabs one, shove it in and fast-forwards until he finds what he's looking for. Finger on the play button, he turns back to waggle his eyebrows at me. "Perhaps you need a tour to decide."

"By all means." Hopping onto the couch, I spread my arms and put my feet up on the coffee table. "Come on, baby. Work it."

He pushes play and the iconic piano chords of "Old Time Rock and Roll" start up. Ben goes total *Risky Business*, doing a pretty impressive Tom Cruise, hip thrusts and all.

In fact, he finishes by flopping across my lap and wiggling there. By that time, I'm laughing so hard I fall off the couch.

The man is a clown wrapped in the body of a prince.

I may not know what it's like to be his girlfriend, but I think I want to find out.

BEN

Puck's sharp bark jerks me out of a sound sleep seconds before a shave-and-a-haircut knock sounds on my front door. Stifling a groan, I roll out of bed and throw on some pants. I do love that my dad is taking Puck on walks regularly now. The exercise and Mrs. Rosen's company are good for the old man's heart. But it's not even seven a.m. On Sunday morning.

A squeaky whimper sounds from under the wild nest of Lucy's hair. I kiss her shoulder before whispering, "It's my dad."

I can't help but laugh at the panicked look in her eyes. "Don't worry, he won't come in. He's here to take Puck for a walk." Just to be safe, I cover her with the duvet. "I'll be right back."

A hand darts out to grab my wrist. "With coffee?"

I kiss her hand before tucking it back under the covers. "With coffee."

Puck's whine keeps me moving toward the front door. After peeking through the window first—just to make sure it is indeed my dad—I open the door.

"Hey, Dad." He holds out his hand, and I hand over the leash.

He salutes me. "I'll be back in an hour or so. Vera's making breakfast after our walk."

Dog and man practically skip down the steps. My dad actually seems happy.

Stretching my arms over my head, taking in a big breath of the crisp morning air, I realize *I'm* happy in a way I've never been before. Everything I need and want is right here, behind me in my bed and in front of me trotting down the driveway.

It seems like Lucy's pretty happy, too. Wanting to keep her that way, I head back inside to make coffee.

I want to plan our first real date.

Having planted the idea that she could join me out west, I'm now determined to convince her that we can be good together outside of this apartment as well as in my bed, where things couldn't be better.

As I wait for the coffee to brew, ideas for where to take her are joined by nagging thoughts. Friday night, I agreed that there'd be no more secrets. She meant keeping *us* a secret, but before we go too far down the path of a real relationship, I should tell her everything about the accident.

On the other hand, ruining this time together would be a waste... at least that's what I've been telling myself all weekend.

I will tell her. I just have to find the right time.

The coffeemaker beeps. I add cream and sugar to hers before carrying two full mugs back to the bedroom, where I find her curled up, sound asleep.

Setting the coffee down as quietly as I can, I snuggle in next to her and relax from my toes all the way to my busy brain. I'm home.

Chapter 20

"Take Me I'm Yours" - Squeeze
Lucy's Copacetic Shagadelic Mixtape, Song #9

LUCY

"Do you go to church, Roxy?"

I'm sifting through dresses on a rack in Roxy's store, looking for something to wear to the fancy restaurant Ben's taking me to. I was going to just wear a church dress, but after my second client canceled this afternoon, I somehow ended up here.

That red dress upended my world. In a good way, I think. Maybe there's another one that'll help me figure out what's next. Or at the least, make Ben proud to be out with me if a photographer catches us.

"I do go to church, darlin'. Do you?" She's working through the other side of the rack, methodically considering each dress by pulling it, turning her head one way then the other and then either holding it out to me, or shaking her head and returning it to its spot.

I continue with my own more impulsive survey as I answer. "I do, or I did. I mean, I was raised Catholic, so I went with my family every Sunday growing up whether I wanted to or not. Lately, I'm having some doubts. What religion are you?"

She holds up a green dress, similar in shape to the red one I wore to the party.

"The dress religion?" I tease.

She starts to shake her head, but it turns into a slow nod. "Well, yes, fashion is a kind of religion for me." She looks at the dress, then back at me. "I don't think this green is for you." She hangs it back up carefully, creating space between garments and smoothing the fabric. "I was raised Baptist, but I don't follow any particular religion these days. My church right now is just about a preacher and a community that makes my soul sing." She studies another fifties-era dress before sliding it along the rack, shaking her head. "You're going to dinner. You don't want to be all pinched in at the waist." She swirls her hand in the air like she's whisking away a fly. "I'm going to the forties section."

As I continue to push dresses along the rack, I mull over her words. To me, church has always been the place where you go to get that slap on the wrist, the reminder that you're a sinner and you have to work hard to keep that in check. Where you contemplate all the things you did wrong that week and beg for forgiveness. I don't think my soul has ever sung anything there.

I haven't been to church in a couple weeks, and I don't miss feeling like I'm always on the verge of fucking up.

Yes, fucking up. That's what I said, God.

Do you really care if I swear? Do you care at all about anything we do down here?

Instead of begging for forgiveness from Father Signorelli, I'm going with Father Krausnick's words, which honestly make more sense to me. *It's a sin to ignore the gifts he's blessed us with. It's a sin to forgo the simple joys of life. And it's a sin to deny love.*

Working with Ben and Puck has allowed me to see that I have a gift. The publicity from the interview is allowing me to share that gift with others.

I've certainly enjoyed more simple joys lately, if sex counts. I mean, why shouldn't it? His kiss is like heaven, after all.

And love? How can I deny my love for Ben? Or even my family's love? By playing the Cinderella role, I've been atoning for my sins. But I think I've also been trying to keep everyone safe—including myself—by keeping us all close. But like Ben said, it's a normal part of life for kids to leave the nest.

"Lucy?" Roxy's voice breaks into my thoughts.

Across the shop, a dark blue something shimmers on its hanger as she dances it in the air. "I have found your dress."

Roxy's smile, the joy in it? *That's* what life is about.

Thank God for that substitute priest.

BEN

Tuesday night, standing on the Minolas' doorstep, I have to make myself press the doorbell. I starved myself all day so I can actually eat dinner tonight, but the tightness in my gut has more to do with the fact that the last time I stood here, I was on crutches and Tony's wake was on the other side of the door.

Shaking that off, I focus on tonight's plan. I'm taking Lucy out for our first real date. My leg isn't broken and neither is my heart. Checking the curb, where the town car and driver I've hired for the evening wait, I remind myself that she, at least, deserves a night to remember. My dad's delivery van would not have worked for a romantic evening, and having a driver will allow us to enjoy the fine wines L'Espalier is known for. I owe Randall big-time for this. He waits tables at another fancy place and somehow used that connection to score a last-minute reservation at the award-winning restaurant.

I don't hear any movement on the other side of the door, so I'm about to try knocking when Mrs. Minola flings it open. "Ben! Don't you look nice all dressed up."

"Sofia, let the boy come in and stop letting all the warm air out." Mr. Minola reaches around her and extends a hand. "Good to see you, young man."

"Good to see you too, Mr. Minola." His warm handshake eases my anxiety a bit. Once I'm in the foyer, my hand goes to the worn newel post, which I grabbed hundreds of times as a kid as I flew down these stairs on the heels of my best friend.

Mrs. Minola whaps me on the upper arm. "What? I don't get a hug? You're too famous for that now?"

Her expressive face tells me a complicated story: a bit of Minola fire, some hurt, but mostly love. Demanding, expectant maternal love. Love I never really knew until I met her. As a kid watching Tony and Lucy with her, I ached for the kind of attention they were already ducking. One day, after a ball game where I'd made a bunch of stupid errors, she turned it on me full force, squeezing me tight and telling me it was okay, I'd do better next time.

Until this moment, I didn't realize how much I've missed her. It isn't just Lucy I love, but this whole family.

Now she's waiting, arms open. Stepping into her embrace, I rest my cheek on the top of her head. That's different, but the affection is the same.

"Thank you," I whisper. She gives me one more squeeze before stepping away to hold me at arm's length.

She shakes her head. "You're too skinny."

"You're pretty skinny yourself," I lob back.

She whacks me again before waving me toward the living room.

Mr. Minola's hand settles on my shoulder. "Lucy will be down shortly. I hear you two have a date."

I clear my throat. "Yes, sir." I'm not sure what Lucy has told them, so I play it safe. "I owe her a special thanks for all the work she did for the play."

"Come on, take a load off while you wait." After Mrs. Minola sits on the couch, he sits next to her. "Doing that play was a good thing for her. She gets new clients every day. She's hardly home anymore."

As I perch on a chair, my eyes devour the room. It's time in a bottle, just like the kitchen. Flowered chintz covers the sofa; crocheted antimacassars protect the matching armchairs. At Tony's wake, every inch of this room was filled with people eating, drinking, telling stories, laughing and crying.

Pictures on the crowded fireplace mantle have me on my feet again. Lucy in a lacy white confirmation dress, a formal family portrait that must be over ten years old, and Tony in his high school baseball uniform, bat in hand.

I pick up one I haven't seen before. "Wow, Sal and Vinnie got big."

"Taller than the rest of us, both of them," Mr. Minola says.

Lucy's mom pats the arm of the chair next to her. "Sit down, Ben. We want to hear what you've been up to."

I give a brief summary of my dad's heart attack and my subsequent return from California and the work I've been doing at Shakespeare Boston.

"Will you go back to California?" she asks.

"Well, I do have a career out there, an apartment and everything. But I don't want to spend so much time away from my dad." *Or Lucy.* "So, I'm still figuring out what's next."

She nods, an inscrutable look on her face. I'm not sure what else I should say. Am I supposed to ask permission to date Lucy? *Why didn't we talk about this?*

Mrs. Minola looks like she wants to pry further, but before she can, Mr. Minola reaches over to squeeze her knee as he says, "It's good to have you back, Ben."

My jaw's a roadblock my words can't get past, especially when tears pool in Mrs. Minola's eyes, but I finally manage a weak, "I'm sorry."

Her watery eyes meet mine. "I know," she says quietly. After a sharp nod of her head, she adds, "We've missed you too."

THE LIMO DRIVER opens Lucy's door, and when I hop out to meet her on the other side, I half expect to hear the pop of camera flashes. For once, I wouldn't mind. I'd love a photo of Lucy in this sexy dress, a shimmery deep blue with tiny polka dots and a bow at the waist, like she's a package just waiting to be unwrapped.

As I help her out of the car, her dark curls cascade in soft waves above a cleavage supported by the wrap of the bodice. When I catch the driver admiring the way the dress flares out over her curving hips, I guide her away from the car with a territorial arm around her shoulders. Eyes finally on mine, the driver murmurs that he'll be nearby, reachable by the restaurant's valet staff when we're ready to go. I make myself smile and thank him before escorting Lucy inside. After we check our coats, the host seats us at a corner booth with the perfect romantic setup, curved so I can sit close enough to touch her, but angled so I can see her face.

That face glows in the candlelight, her cheeks round and pink. When she looks over the menu, her brow furrows. "There aren't any prices."

"That's 'cause this place is fan*cy*." I put the emphasis on the wrong syllable and waggle my eyebrows. "You think I'd take you to some chintzy place with prices on the menu on our first real date? This ain't the Ground Round, baby."

She rolls her eyes and studies the menu again. "Hmm. No seitan or tofu or steamed vegetables here." Her grin is wicked. "What will you eat?"

I shake my head. "I literally ate nothing today, so I can pig out."

She shakes her head. "Sucks to be you."

"Tell me about it."

Our waiter materializes, answering questions and suggesting wine pairings. After a brief discussion, we decide to go for the tasting menu. When the amuse-bouches arrive with glasses of champagne, I lift mine in a toast. "To reconnections."

"To reconnections." She clinks my glass and takes a sip, wiggling in her chair as it goes down. "Ooh, yummy. Bubbles." Setting the glass down and picking up a fork, she pokes at tiny mounds artfully arranged on the plate set between us. "I don't think you're going to have to worry about your diet if the servings are all this small."

I lift what the waiter called an "autumn squash financier" to her lips and enjoy the moan she makes when those lips close around it. "You keep making sounds like that and I'm not going to make it through dinner."

She shakes her head, her eyes closed. "It's just so good." Her hand reaches out to grab my wrist. "Let me just savor this for a bit before you try yours." After another little whimper of pleasure, her eyes pop open. "Okay, your turn. I want to watch."

"You're killing me here," I say before trying it. "Oh my god, that is good."

"See?" Her hand travels to my thigh to squeeze it. "This is special, Ben. Thank you."

Our date is filled with laughter and stories and explosions of taste and, best of all, Lucy. I can't wait to get home and get my hands on her. Not that I've waited. I'm pretty sure we've been in contact one way or another the entire night.

When Lucy excuses herself to visit the ladies' room, I give the waiter my credit card and ask him to tell the valet we're ready for the car.

He bows. "Of course, monsieur."

It is nice not to have to worry about money. That will change if I give up my career out west. Thankfully, the spiral of worries about the future is interrupted when Lucy reappears. I'm just so happy that she's given me a second chance.

I take her arm. "Ready to go?"

At her nod, I lead her through the restaurant, aware that eyes are on her as much as they are on me. Out front, our carriage awaits.

Lucy giggles, obviously as buzzed as I am—with alcohol, yes, but also with the simple joy of being alive. "I feel like a princess!"

I bow and help her inside. "After you, milady."

I tip the valet before heading around to my side. As soon as the driver closes the door, I pull Lucy in close. I want as much of her pressed up against me as is possible within the realms of decency.

She obviously feels the same because her hands are roaming. One worms its way in under my shirt to skim across my belly, then further south. My answering gasp is caught by her hungry mouth.

Afraid I'll lose it in the back of the car if her left hand stays where it is, I clasp it to my chest, nipping at her pouty lower lip to slow her down.

"I want you, Lucy," I whisper. "But I want everything from champagne with an amuse-bouche to brandy and chocolates. Not fast food."

Her forehead drops to my chest, and she groans. When she looks up again, her eyes are filled with wicked intent. "You can amuse my bouche anytime you want, but if you're going to make me wait, it's going to cost you."

Grinning in anticipation, I say, "Take me however you want me. I'm yours."

Chapter 21

"Talk of the Town" - Pretenders
Lucy's Totally Tubular Tuneage, Song #8

BEN

Just as I cross the threshold of the basement rehearsal room, Bella jumps into my path, arms spread wide. "Danger, Will Robinson!' There's a review posted of the show."

I stop so abruptly that Puck gets tangled with my legs. "Is it that bad?"

She braces a hand on the wall and drops her head, shaking it slowly and clucking her tongue. After a deep sigh, she raises her head to look me in the eye. "I don't know, I haven't read it."

"You asshole." I swat at her with the end of Puck's leash. "You had me worried."

"Sorry, I couldn't resist." She grins impishly, looking more like a six-year-old herself than the mother of one. "But to my credit, I didn't want you to accidentally read it when you signed in, if you have a problem with reading reviews."

We're the first ones here for the Thursday performance. On purpose. Three days off feels like a long time when you've been rehearsing six days a week. Bella and I plan to run all of our scenes to make sure all the lazzi—a fancy word for comic bits—are still in working order.

Bella squats to greet Puck. "How are you, sir? Did you enjoy your days off?"

Puck plants a thorough round of kisses on her chin while I strip off my bag, coat and hoodie.

She stands suddenly, feet planted and arms crossed. "So?"

"So, what?"

"Should we read it?"

Clasping my hands on the top of my head, I search the tiled ceiling for an answer. Good or bad, reviews can be a distraction.

The call-board's at the other end of the room. A newspaper clipping's taped to the painted concrete wall right next to it. I can't quite identify the typeface from here. "Is it the *Globe*?"

She squints at it. "I think so." Facing me again, hands on hips and head tilted, she says, "Maybe better to read it now so we can digest it and not be distracted right before the show?"

I nod slowly. "Yeah, that's exactly what I was thinking."

"Alright. Let's do it. One, two, three… go!"

I yelp when she tags me but put my all into the race, and Puck does, too. Bella brings out the kid in everybody. Side by side, we slide to a stop, each of us bracing an arm on the wall, framing the clipping. Puck stands on his hind legs as if he wants to read it.

Bella takes a deep breath and begins to read in a news-anchor voice. "'Shakespeare Boston delights with a fun and fresh *Two Gentlemen of Verona*, its first indoor production since the company's inception five years ago. Director Nick'—blah, blah, blah, let's skip to the important stuff: us. Uh, here we are. 'Shakespearean fools Launce (Benedick Porter) and Speed (Isabella York, cast against gender and type) take the show on a vaudeville turn. Crisp, clown-like renderings of the scenes delight. Porter is almost unrecognizable, and some fans will likely be disappointed to hear that his famous physique is not on display.'"

I groan. "Will I ever live that down?"

She covers my mouth with a hand. "Shush, there's more. 'Kudos to the animal trainer credited in the program, Lucy Minola. The scenes that include Launce's dog Crab are a highlight of the show. The interaction between man and beast are organically woven into the dialogue, resulting in rollicking laughter from the audience.'" She dips her chin. "Lucy'll be happy, huh?"

"Yeah, she'll probably get a fresh round of clients from this."

I drag a finger down the rest of the review, scanning it quickly. "Pretty good all around. Phew. Congrats."

"You too." She holds up a hand for a high five. "We'd better get to work. Now the audience is gonna have expectations."

"Ugh. You're right. Sometimes that's worse."

Even with taking time to read the review, we manage to run through our scenes twice before the other actors trickle in. I talk Will and Randall and Jess into running lines as well, which keeps me busy right up until it's time to get into costume.

When I take Puck out for a walk just before the show starts, the pay phone by the back door is a reminder that I should call Lucy to tell her about the review.

Or maybe I'll surprise her with a copy on my way home tonight instead.

IT'S after ten by the time I get to the Minolas'. Not sure what my plan is. Throw rocks at Lucy's window? There are lights on inside. Maybe she's still up?

After knocking as softly as I can a few times, I'm about to give up and head home when the door opens.

It isn't Lucy, though. It's her mom. "Ben? Is everything okay?"

"Yeah. I'm sorry, Mrs. Minola. I hope I didn't disturb you or anything." I hold up a photocopy of the review. "I just wanted to give this to Lucy. She got another good mention in the paper. Lights were on, so—"

"Come on in sweetie, it's too cold to stand here. It went from summer to winter in just a couple of days." She shivers, wrapping her cardigan more tightly around her slight frame. "You too, little dog."

The house is quiet. "Are you sure?"

"Everyone else is asleep, but I needed to finish some paperwork. Have some tea with me."

I follow her to the warm kitchen, and she waves in my direction as she lights a burner and pulls down some boxes of tea. "Sit down." She points at Puck, who is sniffing at the back door. "You too, dog." He sits immediately, and she smiles. Eyes back on me, she says, "I think it's time you called me Sofia."

My head shakes involuntarily. "Really? That just feels… wrong."

She nods slowly before tipping her head to the side, a wistful smile crinkling her beautiful face. "Unless you want to call me Mom?"

I always wanted to call her Mom. Wished that she was my mom. But I can't go down that path. I'm sleeping with her daughter outside of marriage, something no Catholic parent would be happy about. But there's more. I have to tell her, and not just as practice for telling Lucy.

She sets a china teacup in front of me, and it clinks softly as the cup shifts in the saucer. "Chamomile? Peppermint? Both?"

"Both, please." My vocal cords scrape against each other getting just those two simple words out. She drops two teabags in the cup and pours water over them. Steam swirls in the air.

"Sugar?"

"No, thank you."

She tops off her own cup with hot water before returning the ancient kettle to the stove. Sitting down across from me, she straightens a pile of papers and moves them to the side. "Lucy wasn't feeling well and went to bed early." She sits back in her chair, hands cradling her teacup. "I don't think she's been getting enough sleep."

"I'm sorry, Mrs. M. I know you probably disapprove of her… staying over… with me."

Surprisingly, she waves that down. "I'm fine with it, actually. Gio, that's another matter. To him, she's still his little girl." A soft smile takes over her face as she looks down the dark hallway. "But I'm just happy to see her... alive again."

Puck rests his chin on her thigh, and she strokes his head. "When Tony died and you disappeared, she shut down." She shakes her head. "She covered it by keeping busy." She flashes an uneven smile at me. "Like I have. But when you two showed up, Lucy came back, too."

The house is so quiet that the clanking pipes from the furnace are startlingly loud. I don't think I've ever been here when it was like this. With four kids, three of them boys, someone was always pounding up and down the stairs, blowing through the back door, laughing or fighting. The complete opposite of the house I shared with my dad, so hushed and still you could sit and watch dust float in a patch of sunlight without hearing a single sound beyond the ticking of the grandfather clock in the hall.

Here, now, the quiet is welcome.

But I don't deserve to enjoy it until I come clean. "The day of the accident? The day Tony..."

Her hand stills on Puck's brow. When she smooths it over his fur again, I blow out a breath and make myself keep going. "We were fighting. Me and Tony. Because... Lucy and me, the summer before— before she went to UMass?" I'm doing this all wrong, all out of order, but I stumble on. "We were seeing each other. When we told you she was giving me cooking lessons, that's not all we were doing." Her eyebrows rise slightly but she doesn't say anything. "I was in love with her, Mrs. M—I was in love with her, but I didn't want to hold her back when she went to school. So I convinced her we should date other people. But I regretted doing that. I didn't tell her, though. Instead I told Tony, but it didn't come out right, kind of like how this isn't coming out right right now."

There's a lump in my throat I can't swallow past. But I'm halfway through this dress rehearsal, so I press on. "And he got mad. Really mad. He always said I had to stay away from her, protect her while he was gone. So we were yelling at each other when that guy hit us. And I think—"

My throat's completely closed now, my face wet, but I push to the finish. "I think, if we hadn't been arguing, Tony might've—I'm sorry. It's my fault. That guy was—I know he was going fast, but if Tony hadn't—" I drop my head into my hands. I'm not even making sense.

A warm hand squeezes my arm. I can barely hold my head up, but I force myself to meet her eyes. "I'm sorry," I whisper.

Her hand slides down my forearm to grasp my hand. "Oh, Benny." She shakes her head. "It wasn't your fault. It wasn't anybody's fault. Not even that man who drank too much and decided to get in his car. So many little things led to you all being in that place at that time." She takes my other hand and squeezes both. "I'm sorry you feel this way, or—have you maybe felt this way for a long time?"

I nod, snot running out of my nose, lower lip trembling like a three-year-old.

"Is that what kept you away from us?"

I nod again.

She gets up abruptly, grabs a tissue box from a drawer and plunks it down in front of me. "Well, then. Stop it." Her hands fly in the air, and she looks ten years younger. "You need to just stop it. You need to be back in our lives. We all need to let Tony go and live again. Every single one of us."

She takes her cup to the sink. When she comes back, she looks me up and down, hands on hips. "All you need to worry about is making my daughter happy." She holds my gaze until I nod. "But right now? Go home and go to bed. I think we all need a good night's sleep."

Nodding again, I let her guide me and my dog to the door. That was not the reaction I'd expected from Mrs. Minola. Even though I did a terrible job telling her, she doesn't hate me.

Maybe it won't be so bad to tell Lucy, after all.

Chapter 22

"Under Pressure" - Queen & David Bowie
Lucy's Right On Rock On Mixtape, Song #1

LUCY

Despite the fact that I'm only getting a few hours of sleep these days, I can't stop smiling—even stuck in Boston traffic. Who cares? I'm car dancing to an old mixtape I stole back from Ben, and life is good. I'm helping people and their pets and getting paid well to do it. So well that my savings have doubled in the past couple weeks, making getting out of bed at oh dark hundred a little easier.

Plus, knowing that I'll be with naked Ben at the end of the day—in person, not on the pages of a magazine—puts extra pep in my step.

Good thing, because I'm signing on new clients practically every day. The feature in the paper started the ball rolling, but now it's referrals from people I'm already working with or people who read the review or saw the show. I had to get a pager and answering service so the calls don't clog up the vet office's or my family's phones.

I'm just not sure how many more I can handle. I'm working the earliest morning shift so I can fit in two or three or even four training appointments in the afternoon and evening, depending on where people live. I've completely monopolized our second car. Luckily, the boys have been resourceful about getting where they needed to be on their own, and my dad always drives my mom to work.

Since traffic's at a standstill again, I check the notebook I use to keep track of everything: client names, issues, what we've done so far, homework, as well as directions to each house. Or business. Right now I'm trying to get to a small architecture firm in Brookline where a nervous spaniel spends an uneasy day. The Blickners don't want to leave their dog at home, but he's unreliable around customers, so we're working on safe ways to introduce him to new people.

The first time I visited their office, I drove from Back Bay on the weekend. Now, crossing town at two-thirty on a weekday, there's so much more traffic.

Craning my neck, I realize I'm stuck in a line of parents picking up kids from school. Thinking that there's got to be a way around this, I scrabble in the glove compartment for a map, and almost rear-end the car in front of me.

"Shit!" I yell, slamming on the brakes. Even though I'm going to be late, I make myself wait until I can pull over on a side street before trying to read the map. Just as I find a place to double park—a fine Boston tradition—and fish out a map—which rips—the tape in the player stops. When I push the eject button, the cassette comes out, but the tape sticks, unspooling. And I lose it. On a long "AGHHH" I rip out the tape, wad it up and throw the damn thing in the back of the car before bouncing my head on the steering wheel with a few more yowls of frustration.

If only clients came to me so I could spend more time training dogs and less time in this goddamn car.

Blowing out a breath, I carefully unfold the map so as to avoid further damage and figure out a way to cut away from the school traffic. Settling for some tape of Vinnie's I find on the floor—*Beastie Boys*, not my favorite but it'll do in a pinch—I take a quick left and steer my way across town.

I'VE BEEN GETTING HOME MUCH LATER than usual lately, but Friday evening, it's after eight o'clock by the time I open the back door, expecting to find a cold kitchen and a hungry family. Or worse, the scent of fast food, which is what I came home to last night.

"Papa, I'm so sorry I'm late again." I call from the mudroom. "Traffic is killing me."

"Don't worry about it, sweetheart."

In the kitchen, my dad and brothers are seated at the table, half-empty plates in front of them. No takeout containers, though. "Something smells good."

"There's plenty left," my dad says.

"We even made salad. Yours is in the fridge," Vinnie adds. My dad pokes him in the shoulder, and he hops up. "Sit down, I'll get it."

"Who cooked?"

"We did," Sal says proudly. "Well, Pop did. But he taught us some stuff."

I take my seat, which is set with a napkin and everything. My dad fills my plate with chicken parmesan. Vinnie sets a salad in front of me, and Sal pops out of his seat. "Can I get you a drink?"

Tears prick behind my eyes. "What's going on? Did something happen?"

My dad shakes his hand. "Nothing's wrong. You've been working late a lot and—"

"I know, I'm sorry. It's just—I feel like I have to take advantage of the publicity from this article. But I think I can—"

My dad captures my flapping hand. "Lucy, we're the ones who need to apologize."

I swipe at the tears leaking out of my eyes. "What do you mean?"

"Until you started taking on these extra jobs, which we think is great"—he adds before I can protest—"we had no idea how much you were doing around here. Shopping, cooking, cleaning. You were doing it all. Even when you took on the extra work for the play, you were still making sure dinner was on the stove every night."

"Well, you and mom are working and the boys are still in school and—"

"And you have a full-time job. Now you have a chance to build a business of your own. You've taken care of us for far too long. These boys—"

"Men. We're men now." Vinnie pounds on his chest, a goofy grin on his face.

My dad rolls his eyes. "These *young* men need to learn how to fend for themselves."

Sal lifts a fork loaded with pasta. "Pop's a pretty good cook, too. Who knew?"

"Yeah, who knew?" My dad smiles, and the crinkles around his eyes deepen. It's good to see that smile. He doesn't look as tired as usual, either. "The three of us have decided that we are officially taking over dinner. I'm teaching Vinnie and Sal how to cook."

"You're not allowed in the kitchen anymore," Sal says. "Except to eat."

"So, eat!" Vinnie says, sounding just like my mom.

Blowing my nose in my napkin, I look down at the beautiful meal in front of me. Suddenly ravenous, I pick up my fork and take a bite. "Wow. This is yummy."

"Yeah, we did pretty good," Vinnie says before stuffing a huge mouthful of garlic bread into his mouth.

"Yes, you did," I agree, smiling at my dad. "Thank you, Papa."

"You're welcome, sweetheart." His eyes are a bit damp too. "Now eat up. If you're not quick, Sal there'll start stealing from your plate."

LYING next to Ben in his bed later that evening, I say, "This is almost perfect." We're fully clothed and have just been chatting about our respective days, but it's nice. We never did this before.

He rolls over to his side, flops an arm across my waist and hauls me in to spoon my body. "Almost?" he huffs. "Seems pretty perfect to me."

"Well, there are a few things I wish were different."

He bends his elbow and rests his cheek on his palm. "Like?"

"Oh, that I didn't spend so much time in the car. That I wasn't going to lose you to the theater all weekend—"

"Or that you didn't have to get up at the crack of dawn to go to work tomorrow?"

Just the thought of it has me yawning. "There's that too."

He strokes a finger across my furrowed brow. I'm about to add *That I wasn't worried about what happens next*, when he says, "Remember how Tony used to wrestle me to the ground and fart in my face?"

"Ugh. He did that to me too. It was disgusting." Even as I shudder at the memory—which unfortunately hits me in Sensurround—another follows it. "What was that he used to call you in middle school? After he had that growth spurt but you were still short?"

Ben flops onto his back and throws an arm across his face. "Oh god. Beanie. His little Beanie." He grunts. "He said it was to stop kids from calling me 'Been-a-dick,' but..."

I peek under his elbow. "But it backfired?"

He nods. "Kids just started calling me Teeny-Weeny Beanie." With a sigh, he shakes his head. "Tony could sometimes be kind of a dick."

I sit up. "Kind of? Sometimes? He was a jerk. I mean, I loved him, but I also hated him half the time." Tears gather in the back of my throat. Swallowing past them, looking at the ceiling, I say, "He was such a protector, you know? Like nobody else could say anything bad about me. But at home, especially when my parents weren't around, he would do the meanest things."

Ben brushes a curl off my forehead. "Like what?"

"I don't know." I shrug. "Call me Pizza Face when I had a pimple.

Or remember when he chopped the heads off my Barbies, one by one? He'd leave the naked body lying in gross positions in the yard and he'd hang the heads by the hair. And he never got in trouble. He'd tell my parents that I'd left it outside and some animal had gotten to it. They always believed him."

Ben sits up to face me. "He used to make me stand at the end of your upstairs hall with a pillow strapped to my front. He'd shoot tennis balls at me with a lacrosse stick. Supposedly it was good for me."

Weird giggles escape past my lips. "I'm sorry I'm laughing. But I think I remember that. You made some weird sounds."

He coughs out a laugh. "Yeah, especially when he'd hit me in the balls."

"He was an asshole!"

"He really was."

Suddenly we're both laughing hysterically, but we can't stop coming up with things he did to us.

"When I was seven, he told me that Santa died in a terrible sleigh accident!"

"When we started high school, he told me that the water fountains would give you venereal diseases." He shakes his head. "I was thirsty all the time."

Our laughter fades eventually. After a few beats of silence, Ben takes a deep breath. "Lucy, I—"

Before he can go on, Puck starts barking his head off. We both sit up. He usually sleeps on the couch, but right now he's scratching at the door and howling.

"What the fuck?" Bens jumps out of bed, and I hear him shushing the dog before opening the door. The door closes behind him, and Puck whines. I'm starting to get worried, when the door opens and closes and Ben says, "Good boy."

"What was it?"

"Raccoons. They had the lid off of the garbage can, but I got there before they made too much of a mess."

"He was a good boy to scare them off." Shucking off my clothes quickly, I flip the covers down and climb in. "Lose those clothes and come snuggle."

Doing just that, he says, "You have me well trained."

"Yeah, I'm good that way."

We get back into the comfy spoon position again, his warm body relaxing mine. With a yawn, I say, "He wasn't perfect. But he was the best big brother I had."

Chapter 23

"Girl U Want" - Devo
Lucy's Catch You on the Flipside Mixtape, Song #9

BEN

Sunday evening, after parking in the driveway at home, I'm not sure I have the energy to get out of the van, let alone walk up the stairs to my apartment. A yawn stretches every muscle in my face, and a rumble sounds from my belly. Puck's impatient bark eventually gets me moving. He's had a long weekend too. While he makes a sniffing tour of the dark yard, I sift through happy memories of the six shows we packed into the past four days. I'm exhausted, but I wouldn't trade a minute of it. Even if audiences had high expectations from reading the reviews—there's a good one in the *Boston Phoenix*, too— they lapped up everything we served up.

I only wish Lucy had been there. She'd be proud of the standing O Puck gets every night, but she's stayed away from the show and me to avoid giving any of us a cold she's suffering through. Since she goes to work before I get up and is already in bed by the time I get home from the theater, some days we can't even talk on the phone, so I send her little pager messages to at least let her know I'm thinking about her. I don't know how I lived without her for seven years. Four days and I'm going crazy.

Unfortunately, the clock is ticking down. Too soon, we'll have an entire country between us. Problem is, I don't feel like I can talk to her about a future together until I've fessed up about what really happened the day Tony died. I almost did it the other night when we were reminiscing about him, but the moment passed. Even though her mom took it well, I did such a bad job of telling it I'm afraid of ruining what little time Lucy and I have together.

Plus, part of me thinks that maybe Bella's right, maybe I don't need to tell her at all. So I'm chasing myself in circles, here.

"What're you two doing out here in the dark?" At the sound of my dad's voice, Puck runs to greet him. I think *somebody* must be giving the dog extra treats.

"You eat?"

"Uh, not really. Just a little between shows."

He hooks a thumb over his shoulder. "Roast chicken in the oven. It'll be ready soon."

"Sounds perfect." Following him and Puck inside, the warmth of the kitchen releases a few of the knots I've tied myself up in. "It smells great. Did Vera make it?"

He waves a hand in the air. "I did most of it. She's determined to teach me to cook."

My dad is not known for his cooking beyond hamburgers on the grill and Swanson's frozen dinners, but when I peek inside the oven, a bird is browning beautifully. "Looks like she's a good teacher." I sit in my usual chair. "Is she coming for dinner?"

"Nah, this is for you and me." He sets plates on the table. "That is, if you're eating real food."

I pat my empty belly. "I think I can handle it."

He nods at the fridge as he pulls the chicken out of the oven. "There's stuff for salad in there if you want to have something green."

"Sounds good." I put together a salad for each of us while he fusses with the bird and a thermometer.

"You and the dog were funny in the show."

His eyes are on Puck, collapsed on the mat by the back door.

"You came? Which show?"

He shrugs. "This afternoon. I figured I wouldn't tell you, make you nervous."

When I did plays in high school, I didn't want my dad to come at all. It was embarrassing to share that part of me with someone who knew me so well. He always snuck in, though.

"I'm glad you liked it."

He points at Puck. "Lucy trained this guy?"

"Mostly she trained me, to be honest, to give him commands in a way that would be clear to him. She could get him to run into a burning building. Me, not so much."

"What ever happened with you and her?"

My head snaps up, and I nearly slice off a finger instead of a piece of carrot. "What do you mean?"

He shrugs. "You and Lucy. You were dating her that summer and she went off to college and that was it?"

"Uh." I put the knife down. *How did he know about me and Lucy? And how much did he know?*

He dips his chin and gives me a wry smile. "You were sneaking around, but it was pretty obvious. Lucy was giving you 'cooking lessons'?" He makes air quotes. "I'm not a complete idiot. Even if you don't tell me anything."

I'm speechless. I mean, he's right. But it's not like he ever asked. He is asking now, though. "Well yeah, we were seeing each other that summer. We didn't tell anybody because she was a lot younger than me."

"Three years."

"Well, at eighteen and twenty-one, it felt like a big difference."

"Uh-huh."

His tone is tough to read, but there's something in his eyes that makes me keep going. "Anyway, we didn't exactly break up at the end of the summer, but we sort of decided to date other people." Looking out the kitchen window, I go over what happened that fall. "I regretted it the minute she left for school. I was jealous of all those people, of the guys who were probably lined up outside her dorm room, dying to get in."

"She was a beautiful girl."

"She still is."

"And then you had the accident and moved away."

I look up, wondering exactly how much of a connection he's made. "Yeah. But there's more to it." Gripping the edge of the counter, I breathe deep and keep going. "I was going crazy with missing her by Thanksgiving. I didn't want to date other people, and I didn't want her to either. I wanted to tell our families." A half laugh stutters out. "I thought nobody knew."

Meeting my dad's gaze briefly, I power on. "Tony, however, definitely did not know. He'd warned me away from her, said it was my job to protect her from lecherous assho—uh, jerks. I needed him to know that it wasn't like that for me. But I did it wrong. Tony lost it. He was screaming at me when we got hit." I take in a deep breath. Unfortunately, the scent of cooked meat suddenly makes me nauseous, and I have to swallow back rising bile. "I never got to—to… explain… that I…"

"That you loved her?"

What I see in my dad's eyes drops my jaw and frees my voice. "Yeah. That I loved them all. I lost him before I could tell him. And it was all my fault."

"What do you mean it was your fault?"

"The accident. If Tony hadn't been yelling at me, he could've braked in time."

He shakes his head once, sharply. "Not from the police reports I read. Nobody anywhere in that intersection could've avoided that guy."

"But if—"

His hand stops my words. "Listen. A thousand things could've happened, things you could've done different, that might have made things turn out differently. I know that kind of logic. I went through that with your mother."

"What do you mean? She had cancer."

"Yeah." His hands dive into his armpits and his eyes fall to the floor. "But if I'd made her go to the doctor when she was eating Tums like they were candy and complaining about pain in her belly?" His jaw twitches. "I'll never know if it would've made a difference. So I get it.

"Don't be like me. Don't spend half your life trying to punish yourself for one mistake—a mistake that probably didn't make a difference, anyway—while you neglect the person you care about most." When he looks up, walls that have separated us for as long as I can remember just tumble down. "Live the life you've been granted. Not the one you wish you had."

We just stare at each other for a while. My burning throat and eyes slowly relax, and I release the breath I've been holding. "Okay."

The silence between us is easy by the time the buzzer sounds on the stove. My dad opens the oven and checks the chicken before pulling it out. He fills plates and hands one to me.

"Let's eat."

IT'S MONDAY, the first wide-open day off I've had since I don't even know when. Since I'm leaving soon, my dad replaced me with some kid who I guess is doing a decent job with deliveries. In any case, I'm out and I have nothing to do.

Lucy's not available. We chatted on the phone last night, and she sounded terrible but claimed that she felt better. Still, she's got work this morning and clients later. I'll see her tonight, but there are too many free hours between now and then.

Lots of things I could be doing. Work out. Laundry. Clean the apartment.

I just can't seem to get out of bed.

But then I have an idea that gets me moving: *Mixtape.*

Lucy used to give me shit about how she was the only one who ever made the tapes we listened to together. I always thought of it as her territory. She was so artsy with the covers and would spend hours working out which songs to include and the order they should go in. She took a few back to listen to while she drives around town, so maybe she doesn't have time to make them anymore.

I do have time, and I could make her a mix that'd let her know how much I love her. Maybe it could even communicate how sorry I am about Tony without me ever having to spell it out.

Yeah, that's asking a bit much.

But I could give it to her tonight and then tell her.

Or tell her after she's had a few days to listen to it.

First, though, I have to make the thing.

Moments later I'm dressed and staring at my small collection of albums and cassettes. I'm not really sure how to get started.

A couple hours later, I'm ready to throw my stereo across the room. Lucy always made this seem so easy. After two trips and a great deal of condescension from the dude at Radio Shack, I've finally eliminated the terrible hissing sound. I have a series of songs recorded without cutoffs and long pauses. But the tape just ran out halfway through a song! That never happened with Lucy's mixes. She must've somehow figured out how long each song was and done some serious math to make it all come out perfectly.

Turning the damn stereo off, I flop onto my back. Puck takes this as an invitation and takes a flying leap off the couch and onto my chest. After a good wrestle, I haul my body off the floor.

Time to work out.

I'll have to figure out another way to tell Lucy the truth.

Chapter 24

"Just What I Needed" - The Cars
Lucy's Catch You on the Flipside Mixtape, Song #1

LUCY

After a long weekend of avoiding each other because I had a cold, it's fun to be out with Ben like a real couple again.

Tonight, we're on a sort of double date with Ben's actor friend Will and Will's girlfriend Kate. They made us a very impressive Indian meal, spicy and flavorful and not too heavy. I might have to branch out from Italian someday.

Kate, who does something in finance, sets down her post-dinner coffee. "So, how does being a dog trainer work, Lucy? Do you have your own business? Or do you work for someone else?"

Her cat is on the sofa between us, purring away. I wish we could have a cat, or a dog, or any pet. Sal is so allergic we had to give our dog away when my brother was little.

"No, I'm not really a dog trainer. I actually have a full-time job as a vet tech." Kate has a degree from Harvard, so I'm not telling her that I didn't even finish a semester of college. "I've always helped the practice's clients with behavioral issues when they've come up, but having my own clients just kind of happened because of publicity from the play."

"It's pretty amazing what you did with Puck for the show," Will says. "I'd always heard that working with animals is a nightmare."

"They do tend to upstage everyone," Ben says. "It's not fair. All he has to do is cock his head and people laugh. Let him try to make words like *pillory* and *farthingale* funny."

Will shakes his head. "*You* try being the straight man—the asshole straight man at that—with the two of you onstage. I swear I get booed every single time when I chase you offstage."

Ben dips his chin and pushes his bottom lip out. "I'm sorry we steal the show from you."

Will throws a pillow at him. "No, you're not."

"Yeah, you're right. I'm not." Ben laughs, chucking the pillow back.

Kate rolls her eyes at them. "Do you train cats?"

I scratch her Persian under the chin. "I haven't even tried. I've heard that some people train cats to use the toilet, but come on. It's a cat. Doing what the heck they want is part of their charm."

She gathers hers onto her lap. "That's right. Frankie here is perfect just as he is." She uses the babytalk voice that most owners use with their pets. "Though it would be nice if he'd go for a run with me."

"He could lose a little weight."

Kate gasps and covers his ears. "Don't make him feel bad. He's just big-boned."

At my expression, she drops her hands. "I know, I know. Typical pet owner, I'm sure. My baby can do no wrong—ow!" she yelps when he starts kneading her thigh with his claws out.

Grabbing a toy from the floor, I lure him off her lap. She laughs as she rubs her leg. "You can train cats, see?"

Still dangling the fake mouse on a string for Frankie to swat at, I ask her about her work.

"Oh, I just started a new job at a nonprofit." Her smile is huge. "We help women create their own businesses."

"Really?" That has my ears perking up.

"Yeah." She kicks off her shoes and sits cross-legged so she can face me fully. "I'm supposed to be focusing on our SRI funds—socially responsible investing funds. That's my background—working with funds, anyway. The socially responsible part is new to me. Anyway, right now, the company only works with women in third world countries, giving them microloans so they can start small businesses that make a huge difference in their communities. Even more important, it empowers the women themselves."

She goes on to explain how she'd like to also support women in this country, women living in poverty because their jobs have moved overseas or been lost to automation. Even though I'd love to get some help myself, I can't keep from yawning.

Kate laughs. "I know, I talk too much, and this stuff can be boring."

"No, I'm sorry." I wave a hand in the air. "It's me. I'm burning the candle at both ends these days, going from the early shift at the vet to training clients in the afternoon and evening, and then that guy"—I point at Ben, who is now looking over Kate's CD and album collection with Will—"keeps me up half the night."

My cheeks heat. I can't believe I just said that to a girl a hardly know.

She sighs, her eyes on her own guy. "It's worth it, though."

From the look on her face, she's as in love with Will as I am with Ben.

She hops up. "Ben, time to take this poor woman home. We women have work in the morning, unlike you slacker actors."

Will chases Kate around the room as Ben pulls me up to my feet, half yawning, half laughing. Goodbyes go by in a tired blur. Once my butt hits the car seat and my skull the headrest, I can't keep my eyes open.

The next thing I know, Ben's waking me with a kiss. A kiss that not only has me purring with desire, it lights up the tiger in me. Suddenly I can't wait to get this man inside.

Who needs sleep, anyway?

BEN

Kirk's timing isn't always good, but this time he's spot on. At least where he's concerned. And me too, if I'm honest. Monday, just when I was going a bit crazy with boredom and right after my subletter called to let me know that he wasn't going to stay at my place for the fall after all, Kirk called with an offer I really couldn't refuse.

Which is why, a few days later, I'm gazing lovingly at a girl who I just met a couple hours ago, while we pretend to stretch in front of a statue of Paul Revere. Ironically, shooting this running shoe campaign is probably going to mean I won't have time to run today.

I'm used to being a clothes hanger, but putting the focus on shoes is strangely awkward. The angles are all different. On top of that, I can't rely on the broody vibe I've been using for years for CK. I have to be all chipper and flirty for this thing, and I'm not sure I have it in me.

In fact, I'm not really sure why they wanted me for this. It wasn't supposed to be me. Another client of Kirk's who'd recently relocated to New York booked this shoot, but the guy found out he had meningitis the day before he was supposed to fly up to Boston. In the scramble to replace him, Kirk suggested me. According to him they were practically drooling at the prospect. But now, the photographer's growling because there's no chemistry between me and the model I'm working with.

She's cute and very nice, but she is super chatty and her high-pitched nasal voice is unbelievably grating. Still, I've got to dig deep and make this work. I said I'd do it, this shoot alone will cover my rent for the next couple of months, and there's a possibility of more to come. If only I can remember how to be a fucking model.

The lighting guy finishes adjusting whatever he needed to adjust and Don the grumpy shooter is back. "Alright, Ben. Let's see if you can look like you want nothing more than to tie Court's shoes."

Not Courtney, Court. I don't know why, but even her nickname is driving me up a wall. "No problem, Don."

I pull out all my sense memory training, and do my best to

impose Lucy's voice, Lucy's scent and Lucy's smile over Court's, but it's no good. I'm stuck in my head, judging what I'm doing, chasing my tail trying to hit my marks *and* stay loose while showering Court with my attention. The scowl I catch on Don's face tells me my fake version of a guy in love without a care in the world isn't cutting it.

Thankfully, Court asks for a break just when my head's about to explode with the effort of trying to look I don't have a care in the world.

"I feel like I'm getting shiny. Am I shiny?" Court waves at Ricky, the makeup artist, who comes trotting over.

"You're gorgeous, darlin' but I'll powder you up." After dusting her, he gives me a swipe and mutters, "There's a girl over by the honey wagon who's claiming to be a friend of yours, but don't worry, we've got her corralled."

"Thanks, Ricky." We've been dodging tourists all day, but thankfully no one has been too obnoxious. "Oh, wait. Does she have a little gray dog with her?"

He purses his lips. "Maybe? I can check."

"If her name is Lucy, then she is a friend—my girlfriend, actually —and she might need to drop off my dog. She's had him all morning." Lucy doesn't have to work at the vet's today—naturally the one morning we both have off this week I end up having to do this—but she has clients this afternoon.

"I'll check."

"Thanks, man."

Moments later, a familiar face peeks around the edge of a lighting flag and she's got a wicked glint in her eye. At first, I'm not sure what she's up to when she puts a finger to her lips and mouths "shhh." Ducking behind the flag again, just her fingertips reappear, followed by stiff arms, and then her torso. She's doing the mime thing where you pretend to be flying, the goof. Looking over at me, she waves like she's surprised to see me and then zooms off again. In the next few minutes, she runs through every cheesy thing I used to do to get her to crack up when we were kids—pretending to walk down stairs, having a pencil stuck in your throat, having your face stuck in the elevator door.

And it's works. When we go again, I'm still smiling.

"There we go! That's what I've been waiting for!" Don's camera cranks and I've got it now. Even though I can't see her anymore, I manage to hang on to the feeling.

It's not just that I love her. In the past few weeks, she's helped me bridge a gap between old Ben and new Ben and right now, I'm riding on a wave of hope that I can bring the two halves of myself—and my life—together. That I can feel pain and guilt but also joy. That it's okay to be alive.

Finally, we get a break and I can't get to her fast enough. When I find her waiting on a park bench, I haul her to her feet and capture her gorgeous face in my palms, whispering, "How did you know I needed that?"

She takes my hands from her face and presses them to her heart. "Because I know you Ben Porter."

She's right. So fuck the makeup—Ricky can fix it—I need my girl so gather her close to kiss her, breathe in her scent, and crush her curves in my hands. The sound of Puck barking and the popping of flashbulbs barely register. All I can think is that I don't want to leave her behind ever again.

LATE THE NEXT NIGHT, after our Thursday night show, after we've made love and I've got Lucy spooning in my arms, just as I'm about to let this long day go and fall into sleep, my phone rings. "What the fuck?" I groan. "It's after midnight."

The answering machine picks up. "Ben. Man, what did I tell you about being careful with your image. There's a photo of you kissing that nobody—"

Sprinting to the kitchen, I grab the phone before Kirk can say anything worse. "Kirk! Shut the fuck up, man. I told you, Lucy is my girlfriend, not some"—I can't believe he's calling her fat again, Lucy had enough issues with that when she was a kid—"random woman. I'm not going to hide that." He goes on for a bit about how we're in the National Enquirer and some other crap until I cut him off, saying that it's late and there's nothing I can do about it now and I'll call him tomorrow.

When I crawl back into bed, I discover that my wish that Lucy slept through the whole thing has not come true.

"Why do you work for a guy like that?" she asks.

Thankful that she doesn't seem to be too hurt by his words, I sigh and take her hand. "I know he's kind of a jerk—"

"Kind of?"

"Okay, he's a huge asshole. Or he can be. He's just got tunnel vision. All he knows is that world out there." I wave in the general direction of California. Taking Lucy's hand, I pull it to my chest. "Thing is, when I first moved out west, I was a mess, and he really took care of me. Gave me a job when my internship ran out, helped me find a place to live, even lent me a car until I could afford to buy one. So I think he still kind of thinks of me as this kid he has to look out for. He forgets that now he works for me." I squeeze her hand. "I forget, too. But I'm going to work on that."

"Is it true what he said? Do you have to be careful about being seen with me?"

I blow out a breath. "I mean, sort of? If I want to try and have a career as a leading man in movies or something, I guess I have to maintain a certain image. But I still don't know if I want to try for that. I want to keep acting—real acting—but I don't know if I can live like the guys here do. Will and Randall, I mean. I don't know if I can bartend to support my acting career. But nobody here can make a living just doing theater."

I smooth the wrinkle that has formed between her brows during my monologue. "I need to figure it out, but whatever happens, you're in on the plan. I'm not hiding us. Not this time, I promise."

After a big yawn, she nods. "Okay, I guess."

Sliding my arm around her shoulders, I pull her in close. "No more secrets, right?"

Except that one big secret that I still haven't managed to spill.

LUCY

Later that week, Kate calls to make an appointment with me, and we find a time to meet for coffee. She and Will are thinking about getting a puppy together, and she wants information on how to introduce a puppy to a cat.

When I give her a rundown of training basics, the look of dismay on her face is a familiar one. "Really? I have to put him in a cage when I'm not home?" Even though crate training is a proven way to prevent separation anxiety as well as accidents, most people see it as punishment.

"Think of it as his den. A dog feels responsible for the space, for protecting his territory. A whole apartment"—I spread my arms in the air—"is way too much for a puppy to take care of. Even too much for some grown dogs."

She eventually gets what I'm saying, and we move on to the fun part. "So, picking a puppy."

Kate bounces on her toes and claps her hands. "I can't wait!"

"And you're going to adopt from a shelter?"

She nods. "That seems like the right thing to do." Rolling her eyes, she adds, "Plus, Will thinks spending money to buy a puppy when we can get one for free is ridiculous."

"Well, you will have to cover the cost of spaying or neutering the puppy, as well as some other fees."

She waves a hand in the air. "Yeah, but those'd be incurred costs, anyway."

"Not to get ahead of ourselves, but there may be other factors affecting your choice besides your cat. If you're planning to have kids anytime soon, that's another thing to add to the mix."

She nods, her smile wide. "This relationship is new, but it feels pretty serious. And I want kids someday, so let's keep that in mind."

After we talk through how to choose a beta puppy from a pack— not the one that charges the enclosure to greet you first, not the one cowering in the corner—Kate folds the legal pad full of carefully printed notes into a pristine leather folder. "Okay, I think I've got everything I need for now. Your turn."

She offered to pay me for this consult, but I suggested we do a trade instead.

"Okay." Where she's organized, I'm a mess. "Obviously, I'm in need of some business advice." I hold up my datebook—stuffed full of sticky notes, checks I need to deposit and scribbled ideas—as evidence.

She pushes her chair back. "I'm actually gonna get a refill before we move on. Do you want more?"

"Sure." Now I'm nervous. I can talk all day about caring for pets and training dogs, but when it comes to financial stuff, I'm at a complete loss.

When Kate sits back down and clasps her hands in front of her, her face is so serious I have to stifle a giggle. "Where do you see your business in five years?"

Not the question I'd expected. "Um... I don't know?"

She nods, no judgement on her face. "Okay, let's back up. What's working for you right now and what isn't?"

This gets the ball rolling. Kate is amazing at teasing out details and organizing my hopes and dreams into what she calls "actionable items." By the time I've finished the second cup of coffee, I have a plan for making a proposal to Dr. Morrissey with a prioritized list of what to negotiate for, including things like liability insurance, which would probably not have occurred to me until I was liable for something.

Looking over my list, I shake my head. "Kate, I can't thank you enough. Even if I spent weeks in the library, I couldn't have come up with all this."

She sits back in her chair and taps her nose with a pencil. "This has actually given me a really cool idea." Pulling out her legal pad, she flips to a clean page and writes as she speaks. "Microloans are good and all, but I think what women in the States might benefit from is a place to ask advice. Or a mentor." She bites the pencil for a few seconds before writing more. "Oooh. Maybe a drop-in clinic for entrepreneurs. We could have workshops, but also times when people like you could come in with questions—roadblocks they've run into. Like an… Entrepreneur Support Center." She makes a face. "That sounds terrible. I'll have to come up with a better name." She grabs my hand. "You want to be the pilot project for this if I can get it going?"

"Uh, sure. That'd be great."

Kate takes more notes, asks more questions, and gets me super excited about my prospects. Now I just have to work up the courage to actually make the proposal to my boss.

Chapter 25

"Start Me Up" - The Rolling Stones
Lucy's Catch You on the Flipside Mixtape, Song #3

LUCY

Saturday afternoon, after a morning of driving and training and meeting new clients, I stop to fuel up. Before I head out again, I use the gas station's payphone to check messages. After giving me information on two new potential clients, the woman from the service says, "Oh, there's one more."

"This is from Ben. No last name, no number," she says in her heavy South Boston accent. "He says, 'I'd love for you to come to the show tonight, and I'd love it even more if you'd come over to my place afterward.'"

Glad she can't see my blush. "Got it. That's it?"

"That's it."

"Okay, thanks. Have a nice weekend."

"Sounds like you will, honey."

She hangs up before I can comment. Ben and I both have pagers now, and sometimes he sends me a "707" message, which kind of reads "LOL" if you look at it upside down, meaning "lots of love," but I do wish we had a more private way to exchange messages.

Hours later, I'm wandering the lobby after the show, waiting for Ben to change out of his costume. When I worked backstage for the drama club in high school, there were only a few performances, and each one was completely different. There'd always be some screw-up: someone forgot lines or a piece of the scenery fell down or someone's costume went missing.

This was a whole other ballgame. Tonight's performance technically matched opening night, but in subtle ways, it was completely different. It's hard to explain, but it was like the actors incorporated the audience's feedback into the show moment by moment by moment. Like we were all in it together.

The theater door opens, but it isn't Ben, it's the woman who plays his sidekick. She's in a dress and has lipstick on, so it takes a moment for me to recognize her.

"Hey, Lucy!"

"Hi, Bella. Great job tonight."

"Thanks! We had fun." The lanky blonde gives me a side hug. "It's so good to see you! I guess you've been busy?"

"Yeah. Who knew there was so much demand for dog training?"

"If you trained kids, I'd hire you." She grins. "Wait, do you?"

I shake my head. "I wouldn't even know how to start."

"Believe me, that doesn't change even after you become a parent." She squeezes my forearm. "So, things are good with you and Ben? Does he know you're here?" She looks back toward the doors that lead backstage. "I think he's still getting notes from the stage manager." She leans closer. "You aren't mad at him?"

"Mad? About what?"

She covers her face with her hands and talks into them. "Um. Nothing." She drops her hands and shakes them out while bouncing on the balls of her feet. "I'm just hyped up on post-show adrenaline."

Resettling her shoulder bag, she hugs me again. "He's one of the good ones. Just remember that." After a long look full of some sort of meaning, she claps her hands. "Okay, gotta get home. Bye!"

Before I can process what just happened, the stage door swings open and the stars of the show appear. At least in my book. Puck's bright eyes find me, and Ben drops the leash. Seconds later, the dog's in my arms and I'm in Ben's.

Puck quickly squirms free, but I nestle into Ben with a sigh. "I've missed you."

"I missed you more." He rubs his scruffy beard into my hair. "Thanks for coming."

A yawn takes over my mouth. "Sorry, it's been a long day. This is way past my bedtime."

"Let's get you to bed." He nuzzles my ear. "Though I'm not sure if I can let you go to sleep right away."

"Get a room, you two."

Will's teasing has me stepping back, but Ben pulls me into his side. "You're just jealous."

"Nah, I'm going home to my own gorgeous woman." He bows in my direction. "Glad to have you back, Lucy. Ben could use a little more training. He's all over the place out there. Puck can barely keep him in line."

"Yeah, yeah. Who got more notes than me tonight?" Ben grabs his bag before leaning down to whisper in my ear. "Will you come home with me? I promise not to keep you up all night. Just part of it."

Taking his free hand, I kiss him on the cheek before answering, "Race you there."

BEN

Sex with Lucy is changing me. Like, literally. I think it started that summer when we were together, but now, every time I'm skin to skin with her, I become more myself, like I've been stuck in this passive, go-along-to-get-along mindset since... well, maybe since my mom died. Definitely since my grandma died. My dad was hurting so much and so overwhelmed I just didn't want to make things worse. Even with the Minolas, I thought that the only way I could hang on to my spot in their family was to be invisible and hope no one noticed I'd wormed my way in. Modeling, too. I didn't go after it. It happened to me.

But when Lucy looks at me like I'm her world, I feel like I'm taking up the right amount of space. Not the space of a nine-year-old kid. That of a twenty-eight-year old man.

My fingers play through Lucy's curls as a slide show of the past day plays through my mind—hours of making people laugh topped off with sex so good that I'll do anything to keep this woman by my side—until she mumbles something into my ribcage.

My hand stills. "Did you say something?"

She rolls away from me slightly, her brow furrowed. "I said, why would I be mad at you?"

"I… don't know?"

"Bella said something about me being mad at you."

My heartbeat pounds in my ears. *Shit.* I take a deep breath, blow it out slowly. *Shit. Shit. Shit.*

"Like she was surprised I was there and that things were good with us."

So much for finding the perfect time to tell her. "Well, there is something—a thing I need to tell you. Have needed to tell you. For a long time, but—but I've been too chickenshit to do it." It's like I'm being squeezed back into nine-year-old me again. But I can't. I can't just give up. I need to stand up.

She scoots away from me and sits up, taking the sheet with her. "Why would Bella know about it, then?"

I sit up too and get ready to give it all I've got. "Well, I told her because—"

"Why would you do that? Is something going on with you two?"

"What? No. Jesus. Lucy. How could I—" I gesture to the space between us, the disheveled bed. "How could I be here with you and even think about anyone else?"

"I don't know. I just don't understand why you'd tell her something you need to tell me."

"It's nothing like that. It's… it's about the day Tony died."

She stills. "Why would you even *talk* to her about that?"

"Because—" Now that I've started I can't stop. "I needed the practice." Saying this out loud sounds so, so stupid, but I power on. "I was afraid that if I did it wrong, you'd never forgive me. So I practiced on a couple people."

"A couple people? What, did you tell Jessica, too? Your Juliet that you spent all summer practically fucking onstage?"

"No—and Lucy, come on, that's my job. It's pretend."

"Who else did you tell then?"

"Uh, my dad and your mom."

"My mom? You're more afraid of me than you are of my mom?"

"It's not that I'm afraid of you, Lucy. That's not it at all. Oh man, I'm doing it wrong. Not quite ready for opening night, I guess."

"I don't see how this is funny."

"Sorry. It's not. I know it's not."

"So, what is it? What are you so afraid to tell me?"

She's so beautiful in this moment, even as anger flashes over her face.

"The accident. The car. With Tony. It was my fault."

"What? What are you talking about? Did you get the guy drunk and give him his keys?"

"No." I take her hand, needing the connection. She starts to pull away, but I hang on tight, begging her to listen with my eyes and my touch. "I needed to see you. I was missing you so much. I didn't want to date anybody else, and I didn't want you to either."

Blinking slowly, she opens her mouth and starts to say something but then presses her lips together firmly.

"So, when Tony came by and asked if I wanted to come along to pick you up from UMass, it seemed like I was being given this opportunity. To see you, but also to go public about us. He probably just wanted us to hang out. We did, at first. It was a beautiful fall day. It should've been a perfect day."

I can still picture every detail. Crisp, cool air. Bluest sky, fluffy white clouds. "I put the last mixtape you made me in his car stereo. The Rolling Stones, The Police, The Cars. I wanted to listen to it when I told him."

"What happened?"

The impatience in her voice cuts across the gulf between us. I have to get her back on my side.

"I was gearing up to tell him when we hit some bad traffic on the Mass Pike. Tony got irritated, decided to get off the highway, take 20 instead. I argued it would take just as long. He started razzing me. Like he always did. But this time it had an edge. I don't know why. He was poking me, saying I was so skinny, what was I doing studying theater, was I a fag or something?"

My free hand fists in the bedsheet. "That pissed me off. So much, that instead of telling him the truth—instead of telling him straight out that I was in love with you—I said something really stupid like, no, I wasn't a fag and he should ask you because I'd been fucking you all summer."

A sharp intake of breath, a flash in her eyes and she jerks her hand from mine.

"I'm sorry. That's not at all how I felt—feel—about that summer. Or you. He started me up, and I set him off. Suddenly we were screaming at each other. I don't even know what we were saying. And then—and then, there was a horrible sound and we were flying through the air."

Drowning in memory, I don't quite register a shift in the room until Lucy's halfway to the bathroom.

Heart pounding in my ears, I scramble out of the bed, shove on my boxers, muttering to myself, "Fuck. Fuck. You are such a fucking idiot asshole."

The toilet flushes. The door flies open and I stumble forward telling her that I'm sorry over and over. She shoves me back, eyes blazing. She's naked but she doesn't seem to notice. She shoves me again.

"You want to hear about my day? That "perfect" day? First off, I was having a really good time at school. I missed you, I didn't want to date anybody else either and I was homesick. But I loved my classes. Loved going to parties. Loved being on my own."

She pauses and shakes her head slowly. When she looks up again, there's an ugly sneer on her face. "Thing was, I wasn't really on my own, was I? I was still a spoiled little princess. I didn't want to have to take the bus home for Thanksgiving break, even though I knew it was a busy season for my dad and my mom was working her ass off to make a perfect Thanksgiving dinner." She mimes crying, twisting her fists in front of her eyes. "Why couldn't somebody just pick me up? So Tony, because he was a good big brother, said he'd do it, even though I'm sure he'd have been happier doing just about anything else."

I step closer. "That's not—he wanted to—"

I freeze when her hand makes a stop sign in the air between us. "I listened to you, now you listen to me." Her finger jabs in my direction with each pointed word, so sharply I can feel it behind my sternum even though she's still halfway across the room.

A shiver goes through her, and she skirts around me to grab the blanket from the end of the bed. Throwing it over her shoulders, she paces around the room as she continues.

"I thought he'd be there at four, so I went downstairs to wait. Watched people leave, getting on the bus, in their parents' cars. No Tony. Finally I go upstairs and find a note on my door, stuck there by whoever answered the hall pay phone. My mom saying he'd left a bit late but he'd be there by around five. So I go back downstairs. Six o'clock, he's still not there. I go back up, but there's no message. I call my house, but no one answers. I start wandering the halls. Find a room with a bunch of international students who have nowhere to go. They're drinking. I'm pissed off, so I decide to get drunk with them. We're doing shots. Playing stupid games.

"At some point there's a knock on the door, a voice saying it's security. Everyone's scrambling to hide shit. This man in a uniform says my name, says I need to come with him. I push past him, run to the bathroom. I throw up for a long time. When I come out, the other students are gone. The officer walks me to my room, and I get my bag. He drives me to their office, offers me coffee, food. I can't even talk to him. And then—I don't know how long it was—my parents show up. They tell me Tony's dead. I tell them it must be a mistake. They tell me it was a car accident. They don't say it, but it's clear they think it's my fault. I tell them I'm sorry, but they won't listen to me. They just bundle me into the car."

She stops moving and stares at me, eyes cold. "On the way home, I vow never to ask anyone to do anything for me again."

"Lucy, you can't think—"

"Fuck you, Ben. And fuck Tony, too. I've been wasting my life mourning the losses of both of you, but the thing is, *neither* of you trusted me. He didn't trust me to decide who I could love. And you still don't trust me enough to tell me the truth."

She drops the blanket and wrestles into her clothes, hands and voice shaking as she struggles with buttons and zippers. "All this time I've been doing penance for what I did wrong, and what good has it done? None. It's done nobody any good, least of all me."

She pushes past me and out of my room. "I'm gonna get my own place where I can have my own dog and play music and dance and eat what I want when I want it, and the rest of you who want to tell me how to live my life can just fuck off."

On her heels, I try to stop her. "Lucy, please. Let's—"

Her hand knocks mine away. "You want to know what it felt like when you left? I'll show you."

Without looking at me, she stuffs her feet into her shoes, grabs her bag and coat, and slams out the door.

Puck runs to the door, barks once, then looks back at me.

I drop to the floor, and he crawls into my lap with a whine. "Yeah buddy, I know. I fucked that up big time."

Chapter 26

"Baby Stick Around" - Joe Jackson
Lucy's Catch You on the Flipside Mixtape, Song #6

BEN

"Lucky!"

Puck takes a flying leap off my lap to skitter across the tile floor of the backstage greenroom. Two little kids shriek as he leaps up to lick them in the face. Janet, the Shakespeare Boston stage manager, dodges around them to hustle over to me.

Still foggy from a between-show nap that included a dream about Lucy—who I haven't seen in real life since she left my apartment a week ago, who won't return my calls to her house or her service—I flinch when Janet places a hand on my shoulder. "I'm so sorry to disturb you, but this family says that Puck is their dog."

She looks back at the small group in the doorway, a quintessential American family: mom, dad, boy and girl. And dog. "They have a picture of him with the kids, and the little girl was crying." I've never seen Janet emotional before, but her drill-sergeant veneer cracks when she turns back to me. "I couldn't say no."

On my feet, my knees taking in the information if my head hasn't, I mumble. "Uh, okay."

Puck's a friendly dog, but there's something about how he's interacting with them that has my battered heart plummeting.

Janet, at least a head shorter than me, pats my upper arm. When I don't move, she steers me toward the family. "Come on. Let's go have a chat with them."

Next thing I know, we're crowded into her small office, and the family is all talking at once, earnestly explaining how they'd lost Puck—Lucky, they call him—and then found him again.

"We were heartbroken when we lost him," the mom says. They introduced themselves, but I can barely take in what she's saying, let alone remember her name. "We were at a cookout in Boxborough for the Fourth of July. There were a lot of people and dogs there, and when it was time to leave, we couldn't find him. We spent hours looking for him that night and put up signs everywhere the next day. We live down in Milton, but we went back the next few nights after work and kept looking for him." Her gaze roves over the kids, then to Puck. "We've had Lucky since Max and Lena were two and three."

The little girl looks up, her brown eyes huge. "He was our combined birthday present."

I don't know much about kids, but these guys look like they're nine or ten. "So… seven years ago?"

The dad musses the boy's hair. "Seven years ago. They grew up with him."

I take a shaky breath. "And you just happened to come to the show and recognize him?"

The dad shakes his head. "We saw the article in the *Globe*. We're not subscribers, but a friend saved it—not thinking it was him, just that it looked like him—and gave it to us when we got together for dinner this week. We didn't think there was any way it could be him since we lost him twenty miles from here and it was so long ago, but we had to find out. The minute he walked onstage, we recognized him. It wasn't easy keeping these two from yelling out his name."

The mom looks up, still scratching behind Puck's ears. Just the way he likes. "Where did you get him?" Her tone is a bit challenging, like maybe I got him on some black market for stolen dogs or something.

I shove my shaking hands in my armpits. "He just showed up at my house a couple months ago. He had an injured paw. I put up signs around my neighborhood…" I trail off, not sure what else to say. Obviously, he's their dog.

The dad clears his throat. "I guess you need him for the performances, but we'd like to take him home as soon as possible. How many more do you have?"

When I don't say anything, Janet answers for me. "One more weekend—Thursday through Sunday. And we have another show in an hour."

The dad looks at his watch. "We could pick him up afterward and bring him back Thursday. Would that work?"

"We can't take him now?" the little girl asks.

"It's just a few hours, sweetie. We'll have dinner somewhere nearby. You'll get to stay up late."

She squats next to Puck, tears in her eyes. "But I've missed him so much!"

"I know, but Lucky has a job here."

Janet bends down to talk to the kids. "He'll be done at nine thirty."

I have nothing to contribute to this conversation, so I just shove my hands in my pockets. All I want to do is rewind my life to a week ago, tell Lucy the right way and run away with her and Puck to Vegas so none of this will have happened.

Janet straightens. "Right now, Ben and Puck—uh, sorry, Lucky— need to get ready." When no one moves, she adds, "Perhaps we can look into some sort of compensation for the rest of the run?"

The mom stands. "Oh, no. We're so grateful you've taken such good care of him."

"In fact, we'll be happy to pay you for any vet bills, food—" The dad's reaching for his wallet.

"No." I finally find my voice, but it comes out a bit harsh. I try to clear the debris from my wreck of a throat. "No, it's fine." I force a smile onto my face. I don't know how the hell I'm going to get through the show tonight. It's been a Herculean effort to keep a lid on my emotions as it is. But hey, that's why they call it acting, right?

The mom gets them moving. "Okay, kiddos. Let's give Lucky one last hug, and we'll take him home in a couple of hours."

Finally, after so many "last hugs" I'm about to roar with frustration, the family troops out the door, leaving me sitting in Janet's office alone with Puck. Lucky. Whoever the fuck he is. He stares after them for a few moments, whining softly, before returning to my side.

"Why the hell didn't you tell me you had another family?"

He doesn't answer.

I FAKE my way through the show and somehow get myself back home. Without Puck riding shotgun, loneliness rips my battered heart to shreds. Instead of going to my place, I really go home. When my dad walks in the back door, I have no idea how long I've been staring at the well-worn surface of the kitchen table.

"I didn't know you were here," he says, looking back toward the den. "Something wrong with the TV?"

There's no television in the garage apartment, so if I want to watch a game, I do it here. It's a good way to spend time with the old guy.

"No. I, uh..." I scrub a hand over my face. "I had a pretty shitty day." I look over at the clock. "I should go to bed, I guess."

Problem is, I can't seem to get out of this chair. "How'd you do it, Dad?"

Instead of answering, my dad plunks down two glasses and a bottle of Scotch, giving us each a hefty pour. "Do what?"

Picking up a glass, I stare at the brown liquid, the exact color of Lucy's eyes. Puck's too, for that matter. "Go on. After Mom died."

He scrapes out a chair and sits down heavily. "I don't know, Ben. I think I was pretty out of it for a long time. You were so little. Thank god your grandmother was there to step in. I was useless. If I'd had to take care of you by myself…" He shakes his head and lifts his glass.

The liquid burns through the numbness in my throat and chest. I wish it'd burn up my heart. Not like I need it anymore.

My dad clears his throat. "I wish… I wish I'd been a better father to you."

Meeting his gaze, I open my mouth to disagree, but he shakes his head sharply. "I know I kept you at arm's length. I see that now. I was just afraid. Afraid to let myself love anyone again. Though I did—I do —love you. I just…" He looks away.

I swirl the liquid in the glass and take another shot. He did do his best. I guess that's all anybody can do. "I know. I get it. I love you too."

After a few beats of silence, he looks around the kitchen. "Where's the dog?"

"Yeah, well, that's part of the shitty day." I tell him what happened.

"What? How can they do that? You've had him for months, paid his vet bills. Don't you have some kind of right to him?"

I swallow what's left of my Scotch and slam the glass on the table. "I doubt it. Anyway, they have two little kids who've known him their whole lives. I can't take him away from them." The dog bed my dad put by the back door looks so sad I want to throw it away. "Gonna miss that little guy."

My dad pours another round. "How'm I going to take a walk with Vera now?"

A laugh puffs past my lips. "I don't know. You'll have to be a man and ask her out without the dog, I guess."

"Humph. I guess that applies to you, too."

"Yeah, I pretty much fucked that up too." I pick up the glass, then put it down again. "I have to go back to LA next week, right after the show closes. I don't know what's going to happen after that, whether Lucy wants me to come back."

My dad looks like he's going to say something but then just nods. "You're always welcome here, for as long as you want."

"Thanks, Dad."

"I missed you, you know, when you were gone for so long."

"I missed you too. Whatever happens with me and Lucy or work, I'll be back more."

"Good, good." He knocks on the table lightly, picks up his drink and checks the clock. "What d'you say we watch the end of Sports-Center? See what foolishness the Patriots are up to."

"Sounds good, Dad."

I MAKE it through Monday by taking the longest run of my life, lifting weights till my muscles scream louder than the mocking voices in my head, and then passing out on the couch. Now it's Tuesday, I have another empty day in front of me and this apartment is too damn quiet.

Then I have an idea.

I have to wait until it's a reasonable time to call, so I go for another run. Not quite so far this time. When I get back, I dial Will's number.

His roommate Pam answers. "Yello."

"Hey, Pam. This is Ben."

"Oh my god, I heard about Puck. That totally sucks."

"Yeah. It does. Listen, is Will around? I need some help with—this is kind of embarrassing—but I need to make a mixtape for somebody and apparently it's a skill I don't have. So—"

"Will can't help you with that."

"But he and I talked about—"

"First of all, he's not here. Second of all, he doesn't own any music. Plus, he knows nothing about recording equipment and is terrible at math."

"Oh, okay, well—"

"I am the one you need to talk to."

Before I can say anything, she gives me extremely detailed instructions regarding purchasing blank cassettes. Thankfully, the guy she tells me to talk to at Tech Hifi knows what she's talking about.

An hour later, before I can even knock, Pam and Deb's dog Rufus barks to announce my arrival. The sound is a painful reminder. However, there's nothing I can do about the loss of Puck, but there is something I can at least try to do to prove to Lucy that I love her. That I've always loved her.

The door swings open, and Pam takes the plastic bag from my hands to inspect the contents. She nods and pulls me inside. "Good job. I've got everything ready to go. We might need to take a trip over to Tower Records, but we'll start with our music collection."

At least I'm doing something. It might be a lost cause. It might make things worse. But it's not like I have anything to lose.

Chapter 27

"Catapult" - R.E.M
Ben's Very First Mixtape, Song #1

LUCY

After exiting the exam room, Dr. Morrissey slams the patient chart onto a metal table in the back hall "Can you believe that guy?" she hisses. "First he doesn't believe me. Then he's pissed at *me* because a breeder sold him a male instead of a female. And then he has the gall to ask if he could talk to the real vet?"

At least Ben isn't a sexist asshole like the owner of the beagle Dr. Morrissey's pissed at. I'm still mad at Ben, though. And I'm embarrassed. I can't believe he told all those other people something that has to do with him and me. But right now, I have to get my boss in a better frame of mind, so I put my game face on.

"You're a girl. You can't be the real vet." I nudge her shoulder with mine. "Anyway, you missed the fun conversation where I had to explain to the man about balls descending."

"Probably made his balls *ascend*," she mutters before shoving the chart through the window to reception and heading down the hall. "Alrighty then, what's behind door number two?"

I pull the chart and hand it to her. "Oh, you're gonna like this one. It's a case of cat scratch fever." I do a little head banging, hoping to cheer her up. Even though half my heart is stuck back in Ben's apartment, I mean what I said to him. It's time for me to stop being a martyr and live my own life. I'm going to make my proposal today, and it'll go better if the doc's in a good mood. "'Cat Scratch Feverrrr.' Come on doc, sing it with me!"

She rolls her eyes. "I hope they know *I* don't do it for free." She does a full-body shake and plasters on a professional smile before opening the door. "Good afternoon, Mrs. Adams, how are you?"

"Well, I've been better." The older woman looks down at the large shorthair in her lap. "I'm worried about my sweet John Boy."

Morrissey scans my notes. "From what Lucy tells me, it sounds like he's got an abscess. Does he get into fights with other cats?"

"Well yes, sometimes. But he didn't have any scratches."

The vet sits on the bench next to Mrs. Adams. "The small puncture wounds from a cat bite heal over quickly, but some pretty nasty bacteria can get trapped underneath. All this?" She points at the swelling on the top of John Boy's head. "Is pus. If we don't treat it, it will be something to worry about, but we can very easily lance it and drain it and give him an antibiotic. We'll take him in the back and take care of it and then send you home with some meds, okay?"

Mrs. Adams grips John Boy protectively. "Do you want me to hold him while you do it?"

"Oh, no. Lucy can take care of that." Morrissey winks at the woman. "He might get a little feisty, and I like you better than I like her."

I grunt out a laugh at her joke, even as the cat growls.

"Will it hurt him?" John Boy's mama asks.

"He'll feel much better once it's over, believe me," I say, my voice soothing. She hesitates briefly before handing him over to me with a resigned sigh.

A few minutes later, I've donned padded gloves and have John Boy pinned. When Dr. Morrissey leans in to open the abscess, pus explodes from the cat's cheek, spraying us both.

"Ugh. So disgusting."

"Gets me every time." She quickly sponges the wound with hydrogen peroxide. "Like a volcano."

"Reminds me of when I used to watch my older brother pop his zits."

"Ha!" She shakes her head as she squeezes fluid from the opening. "I did that too!"

"We're not normal."

"Probably not."

Thankfully, the cat has relaxed into my hold. "Poor kitty," I coo. "You were super swollen. You're a much handsomer boy without all that fluid backed up in your face."

As she gives him the antibiotics injection, I ask, "Hey, could I talk to you about something at the end of the day today?"

She gives me a sharp look, as she drops the needle in the sharps bin. "As long as it's not about you quitting."

"Oh, no, no. The opposite, really. It's an idea I have." John Boy growls. "Easy, buddy."

Looking down, she unbuttons her lab coat. "Gonna have to change this out." She checks her watch. "I'll have some time at the end of the day since I don't have to pick up the kids." She points at me. "But you have to talk Mrs. Adams into neutering this guy."

"I guess one more chat about balls won't kill me."

Ten minutes later, after I make the argument that her cat will be healthier and happier without his testicles, Mrs. Adams goes home to discuss the matter of fixing their cat with her husband.

"I just hate to deprive him of that pleasure," she whispers.

Once she's gone, I clean the exam room with extra vigor, hoping to dispel some nervous energy. I rehearsed my pitch with my parents and brothers last night, so I think I'm ready to present it to Dr. Morrissey.

Then it hits me.

Is that what Ben had been doing?

Maybe it wasn't that he didn't trust me. Maybe he was telling other people about the accident before he told me because when the stakes are high, it's vital to get it right.

AT THE END of the day, as I lower my butt into the chair across from Dr. Morrissey in her office, I mentally go over all the reasons why this is a good plan for both of us. Then I straighten my little stack of papers, clear my throat and start my rehearsed speech.

"There is clearly a demand for canine behavioral services here in Boston, because my answering service is getting calls from new clients every single day. The problem is, I'm spending so much time driving around town to meet with individual clients, I can't take on new ones. I need a home base where I can train dogs and their people one-on-one, but also lead group classes."

When Dr. Morrissey opens her mouth, I hold up a hand. "Just hear me out, please?" At her nod, I continue. "As I said, I don't want to give up my position here. So far, it's been good for both of us."

I slide over a chart Kate helped me create. "There's been a forty percent increase of first-time visits to the practice during the past six weeks. Sixty-nine percent of those were clients of mine."

Giving her a moment to scan the visuals, I take a breath and check my notes. When she looks up, I continue. "If my training facility were close by, I could continue to bring in new patients as well as have a steady paycheck with benefits." Smiling, I take a moment before going on. I'm not so sure about this next bit. "Researching available buildings within a two-mile radius, I was surprised to find that the owner of the old laundromat next door is the same corporation that owns this practice." I'd been under the impression Dr. Morrissey purchased the practice from her older partner when he retired. "I plan to contact the corporation, work out a lease with them for the building and then do a quick rehab so I can use it as a training facility."

My boss cuts in. "The corporation is me." She waves a hand at my obvious confusion. "My best friend is a lawyer. When I decided to buy the practice, she advised me to create an LLC. I bought the laundromat when I had a windfall, thinking it could be a grooming spot." She sits back in her chair and crosses her arms. "I just ran out of time and funds to do that." She nods slowly. "Okay. Let's talk. I'm assuming you have more numbers in that stack of paper you've got there?"

"Yes, indeed I do."

Thankful for Kate's help in preparing for this meeting, I hand over my detailed proposal, and we work through it. By the time we're done, we have a tentative plan for splitting costs, turning the laundromat into a grooming *and* training facility and moving forward with a partnership.

The only thing that could make this day better would be sharing it with someone important to me. Someone who makes my soul sing but who can also make me so angry that I can't be in the same room with him.

That odd priest said something about anger burning out the old to make room for the new. *A cleansing fire leaving room for growth. If handled skillfully.*

I just wish I knew where to obtain such a skill.

HEADING home after my evening appointments, I almost turn down Ben's street instead of my own. I miss him. I miss that glorious body, I miss laughing with him, I miss telling him all about my day, I miss falling asleep next to him and most of all, I miss waking up to those gorgeous green eyes smiling at me.

I love him. I always will. I'm still angry, but I could just march down the path between our yards and work things out with him.

As I park in front of my house, though, I realize something.

A lot of the things I yelled at him on my way out the door are true.

I haven't actually been living my life for the past seven years. I've been hiding from it, serving an endless penance, handed down not by God but by myself. Talk about hubris.

My head drops onto the steering wheel. I'm so full of so many different feelings I can't move. I might be able to have a career that I'm passionate about, that I could potentially make a decent living from. But what if I screw up? What if everyone finds out I really have no idea what I'm doing? I've read books and rented every available video on animal training, but mostly I go on instinct. What if that fails? What if I make a mistake and someone gets hurt?

Rolling my forehead back and forth, I take in a shuddery breath. All I know is I can't go back to how things were before Ben came back and turned my life upside down. To that colorless circle of work and errands. Whatever I have to do, I'm going to start my own life. Once I'm on my own two feet, I'll figure out how to work things out with Ben.

Twisting around to grab my bag from the passenger seat, turn back to open the door and scream at the sight of my brother's face looming in the window.

"Jesus Christ, you scared the crap out of me!"

When I don't open the door, Sal does it for me. "I was wondering what the heck you were doing there. At first I thought maybe you'd passed out or something. But your lips were moving. Were you talking to yourself?"

Fuck. Between my dirty windows and the ebbing twilight, Sal looked like Tony. Hauling myself out of the car, I mutter, "I'm losing it."

Then everything goes black.

"Whoa there, Nelly." Sal catches my elbow. "What is the matter with you?"

Grabbing the roof of the car with my free hand, I close my eyes. It doesn't help. "I'm just dizzy. I think…" I scan through my busy day. "I think I forgot to eat today."

"Man. I could never do that." He puts an arm around my shoulders, tugs me in close and takes my enormous bag. After closing the car door, he guides me toward the house. When did he get so big? No wonder I thought he was Tony.

"There's plenty of minestrone. We ate a couple hours ago, but I'm hungry again. I'll eat with you."

Before I know it, I'm sitting at the kitchen table, Sal's chatting away about his day and I'm staring at an empty bowl of soup I don't remember eating. A warm hand rests on the center of my back, relaxing muscles I didn't know were tense. "Sal said you almost fainted out front because you'd forgotten to eat." My mom frowns. "Are you taking care of yourself?"

I shake my head, suddenly exhausted. "Probably not."

Without being asked, Sal takes both of our bowls to the sink. As soon as he disappears down the hall, the floodgates open. Forehead on my hands, my mom's hand on my back, I cry so many feelings I can't even name them all.

When I finally sit back in the chair, I'm empty of everything but snot. My mom sets a box of tissues next to me, and I go through so many I make a mountain of Kleenex wads, the sight of which has me laughing hysterically until I'm hiccuping. Shaking my head, I mumble, "It's official. I've gone nuts."

My mom sighs, but she's smiling as she hands me a glass of water. "No, my girl. You're just living again. Coming out of a cocoon is a lot of work." She squeezes my forearm. "My beautiful butterfly."

I grab the last tissue from the box, cover my face with it and groan. "I think maybe I'm a moth, like one of those ones that are so stupid they just fly into the porch light over and over again."

My mom stands abruptly and paces to the sink, looking out the window for a moment before crossing to pull a fat envelope out of the junk drawer. "I'm just going to spit it out. Your dad should be here, but I think you need to hear this now."

"Is everything okay?" Now I'm worried about her. My hiccups disappear along with any lingering humor. "Are you—are you sick?"

"No, sweetheart, no. Don't worry." She sits down next to me, her eyes on the envelope in her hands. "Your father and I have been doing a lot of soul-searching recently. You're so passionate about the work you're doing it made us realize that we've been stuck. In our grief." She takes a moment to clear her throat. "We miss Tony every day. But we still have three amazing children." She looks down the hall toward the front door, like maybe my dad might walk in any minute. "And each other."

She smooths the envelope in her hands before going on. "A year ago, we got a settlement from the civil suit we brought against the driver of the car that hit Tony's. We put the money in the bank and just let it sit there. We couldn't deal with it at the time."

She shakes her head. "You and Sal and Vinnie work so hard and achieve so much. It's clear what that money is for. We're giving it to you kids."

She pulls papers from the envelope, sifts through them and hands me a savings account statement with my name on it and a number with a whole lot of zeros. "Mom. This is… too much."

She holds up a hand. "Spend it however you want. Buy a new car, take a trip to Europe, get a pony. Whatever you want. Whatever you need."

I can't quite wrap my head around this, not to mention my heart. Guilt pricks at me. I don't deserve this.

"Lucy, look at me."

When I do, the fierceness there surprises me. "I don't want you to feel badly for focusing on yourself and your career. It's your time." She scoots closer to pull me in for a side hug. "I mean it. We'll be here to cheer you on whatever you choose to do."

Leaning on my mom is good. Even just temporarily. "Thank you so much, Mama. For everything. I love you."

"I love you too, baby girl."

Chapter 28

"Tears of a Clown" - The English Beat
Ben's Very First Mixtape, Song #2

BEN

Our final performance comes way too soon.

Suddenly it's time. Time for me to leave town. Time for me to put a whole country between me and Lucy. Time to say goodbye to my new best friend. Squatting, keeping eye contact with Puck, I force my emotions to sit, stay and behave as I speak. "You have my number. If you ever need anyone to take care of him, I'm your man."

Fred Johnson buckles a well-worn collar around Puck's neck and hands me the collar and leash I purchased with Lucy. "Thanks for everything. You're sure we can't reimburse you for the vet costs?"

I shake my head. "Please don't worry about it."

When I stand, Puck whines and walks his front paws up my legs to snuffle his wet nose into my palm. "I'll miss you too, buddy."

One last scratch behind the ears, a quick shake of Mr. Johnson's hand, and I turn on my heel to head back to the dressing room before I embarrass myself. Thankfully, the rest of the cast has decamped to a bar for a closing party, so I can grab my bags and call a cab in peace. My dad offered to take me to the airport, but I didn't want him to have to deal with the traffic.

After picking up my suitcases from the corner of the men's dressing room, I head to Janet's office to use the phone. When I knock, the door flies open. Janet's office is full of people, and none of them are Janet. Instead, Bella, Will, Jessica and Randall are perched on various surfaces.

Bella crosses her arms over her chest and narrows her eyes at me. "Just what do you think you're up to, young man?"

"What are you guys doing here?"

She rolls her eyes. "Janet told us you were going to call a cab to take you to the airport. You may be a famous model, but you've still got friends who want to see you off."

Will takes my suitcase. "Yeah. I need make sure that my biggest competition is leaving town."

Randall cuffs me on the back of the head. "What he said."

"What about the party?"

Jessica hooks an arm in mine. "Eh, it'll still be going after we drop you off."

Bella looks at her watch as we all troop down the hall. "When's your flight?"

"Seven."

After I heave my briefcase strap over my shoulder, she grabs my free hand. "Perfect! It's only five. That gives us plenty of time to grab a beer on the way and get you to the airport by six thirty."

She squeezes my hand. "And don't worry; I'm driving and I won't drink. But you, my friend, can drown your sorrows all you want."

TOO SOON, I'm on the plane, already missing Boston. When I landed at Logan a few months ago, I figured I'd make sure my dad was okay and within days—weeks at most—I'd be back to my real life in LA.

Now it's that life that feels unreal. Untethered, anyway. Not only did I stumble into the work I do there, I have no lasting connection to it or to anyone I know.

Whereas here, I'm already missing so many things—new friends, colleagues, Puck, my dad. Most of all, with Lucy. That link has never been broken.

Not seven years ago, and not now.

I CAN'T BELIEVE *that big kid, Tony, invited me to play capture the flag. When he caught up to me on the walk home from my first day at my new school today and tapped on my shoulder saying, "Hey, new kid," I was sure he was about to beat me up.*

Instead, here I am in the woods near our house—a super cool park full of giant rocks and trees and other hiding spots—with a whole group of kids my age. Mostly boys. Two girls. One is our age and kind of a tomboy. The other is younger. Pretty sure she's Tony's sister.

Problem is, I'm a captain and I don't know anybody.

And it's my turn to pick.

The other captain already picked Tony. Obvious choice. I scan the group. I mean, probably everybody is good. Except maybe Tony's little sister. I catch Tony's eye, and I get it. I'm being tested. It'll probably doom my team, but I know what I need to do.

"Uh, I don't know any names, but I pick you." I point at Tony's little sister, but her messy hair is covering her face while she digs around in the dirt.

A kid next to her groans and shoves her. "He picks you, Lucy."

When she looks up, I can't stop the smile on my face because hers is lit with a grin that makes me think we're either gonna win this game or get in some kind of trouble.

TURNED OUT IT WAS BOTH.

Blinking awake as the cabin lights flick on and the person next to me shifts, sifting through memories and dreams, I'm suddenly energized. I can't wait to get off this plane and start making changes.

Something about that smile on Lucy's face in my memory makes everything crystal clear.

I left behind my family, my friends, my dog and the love of my life. But this time it's different.

Yes, Tony's gone. Yes, we miss him. When I left Boston seven years ago, I was running from a giant crack in the Minola family foundation that I was sure I'd created. I couldn't face it—couldn't face Boston without Tony, couldn't face Lucy and the many ways I'd hurt her.

But all of that—or at least a lot of that—was fiction.

The reality is that we're all responsible for Tony's loss, and none of us are. Including Tony himself.

All I can do now is take responsibility for my own choices, my own career, my own life. Something new for me, but I'm ready for it.

The minute we land, I'm putting a plan together. Tomorrow, I'll meet my agent and lay it out for him. When it's in place, I'll go back to Boston and reclaim my life there.

Then I'll do whatever it takes to convince Lucy that she should be a part of it.

Chapter 29

"Always Something There to Remind Me" - Naked Eyes
Ben's Very First Mixtape, Song #3

LUCY

"I'm sorry," my client says through gritted teeth. "I'm just so angry."

I blow out a breath. This training session has been a challenge on so many fronts. "Let's sit down for a minute." I ease the leash from her shaking hand and guide her toward a park bench.

Once the puppy is settled at my side, I turn to face her. "How about we go over all your options here?"

She sits back and shakes her head slowly. "I just don't know what they were thinking."

I'm sure her children thought that giving their mom a puppy six months after their father died was a good idea, that she could use the companionship. But that's not how it's working out.

The six-month-old yellow lab whines and starts to get up. "Bear, shht." I give him a sharp tug and release of the choke chain, and he eases back down to the ground with a grunt.

"You make it look so easy. But I just get frustrated with him so quickly, and he's getting so big. If you hadn't been here when he lunged at that other dog, I would've fallen! At my age, that can have serious consequences." She looks up at the cloudy sky. "I've never had a dog. Why would they think I want one now?"

I'm not sure I have a solution for her other than to give the dog away, even though that feels like giving up. "You said they were worried about you being lonely?"

Her hand flies up as she shuts these ideas down. "He's made things worse on that front! I've got neighbors complaining about the barking, and I'm trapped by this puppy's schedule so I can't even do things with my friends." She turns to me. "I'm sorry. I shouldn't take this out on you."

I shake my head. "It's fine." I look down at the dog, vibrating with the desire to move. "Look. He's smart and trainable, but labs tend to stay very high energy for at least the first two years. Sometimes longer."

The dismay on her face makes it easier to say the rest. "You two may be a bad match. Or you and any dog may be a bad match. The good news is he'll be perfect for someone and he's young enough that it'll probably be easy to find another home for him." I hesitate, hoping I'm not pushing her to do something she'll later regret. "If that's what you want."

She slumps back into the bench, her relief palpable. "That is definitely what I want."

We head to her Back Bay apartment—no backyard, a tough situation for such a high-energy dog—and I help her make plans. By the time I've said goodbye to them, I'm wrung out. Ever since the meeting with Dr. Morrissey and then finding out about the money, I've been on a rollercoaster of emotion. Thank goodness Mrs. Wiseman's my last appointment of the day. I just need to get across town so I can crawl into bed.

This widow's anger is completely understandable. Her kids saddled her with a huge responsibility she didn't ask for.

What about my anger? The anger I've been lugging around since Tony died? The new brand of anger I've kept simmering on a back burner since I decided Ben didn't "trust me"?

That shit I brought on myself.

Maybe the problem isn't the anger itself—I had reason to be hurt and angry at Ben for leaving without telling me after Tony died. The problem is the way I held onto it, burying it while I played the role of a "good girl."

And now? Being angry at him for sharing private things with other people, for not trusting me, that's somewhat justified. But it doesn't have to burn the whole relationship down.

The light turns green, and not a second later, the car behind me lays on the horn. I give the guy the finger in the rearview and shout, "Learn some patience, asshole!" Which feels good. Really fucking good. As does yelling "Fucking asshole" as loud as I can for good measure. Maybe this what cleansing anger is, because I'm suddenly hopeful.

Twenty minutes later, my car parks itself in front of Ben's house. Full of all the feelings and too impatient to wait until I have my life in order, I trot up the stairs to his apartment and knock on the door to tell him that I love him and we'll figure it out together.

No bark from Puck.

The van's in the driveway, as is Mr. Porter's sedan. The kitchen light in the house is on. Maybe they're having dinner?

So what if I interrupt? This is important.

Moments after I knock on the back door, Mr. Porter peers through the curtains and then opens the door. "Lucy, this is a nice surprise. How are you?"

"I'm good. How are you?"

"Good, good." He nods.

"Is Ben here?"

His brow crinkles. "He left for California a week ago. You're… not in touch with him?"

"Oh my gosh. Wow, I didn't realize…" Has it been that long since we had that fight? "I knew he had to go back, but I guess I—"

"Do you want to come in? I was about to have some coffee and kugel. Vera Rosen made it. Oh, and before I forget, she asked me to spread the word. She's looking for a tenant for her upstairs apartment, so if you know a nice young woman who might be interested, please let her know."

I nod as he goes on about the apartment. I still can't believe he's gone already. Then I realize that someone else is missing. "So he too Puck with him?"

Mr. Porter gets that concerned, crinkled-brow look again. "Puck's gone. He didn't tell you?"

"Gone? Is he okay?"

"He's fine, I guess. His original family took him back. They saw his picture in the paper and came to claim him. It hit Ben hard to lose him." He looks over his shoulder and sighs. "Have to admit, I miss him too."

I take a step back and have to grab the porch railing to keep from falling down the stairs. Why didn't Ben tell me?

Maybe because you shut him out and he listened, you idiot.

"You sure you don't want to come in, Lucy?"

I shake my head, forcing a smile. "No, thank you. I… need to get home. I'm sorry. I hope Ben's okay."

"I'll tell him you stopped by," he calls as I stumble down the path back to my car, my heart imploding. Followed by my brain.

I try to do something for myself for fucking once, and everything falls apart.

Driving to my house, the questions line up. How could Puck's family have found him after so much time? Why would Ben let him go without a fight? Maybe the same reason he let me go without a fight? After all, he's back in California where neither the dog nor I would fit into his fancy model lifestyle.

But I know that's not it. That's the Ben I conjured up when he showed up at the vet's months ago, not the Ben I knew—know. He's got to be hurting.

Am I so scary that he wouldn't reach out to me, even to tell me about Puck? Or to say goodbye? Maybe he doesn't love me the way I love him.

But I know that's not it, either.

So what do I do now?

I've only just begun to put my life together, but maybe I should at least call him and tell him that I'm not still mad at him. I could page him, send him the "707" message, but then what? This isn't the kind of message you leave with the busybodies at a service. I could ask his dad for his number, but that feels weird. Stopping at the upstairs phone nook, I sit down heavily, pick up the phone and dial 1-555-1212.

"Directory assistance, can I help you?"

"Yes, please. Los Angeles, California."

"One moment, please."

After a few beats, another woman answers. "Directory assistance, can I help you?"

"Hi, yes, I'm looking for a Ben Porter."

"You're gonna have to give me a little bit more than that, honey. I've got hundreds of those. Do you have an address?"

"No. Um, can you try Benedick Porter?" I spell it for her.

"Hm. We only have one of those."

"Oh, great, thank you."

"But it's unlisted."

"Oh, okay. Well, thanks anyway." I hang up, wondering if we'll get charged for the information if I didn't really get any.

In a haze, I stumble down the hall to my room.

Where I still live like a teenager. Or a nun.

It's not exactly frozen in time—I mean, I took down the life-size Sting poster a long time ago—but it's not that of an independent woman, either. White walls, white trim, tan coverlet on the bed, a few framed bible verses… I may as well have habits hanging in my closet. Instead, my drawers are stuffed with scrubs.

Time to get my shit all the way together. Once that's done, I'll have something to say when I leave a message for Ben.

What did Mr. Porter say about Mrs. Rosen looking for a tenant?

Chapter 30

"Pride (In the Name of Love)" - U2
Ben's Very First Mixtape, Song #4

BEN

I've never uttered the words I'm about to say to my agent of six years, so I take a deep breath to make sure they come out without a waver. "This is what I want."

To his credit, Kirk Vancouver doesn't even blink. In fact, he smiles and puts his feet up on his desk. "As long as you're not going to say 'retire,' I'm all ears."

"I'm not ready to retire, but I do want to make some changes. I want to make New York my base, split with Boston. I want to do theater in Boston and transition to film and TV down in New York."

He nods slowly, then his feet drop to the floor and he begins to flip through his Rolodex. "Well, not all of my contacts here will serve you. It's good you did that modeling job for the shoe company. That casting director does all kinds of work. However, you will get some resistance. New York casting directors can be pretty snooty about acting chops. Out here, casting people don't care so much; they just want the eye candy or the fan base." He rolls his eyes. "I hate to say it, but doing those plays at that damn Shakespeare theater might actually work for you."

When I open my mouth to protest, he raises his hand. "I know, I know, it has a good reputation, blah, blah, blah." He dips his chin. "But it's not Broadway. And that's all some of them care about."

I sit forward in my chair. "I know it's not going to be easy. But this is important to me. My family and my... my girlfriend are in Boston. And a theater that I care about."

He narrows his eyes.

I lean forward. I want him to take this seriously, and I do want him as my partner if he can get on board with this shift. "I know the money is crap at the theater, which is why we'll both be better off if I can get some gigs in New York. I'll do whatever I need to. Meet whoever I need to."

"You're going to need new headshots to start."

"Already made an appointment with a photographer."

He nods. "All right, then. I'll start making calls."

"Thanks, Kirk. Thanks for working with me on this."

"That's what you pay me for. Now get outta here. I got work to do." Shooing me away, he pulls a card from the Rolodex and punches a number into his phone.

"Yeah. Me too," I answer.

MY DAYS ARE FILLED with the final CK shoots, meetings that will hopefully launch this career shift, and packing up my stuff to send back east. My nights are filled with making plans for the future.

I just need to figure out how to prove to Lucy that I'm not going to run away again. I should've tried to talk to her before I left. But I think that I need to show her how serious I am. I need her to know that I've always loved her.

A mixtape alone isn't going to cut it.

An apartment in New York isn't the same as one in Boston, but it's a hell of a lot closer than LA. Even if I could afford to retire right now, I don't want to. I'm an actor. Working with Shakespeare Boston has made that clear to me. It'd be a waste of the past seven years to throw away the contacts Kirk and I have cultivated. I just hope that Lucy will be okay with a semi-long-distance thing.

Ripping open yet another box from my storage unit, I pull out a stack of notebooks from college and chuck them into a garbage bag. The plays, I'll keep. Might need to find a monologue or two to audition with. At the bottom of the box, a stack of papers bound by two rubber bands has my heart in my throat.

I completely forgot that I kept these.

One of the bands breaks when I pull it off.

They're all letters, almost all unfinished.

All addressed to Lucy. At UMass Amherst.

No stamps.

No seals.

Never delivered.

Maybe it's time to do that now.

Chapter 31

"Love Plus One" - Haircut 100
Ben's Very First Mixtape, Song #5

LUCY

A week later, at the end of yet another long day, I park in front of Mrs. Rosen's instead of my parents'. I haven't moved, far but I've moved—to one of the prettiest houses in the neighborhood, a Victorian painted butter-yellow and forest-green fronted by a lovingly maintained flower garden.

Passing through the gate in the white picket fence that encloses the yard, front and back, I remember that the Rosens had a dog for many years, a collie named—like most collies when I was growing up—Lassie. Heading up the back stairs to the second-floor landing, I insert my very own key into the lock, and every bit of me sighs with pleasure as I take in the gleaming hardwood floors and the freshly painted walls of my new apartment. It's a bit empty, but everything in it, I put there. I bought a bed the day I signed the lease. It's covered with a rainbow quilt my grandmother made. The walls are robin's-egg blue. Mrs. Rosen gave me an old table for the kitchen, and I painted it bright red.

After a visit to the pink-tiled bathroom—not having to share a bathroom with two teenage boys has been a life-changer in and of itself—I head to the kitchen to heat up some leftover soup for my dinner. As I stir the pot, the phone on the wall taunts me. I haven't set up a long-distance plan, and I still don't have Ben's number in LA. I could ask his dad for it, but something's holding me back.

I mean, he hasn't called or paged me, either. I check my service multiple times a day.

There's no new growth in the burned-out forest between us, but I'm planting my own seeds anyway. I have my own place—check. The laundromat renovation started yesterday—check.

Slopping the soup into a bowl, I sit down with a pen, a legal pad and the folder where I keep everything from building permits to invoices to paint swatches. I might need a file cabinet. Adding that to the list and going over my to-dos for tomorrow, the satisfaction of ticking items off the list warms me even more than the minestrone.

Not as warm as Ben's arms around me or a dog at my feet.

One thing at a time, Lucy. One thing, one step, one day at a time.

"WHERE ARE YOU, YOU LITTLE MOTHERFUCKER?"

I've spent the past twenty minutes digging through my new apartment, looking behind and under the few pieces of furniture, but my day planner is nowhere to be found.

Everything is in there. Not just my actual calendar of appointments—which is complicated enough—but every client profile, all my notes, all my contacts. Rebuilding it will take more time than I can imagine.

Maybe I should check the car again. Opening my front door wide, I yelp, not expecting someone to be standing on the threshold.

"Mrs. Rosen. Is everything okay?"

The tiny woman has one hand pressed to her chest and hangs onto the railing with the other. "Lucy, you startled me."

"Sorry. I lost something, and I'm going a little crazy."

Releasing a breath, she leans over and begins to sort through the contents of a shopping bag. "Was it a... What do you call these things? It's so professional. A fax thingy?" Straightening, she holds up my planner.

"Oh my god, you found it."

"It was in the driveway." Wincing, she hands over my lifeline. "I'm sorry; I think I ran over it."

Despite tire tracks on the faux-leather cover, it's intact. "It must've fallen out of my bag or something." I hug it to my chest. "Thank you, Mrs. Rosen. I don't know what I'd do if I lost this thing."

"Call me Vera, please, dear. We're practically roommates!"

Technically we're tenant and landlord, but she's so lovely I don't want to correct her. "Um, do you want to come in? I could make some tea or coffee."

"Oh, no thank you, sweetheart. It's late. I just got in from a movie with John, and I wanted to make sure you got these things." She hands over the shopping bag. "This is some mail that your mother dropped off."

Hanging onto the planner like it might run away, I take the bag. "Thank you again, Mrs. Ro—Vera."

"Well, I'll leave you to it. Bedtime for me." She waves a hand. "Let me know if there's anything you need."

"I will, but everything's perfect so far. Thanks again."

I watch her descend the steep stairs, making sure she makes it safely to the first floor before going back inside. Closing the door against the chilly evening, I head to my tiny kitchen to heat some water for tea, a nice cup of Sleepytime while I go over my schedule.

Once the kettle's on, I remember the shopping bag, and I dump its contents onto the table—a stack of magazines, something from the city that might be important, junk mail and a large manila envelope. I guess I need to do something about having my mail forwarded. There are so many things grownups have to think about. After tossing the catalogs in the trash and setting the letter and magazines aside, I turn over the larger envelope, assuming it's information I ordered from a behavioral vet tech program. But the return address is Los Angeles. And my name and address are handwritten. In blocky capital letters I recognize.

I'm going to drain the adrenaline well tonight.

Hands shaking, I ease open the envelope. After all, it's only paper, pen and words. Sticks and stones, right?

When I dump it out, I'm a little confused at first. It seems like just a bunch of random pieces of paper rubber-banded together: folded notebook paper, flyers for various campus activities, even ripped-out pages from books. Many of them are wrinkled like they'd been crumpled up into a ball.

As I pull off the rubber bands, one of them snaps, slapping my hand painfully. Hoping that's not a warning of what's to come, I unfold the top piece of paper.

Monday, August 15, 1981
Lucy,
You haven't even left yet, but I want you to have mail waiting
for you when you get to UMass. My dad did that for me
freshman year, and it helped a lot with the homesickness.
So, hi.
I really believe everything we said. I want you to be free to
meet all kinds of people. But I'm already jealous of all those
people.
I don't want you to forget about me and
FUCK

The last word takes up the second half of the sheet of paper.

When Ben never returned any of my letters after we broke up and I went off to school, I was so, so angry. Seems to be a behavior pattern of mine.

Despite all my jumbled feelings about whatever our relationship was or wasn't, I did go out with a few guys. I had fun. Everything at school was so new and exciting, dating was just part of the package. But Ben was always there. Not in a creepy way or like he was looking over my shoulder judging me. Like a guardian angel. I felt safe stepping out of my comfort zone, because if I asked, I knew he'd hop on a bus and come find me.

He was right. Being on my own was good for me.

It just didn't last.

But that wasn't his fault.

Realizing I've been holding my breath, I take in a big one. And then I get up and open a bottle of wine. Herbal tea is not the right beverage for this trip back in time.

The next letter is written on the back of a typed assignment for some history class.

People assume that actors are good at expressing their
emotions.
Well, this one isn't. Maybe I am when it's a character that some-
body else wrote.
But my own emotions? Not so much. For instance.
I'm an expert at keeping what I feel about you hidden down a
deep, dark well, never to see the light of day.

There's a big angry scribble down the rest of the page. The next is on a sheet of fancy stationery, but it's also the most crumpled.

Lucy,
You make everyone around you a better person without even
doing anything. They just soak up your—your spirit, your Lucy-
ness. It reaches inside everyone, and they are just a better person
for having been around you.
I am a better person having had my arms around you.
Having been inside you.
Having

There are a bunch more half-finished letters as well as torn-out pages from plays and novels with notes in the margins say things like "Tell Lucy" or just "Lucy!"

At the bottom of the stack are two letters actually in envelopes.

One I sent to him. I'm trying to decide which to read first, when memories of the day I wrote mine come slamming back.

I'M SO NERVOUS, *I keep dropping the quarters before I can get them into the payphone slot. It's after midnight, but I just need one more hit of Ben.*

I finally manage to punch in his home number—I forgot the area code the first time because I'm not used to calling him long distance—and thankfully it rings. I was worried I didn't have enough money.

"Hello?" Ben's voice is scratchy, like I woke him up.

"Hey, Ben, it's me." He doesn't say anything. "Lucy."

"Yeah, sorry, I was asleep. Wait—are you okay?"

"Nothing's wrong, I just couldn't sleep. I'm here, in my dorm." I realize I should keep my voice low. The phone's at the end of the hall, but people might be sleeping in the rooms nearby. "I just—I just wanted to tell you..."

MY HEART POUNDS EVEN NOW as everything I was feeling that day roars back. It was my very first day. Fear of the unknown battled with the fear of missing out. My body ached from missing his, even though we'd kissed less than twenty-four hours before.

I was afraid that if I told him I loved him, he'd say it back just because he felt like he had to. After all, I was the one who initiated everything between us. So instead of telling him what I was really feeling, I started yakking about every minute detail of my trip here, my dorm room, my roommate, what I'd had for dinner. Before I could circle back to what I really wanted to say, I was interrupted.

"Please insert one dollar for another three minutes," the mechanical voice announces.

"Shit. I don't have any more money, Ben. I used all my laundry quarters already."

"It's okay, Lucy. You're gonna be okay. You know I—"

I'll never know what he was going to say. He didn't have the number of the payphone, so he couldn't call me back. I went back to my room to grab the box of stationery one of my girlfriends had given me and took it to the lounge to write the sticker-covered letter now in my hands.... where I just blathered on some more about mundane crap.

I never told him I loved him. Instead I made it seem like I was ready to move on. Now, as I read my own words, it's clear I was doing my best to convince *myself* of that fact. He never answered my letter, so I assumed I was right and we were over.

Will the undelivered letter staring at me from my kitchen table tell me what he was really feeling back then? Only one way to find out.

I open it.

Wed. Aug. 24 '81
I'm back at school.
I should've told you this in person but I'm such a total barney, I
couldn't.
But I have to tell you - I love you Lucy.
There.
If I'm being honest here, I've loved you since the day I first saw
you, squatting on the sidewalk saving worms.
Yours forever,
Ben

Why didn't he mail this letter? Was he unsure if he truly loved me? Or, did love me but didn't feel like he should?

The biggest question of all: why did he send these *now*?

Checking the envelope and sifting through the papers again confirms that he didn't include a note of explanation.

Maybe it *wasn't* right for us to be together then. Maybe, as tragic as Tony's death was, it really had nothing to do with either of us. Maybe it was just his time.

It wasn't our time to be together, that's obvious. Not then.

I wish he was here so I could shake the answer out of him, but I guess I'll have to be patient. Not a quality I'm known for.

THE NEXT MORNING it's so busy at the clinic and at the renovation jobsite next door that I'm able to successfully play keep-away from the loneliness that has snuck into my heart since I moved into my own place. That blatantly set up camp last night as I read and reread Ben's words.

Maybe that's what going to college is really about—easing kids out of the nest and into their own lives. Now that I've taken a flying leap out of my nest, I'm lost.

Even if Ben comes home for Thanksgiving—which I haven't worked up to asking Mr. Porter about—I don't know why I think my baby-steps independent life will ever stand up to his exciting one. He's already left his nest and soared. I'll just be a weight dragging him down.

A bell rings, bringing me back to my very earthly but demanding life.

I need to get to the patient in exam four, but I also need to stop and coo over the tiny puppy Cindy's lifting from the small-animal scale.

"Can you hold him for a minute?" she asks. "He's so wriggly I'm afraid I'm going to drop him while I record everything."

There's another bell, but I take the puppy anyway. "Of course." He nestles into my chest, and my heart melts. "What's your story, skinny little man?"

Cindy shakes her head. "Skinny is right. Poor guy was found all by himself behind a dumpster."

The receptionist gives up on the bell and yells my name down the hallway. "I'm sorry, cutie. I gotta go take care of someone else." Reluctantly, I hold him out for Cindy to take, but she holds up a chart instead. "If you want to trade, I'd much rather take whatever's behind door number three than deal with worms this morning." She rubs her stomach. "The Mexican I ate last night is not sitting well."

I shrug. "Works for me."

"Thanks."

Securing the puppy under my arm, I scan his chart.

"Looks like you need a home." Tucking the chart under my other arm, I head for the back to give him a flea bath and deworming meds, and I make a decision. "Lucky for you, I have one that needs a puppy. You're not Ben; you're not even Puck. But you need somebody. Turns out, I need somebody too."

ALL I CAN SAY IS THANK goodness for Mrs. Rosen. When I stopped by her apartment after work to make sure she'd be okay with me fostering the puppy, she practically grabbed him from my arms and declared that she'd be his co-foster parent. I guess she and Mr. Porter have missed Puck too.

Good thing, because I had not thought this through. Talk about the cobbler's son having no shoes—this pet behavior specialist can't take care of a puppy without some help. There's no way I can haul him all over town with me or keep him at the vet's all day. Too many germs, not enough immunity built up.

So he's been spending his days in the lap of luxury.

When I knock on her door, she doesn't answer right away, but I can hear her talking on the other side of the door.

"Sit, dog. Sit. What did I say to you? No, I said sit, not chew on the carpet!"

Eventually the door opens a crack, and Vera peeks out. I hardly recognize her without perfect hair and makeup. "He is a very naughty boy," she whispers.

I wince. "What did he chew today?"

She sighs. "My favorite shoes."

"I'm sorry. Listen, if this isn't going to work, I can—"

She holds up a hand to stop me, looks behind her, groans and whips around to pick up the puppy. "No! Bad dog. That is for Lucy."

I step in, closing the door behind me. Vera's doing a tug of war with the puppy and a package. "Your father dropped off some more mail today."

Sweeping the little demon into my arms, I pry a large, taped-up envelope out of his mouth. "Seriously, Vera. If he's doing damage—"

She sighs. "I think I just need some more training."

"Puppies can be tough, especially ones like this guy, who likely got separated from his litter way too young. He needs firm, consistent curbing. But you also can't expect too much. It's way too early to teach him to sit."

We talk about redirection, and I promise to get more chew toys. She promises to keep him in his crate when she can't supervise him directly. I take him out to practice doing his business before climbing the back stairs up to my place. Once he's settled behind the baby gate to keep him in the kitchen, I go through the mail. No letter from Ben. I've gotten nothing from him since the package of old letters. But then I remember the package that I'd stuffed in my bag to keep it away from a curious little mouth. Luckily, his sharp puppy teeth only got through the first layer of heavy-duty packing tape. Turning it over, the return address makes my heart skip.

And has me pouring a glass from the bottle of wine I opened the other night.

A couple of healthy sips later, I'm wrestling with the tape. Ben must've used an entire roll on this thing. Maybe I should just hand it over to the pup and let him do his worst.

Instead, I hunt for scissors, finally find them in a box of not-yet-unpacked stuff and manage to pull out something wrapped in a lot of bubble wrap, held together by yet more tape. Resisting the urge to throw it across the room—is Ben trying to make me even more mad at him?—I cut through the layers to find a cassette tape with a hand-decorated cover. "FOR LUCY" is written on the spine.

A smile stretches my face and my heart.

Ben Porter made me a mixtape.

About time, the bastard.

No note from him to be found anywhere—not on the ground, not stuck in the wrapping—just block printing of song names. Ben really has a thing about sending actual finished letters.

But I'll take it.

Ten minutes later, I'm back in the car. The puppy I can't settle on a name for is in his travel bag next to me, and the stereo's cranked up to eleven. Driving is the best way to listen, so I head west on Route 2, music filling my car and my ears and my heart, quaint New England towns a blur in my peripheral vision.

When the first side ends without cutting off a song, I'm impressed.

As I turn the cassette over, the fuel indicator catches my eye. The bright red light jars me back to reality. I don't even know where I am. I push eject instead of play.

By the time I find a gas station, the needle has dipped below empty and both the car and I are running on fumes. While the tank fills, I take the dog on a little walk so he can relieve himself as I read the song list carefully printed on the case liner. I can picture Ben choosing each one, feel his need to tell me something about us.

"Catapult" might be about how him finding Puck launched us both into new territory. "Tears of a Clown" is an obvious reference to Launce, and maybe how playing that role helped him process some of his own pain. "Always Something There to Remind Me," by Naked Eyes. Well, if it's as true for him as it's true for me… "Pride (In the Name of Love)" is next on the list, and I hope it's about us in a good way. Haircut 100's "Love Plus One" follows. Maybe Puck is our plus one. Or Tony?

The last song on side one is "Don't You (Forget About Me)." I may be simpleminded about some things, but I'm taking that message literally.

When the pump *thunks*, I replace the handle and gas cap and head back home. The other side of the tape is full of songs all about love and its complications. Delighted, tortured, sexy, sensual. It's all there.

Back in Arlington, I park the car and put the puppy and myself to bed. I just wish I could drive to Ben's apartment and yell at him. And then make love to him.

Chapter 32

"Don't You (Forget About Me)" - Simple Minds
Ben's Very First Mixtape, Song #6

LUCY

The night before Thanksgiving, as I'm brushing the last dab of egg wash on the crust of a towering apple pie, Mr. Porter dries his hands and clears his throat.

"May I be released from KP duty, dear? I've got to be up early tomorrow."

Vera smiles as she reaches around to untie the frilly apron stretched across his belly. The affection in her crinkled eyes makes my heart ache. Silently blowing out a sigh as I open the oven door and slide the pie inside, I know I only have myself to blame. If I'd figured out a lot sooner that my love for Ben was bigger and longer-lasting than my anger at him, if I'd accepted that we both made mistakes in the wake of Tony's death, I wouldn't be alone tomorrow, on the worst of all holidays for my family.

Closing the oven and hoping that my landlord and Ben's dad are finished with their canoodling, I face the happy lovebirds and paste a smile on my face.

Anyway, I won't be alone. My parents are coming here for Thanksgiving dinner since my brothers did end up escaping with their girlfriends. On top of that, I have a new puppy to take care of.

Mr. Porter pauses in the kitchen doorway. "I'll be over to help out as soon as I get back tomorrow morning."

"What time do you have to leave for the airport?" Vera asks.

My heart skips a beat.

Mr. Porter squints, as if picturing a calendar. "He's on a red-eye that lands at six a.m. There shouldn't be too much traffic that early, especially on Thanksgiving, right?"

Since it's pretty clear that I'm watching a performance put on for my sake, my head swivels back to Vera.

"I think five-thirty would be fine." Vera crosses her arms, leans back against the sink and sighs dramatically. "I do wish you could be here all morning. I'm going to need help getting the fire started in the smoker."

"Hmm." Mr. Porter nods and shoves his hands in his pockets. "Well, dinner may have to be late if we run into traffic on the way back."

Two pairs of eyes ping-pong to mine, reminding me of the way Ben and Bella played their scenes.

"Unless…" Vera begins.

"Lucy might be able to make a run to the airport?" Ben's dad finishes.

Closing my eyes, I take a deep breath before taking on the role they've written for me.

Opening my eyes, a smile stretches my cheeks so wide that it's almost painful. "Why, I'll be happy to do an airport run. Just let me know who I'm picking up and the flight information, and I'll go now and set my alarm."

BEN

My hand isn't big enough to cover the yawn I make as I trudge up the jetway. The red-eye's never pleasant, but this flight was full of babies.

As soon as one settled, another would start up. Of course, the package I'm carrying wasn't exactly quiet, either.

Once we get to the end, I cut to the right, past the other deplaning passengers, and begin scanning the faces in the crowd waiting to meet us.

No sign of my dad, though. Maybe I misunderstood the message. Maybe he's meeting me at baggage claim instead.

Little kids squeal before running into the arms of grandmas, guys in uniform slap the backs of older versions of themselves, and whole families erupt in cries of recognition and love.

When I'm tackled from the side, I don't see it coming.

LUCY

Quickly checking the monitor next to the gate, I hope I don't have the wrong flight number. Or worse, the wrong airline. I barely slept last night, my mind running through scenarios of what might happen at the airport, my body restless and hungry for his touch. How many red-eye flights can there be from LAX to Logan? But none of the faces emerging from the jetway is the one I'm looking for.

Thinking—hoping—that I missed him somehow, I scan the crowd around me. My eyes trip over a chiseled face I almost don't recognize without a beard. Of course, he would've shaved it for the shoots he went back for.

I could've been hired by the Patriots, I dodge and weave through the crowd so quickly, muttering an apology when I almost take out somebody's grandpa. Before my heart beats twice, I've tackled him. His entire body tenses for a moment. But when our eyes meet, his arms have me, and he somehow manages to keep us both from ending up on the ground. Before I can babble a single word of regret or apology, he covers my mouth with his. Lost in the familiar taste and feel of him, I don't want to ever let go. At some point, though, his strong hands grip the sides of my face, and he breaks the kiss to whisper in my ear, "Do you forgive me?"

"Yes, Ben. Yes." I squeeze him tight. "I'm sorry too."

His brow rests on my shoulder briefly, but when he meets my eyes, his are steady and his voice is firm. "I left. Again. I told myself you were done with me. But then I realized I did it again. If you forgive me, I promise I'll never leave without making a plan with you first."

"I was hurt, but I…" Sucking in a deep breath, I lay it all on the line. "I was wrong too. Before, when Tony died, you left, but I could've tried to find you, written you letters. It was easy to stay mad at you because you weren't there. I'm working on breaking that habit." He opens his mouth to speak, but my hands grab his shirt and pull him closer. "Besides, you've spoiled me. No one can come close to making me feel the things you do." I lean in close to whisper, "So you'd better take me home and make love to me before Thanksgiving dinner, or I'll really be mad at you."

Shaking the disbelief from his face, he kisses me until the flashing and popping sounds of cameras bring us both crashing back to earth.

I try to cover his face with my hands. "Shit. We've been caught."

His arms tighten around me. "I don't care."

"But your agent—"

"Lucy, I don't care."

I start to tell him that I don't want to make a scene, but suddenly he's on his knees. "Lucky for you, I've been learning lines for an audition for *The Tempest,* because if you got those letters, you have evidence of how bad I am at expressing myself."

He spreads his arms wide and his voice fills the terminal. "'Hear my soul speak, the very instant that I saw you, did my heart fly to your service; there resides, to make me slave to it; and for your sake am I this patient'"—he holds up his carry-on as he finishes—"*dog man.*"

The crowd goes wild.

And I think Ben's bag barks.

BEN

The entire car ride from Logan Airport to Arlington, I'm in contact with Lucy. But it's not enough. Good thing the holiday makes it an unusually short trip. If I had to sit through regular Boston traffic, I'm pretty sure I'd explode. I need this woman more than I need to breathe.

The moment she parks on the street in front of my dad's house, I take her gorgeous face in my hands and kiss her hungrily. "I need to be skin to skin with you in minutes."

"I'm with you," she breathes between kisses. "But I've got to take care of something first."

Groaning, I run a hand down her luscious thigh. "I thought you were letting other people do the caretaking these days." I can't keep the frustration out of my voice. During the car ride she told me all about her plans for the new training center. I'm on board with her staying focused on herself. But I'd like to be second in line.

She takes my hands in hers and squeezes. "I am, but I couldn't say no to this."

Before I can make any kind of argument, she stops me with a finger over my lips. "I promise this will only take a few minutes and then I'm all yours till Thanksgiving dinner." She looks pointedly to the bag at my feet. "Besides, don't you have something to take care of as well?"

I make an over-the-top face no acting coach would ever let me get away with. "All right. But let's get to it. I don't want to waste another minute."

Heaving myself, my bag and my special carry-on out of the car, I follow her a few steps before I realize she's heading across the street, away from my warm apartment where we can be naked. "Where are you going?"

She reaches back to grab my elbow. "You'll see."

With a growl Puck would've been proud of, I let myself be pulled along as she opens the gate to Vera Rosen's backyard, practically skipping down the brick path along the side of the house and up a set of outside stairs. She opens a door without knocking. Dropping my hand, she disappears inside. When she reappears, she has a wiggly and whimpering ball of fur in her arms. "Meet my new responsibility."

Before I can say anything, my carrier erupts with a series of yaps.

Lucy heads back outside. "I've got to take him outside to p-o-t-t-y. Come on."

Moments later, I'm next to her again, shivering in the cold morning air. Lucy's doing her high-pitched "Go potty!" and "Good boy!" routine. Thankfully, I don't have to do the same.

She looks over with a raised brow. "You said you'd explain when we got back here."

"I guess we both have some 'splainin' to do. But first, I need another kiss."

I hope Mrs. Rosen isn't up yet, because my hands can't get enough of this woman.

"Can we go inside?" I manage when we come up for air. "It's freezing out here."

"A couple weeks in California and you've lost your New England edge," she teases, punching me before scooping up my new friend. "If I can't get your story, can I at least have your name, little dog?"

"It's Tuck." I pick up her dog and head for the stairs. "And I promise I'll tell you her story if we can go inside and get naked."

Thankfully, she not only follows but agrees to let the dogs have a quick nap in their respective crates while I show her just how much I missed her.

Every damn inch of her.

Clothes thrown back on, we release the hounds and sit with them on the floor. As they get to know each other, I tell her about my new career plans and new apartment.

"New York, huh?" she says when I'm finished.

Taking her hand in mine, I press it to my heart. "You and this relationship are my first priority. But we're young. We both have careers that could really take off. Moving to the east coast means I can build on the career I've started without being so far away.

"I know your new venture will take a lot of your time right now, but I hope you'll visit me in Brooklyn sometimes. When I don't have to be in New York for work, I'll be back here."

She just nods slowly.

"I know it's a lot to take in, and maybe I should've talked to you first before moving ahead. But I also felt like I needed to show you—and me, I guess—that I'm taking charge of my own life and career. That I'm in the driver's seat for once. I just hope you'll always be there next to me."

Finally, she pulls me close for a quick kiss. Then, hands on my cheeks, she separates us an inch. "Okay. I get it. I did the same thing with the training center. From now on, though, we are partners in all things. We talk about the big changes."

The dogs decide they need to get in on the action. As they wriggle in between us, Lucy picks up my new friend. "New pets are an example of big changes. How did you end up with this little girl?"

I tell the story of the model on my last shoot who discovered she was allergic to dogs after her boyfriend got her a dog. Something about the tiny terrier reminded me of Puck—not just the rhyming name—so I impulsively offered to adopt her. Full-grown, she only weighs ten pounds, so I figured she'd be easy to bring along on my new, nomadic life plan.

Lucy tells me all about adopting the puppy now curled up on my lap, who's got to be a distant cousin of Puck's. Same tufted eyebrows, same whiskery mouth, same alert triangular ears.

Likely reading my mind, she leans on my shoulder. "Neither of them can replace Puck. No dog ever will. But they need a home, and I think we can give them a good one."

"We?"

"Yes, we." She looks up, her smile wide. "Together we have so much love to spare we might have to adopt an entire shelter full of animals."

Hugging her close, I breathe in her comforting scent. "Sounds good to me."

LUCY

The chairs around Vera Rosen's table don't include everyone I love. They never will. Sal and Vinnie will be back another year, but maybe some souls are only meant to visit your life. Even a brief encounter can make a profound change.

Letting go is a big part of the healing process. Catching Ben's eye as he passes yet another dish piled high with food, I'm thankful that this man came back to me again. A smile stretches lips that only an hour before worshipped every inch of my still-tingling body. The hand that caressed my face and pulled me close now lifts a wine glass while his free hand finds mine to hold on tight.

"Thank you, Vera, for bringing us all together for this meal—which I can actually eat now that my CK contract is complete," he begins, sweeping his gaze around the table. "I'd also like to say that I'm thankful for Puck. Although he's not with us on a daily basis anymore, I'm grateful that he brought me back to Lucy and reminded me that love and loyalty are easy to give." He gestures with his glass at his canine co-star, who showed up right before dinner and now shares a cushion with Tuck and my puppy in the corner. "And that his first family decided to go out of town so we can have him here for the holiday."

Mr. Porter lifts his glass. "I'm very grateful for new friends." Eyes on Vera, a sweet blush tints his cheeks. "It takes some of us longer than others to recover from loss, so I am glad for patient neighbors." He lifts his glass in Ben's direction. "And sons."

My mom dabs a napkin to her lips and takes a big breath. "I'd like to add that I'm thankful that we had Tony in our lives. I would've rather had him for more than twenty-one years, but I'm glad we had him as long as we did."

My dad's chin wobbles, so I dive in. "To new friends and old, whether they walk on two legs or four, whether they grace our lives for a brief time or for the rest of our lives, I am grateful for you all."

"Well, I don't know about the rest of you, but I'm grateful for this feast, prepared by one and all," my dad manages to say.

"Except for Ben," Mr. Porter adds, grinning.

Ben gestures at the platters of food. "You should've told me no one was making seitan!"

His dad coughs out a laugh. "I, for one, am thankful no one did."

Vera's the last to lift a glass. "I'm grateful to have a new family to make new traditions with. So let's drink to that, and then, John, please pass the stir-fried rice."

"Happy Thanksgiving!" echoes as we continue to pass dishes that span the cuisine of the globe, each one more tempting than the last. Who needs turkey and fixings when you can eat Chinese, Italian and good old southern barbecue?

A whimper under my chair has me leaning down to whisper, "I'm thankful for you, too, Bruin."

Ben shakes his head. "I don't know what this woman is thinking. Bruin is a ridiculous name."

"I suggested Patriot, Celtic and Sox, but she'd have nothing of it," Mr. Porter says around a mouthful of chicken parm.

"There's a whole canon of names to choose from!" Ben puts down his fork and picks up my puppy. "If you want to stick with the first letters of Bruin, you could go for Brutus. But he seems like more of a lover than a general, so there's Romeo, of course." The puppy whines. "No? How about a clown name?" He looks over at Puck and Tuck. "What do you two think? Not Launce, but maybe... Touchstone? Bottom?"

I whack him on the arm. "I'm not yelling Bottom out the back door."

He ignores me. "Dromio? No—I've got it. Dogberry!"

The puppy barks enthusiastically. Ben waggles his brows at me. "I think he likes it."

I roll my eyes. "Dogberry. That's ridiculous. You're lucky I'm in love with you."

At these words, the clinking of cutlery against dishes come to a halt, and everyone stops chewing to stare at me. I look down to take a moment to steady myself, but then I realize that I don't need to. "Yes, I am in love with Ben. I have been for a very long time." Then I turn to the man next to me, who I hope will be by my side for as long as we're alive. "What do you have to say to that?"

Ben closes his eyes and takes a breath, making my heart skip a beat. But when he opens them again, the love there is so pure and deep that I know I'll never question it again. "No matter where our work takes us, I always want to come home to you."

Clearing his throat, he pushes his chair back, puts the puppy on the floor and gets down on one knee. All three dogs take this as an invitation to play, but he fends them off as he pulls a small velvet box from his pocket. "Luciana Maria Minola, with these people—and dogs—as witnesses, will you marry me?"

There's no question in my mind. I don't want to spend another moment of my life without him in it. All the emotions in the world seem to be clogging my throat, however, so I just nod as enthusiastically as I can and pull him up to standing to throw my arms around him.

Ben kisses me, the table erupts in applause and Puck, Tuck and Dogberry add a chorus of happy howls.

Afterword

Thank you so much for reading Ben and Lucy's story! To rock on with Jess and the radio DJ she falls in love with over late-night phone calls, check out *You Spin Me* at books2read.com/YSMKGrey.

To get a FREE prequel of Ben & Lucy's story along with deleted scenes from this book and other bonus material, sign up for my newsletter by visiting followkarengrey.com.

If you loved this Boston Classics novel, leaving a review is the absolute best way to support an author. You can leave one wherever you downloaded the book, or on Goodreads or Bookbub.

Also by Karen Grey

What I'm Looking For Boston Classics Book 1

The course of true love never did run smooth, but in this smart and sexy retro rom-com with a finance-nerd heroine and a drama-geek hero, returns on love can't be measured on the S&P 500. books2read.com/WILFKGrey

You Spin Me Boston Classics Book 2

If two lonely people fall in love over late-night phone calls, will meeting face-to-face make them, or break them? In this heartfelt, slow-burn retro romcom, it may be the end of a decade, but it's the beginning of a love story. books2read.com/YSMKGrey

Child of Mine Boston Classics Book

A single mom gets a job offer she can't refuse but has to work side-by-side with the one-night stand that doesn't know he's a father. Of her daughter. books2read.com/COMKGrey

You Get What You Give Carolina Classics Book 1

When a fiery redhead and the guy she thought was a one night stand turn out to be rivals, his family feud causes shockwaves bigger than the surf stirred up by the latest hurricane. books2read.com/YGWYGKGrey

Hold On To Me Carolina Classics Book 2

In this slow-burn, boss-assistant, entertainment biz romance, a bad cop movie production chief takes on a sexy assistant who challenges her every assumption. books2read.com/HOTMKGrey

I Want It That Way Carolina Classics Book 3

She's a driver to the stars who just wants to get her tubes tied. He's a former child actor who needs to get back behind the wheel. A fake relationship seems like the perfect solution. books2read.com/IWITWKGrey

Acknowledgments

My first two novels released in the summer and fall of 2020. The events of this year have made my personal privileges clear. I am fortunate in so many ways, especially in terms of resources and support. I've always known that the work I do (actor/audiobook narrator/writer) is the icing on the cake of life, but that is evident now more than ever. I am so thankful for each person who puts life on the line so that the rest of us can not only survive (e.g., health care workers, food production workers, firefighters—the list is long), but enjoy all the things we think we can't live without (e.g., books, the internet, Netflix, chocolate—the list is way too long).

Additionally, while I hope this book provided some escape from the stresses of life, with a few laughs along the way, the story is obviously rooted in grief. A kernel of its origin lies in a drunk driving accident that affected the family of someone very close to me. Additionally, the audio production of this book was narrated in part by a hugely talented young man who lost his life after a long struggle with depression. Books can help us cope with life's stresses—even those served up by 2020—but I am thankful every day for dear friends and family that I can turn to for support. If you are struggling or know someone who is, I have some resources listed at the end of these notes.

That said, I so appreciate YOU, dear reader, for spending some of your hard-earned cash and precious time with me and my made up people. We all hope that we've brought you a needed escape and a laugh or two.

Getting this book to you has, of course, been a collaborative effort. Editor Sarah Pesce and proofreader Jax Hinson questioned choices, made suggestions and cheered me on through the process. My local writing group, Kelly Goss, Andrea McNair and Hayley Swinson helped get early drafts in shape. Anne Pakulniewicz and Laurie Janus did last minute reads for me and gave invaluable feedback.

For help with the details of Lucy's job, I turned to two veterinarian friends who both happened to work as animal techs in the 1980's: college housemate Fran Merritt and sister-in-law's sister-in-law (no idea what that makes us) Rose Oppenheim. All the good vet office stories are theirs; all errors are mine.

For Ben's modeling job, I have a teensy bit of experience with modeling but I mostly did research by reading. With regards to his acting work, especially the clowning in Two Gents, I thank all my teachers (yes, studying clowning is a thing—not only at Ringling Brothers but in serious actor training programs), especially Karen Beaumont as well as co-conspirators Pat Buckley and Lindsay Pontius.

Lana Pecherczyk of Bookcoverology has created *another* beautiful cover, as well as the adorable mixtape drawing for the chapter headings. This time around, Jennifer Watson and the other ladies at Social Butterfly PR may have helped you find this book, as they put many hours into getting the word out.

I am lucky to have so many amazing friends spread across the world, but my Wilmington book club members, the Brandeis MFA '92 Anti-Wonderwomen, the Better Cheddars, and the Ladies Who Are Lunch are all women who inspire and challenge me.

I am especially grateful for my family during this crazy time. I wouldn't want to quarantine with anyone else but my two girls (and even their significant others), my many pets and especially, my husband, James. Here's to more nature walk bingo!

- Mothers Against Drunk Driving www.madd.org/history
- Substance Abuse and Mental Health Services Administration www.samhsa.gov
- National Alliance on Mental Illness www.nami.org
- GriefHealingDiscussionGroups.com

About the Author

KAREN GREY is a *USA Today* bestselling and award-winning author of vintage romantic comedies with smart heroines and hunky heroes. Drawing on a long career as a performer, her retro 80's and 90's romances are populated with characters working both on- and off-stage in theater, TV and film. When not reading or writing, she's lounging at the beach or hiking in the mountains. Or dreaming about both with an IPA in hand and a dog or a cat nearby.

(Author photo: Celestial Studios)

For the latest news and bonus materials, join her free VIP club at:
followkarengrey.com

facebook.com/karengreyauthor

instagram.com/karengreyauthor

goodreads.com/karen_grey

bookbub.com/profile/karen-grey

tiktok.com/@karengreyauthor